I0729234

AMANDA BOOLOODIAN

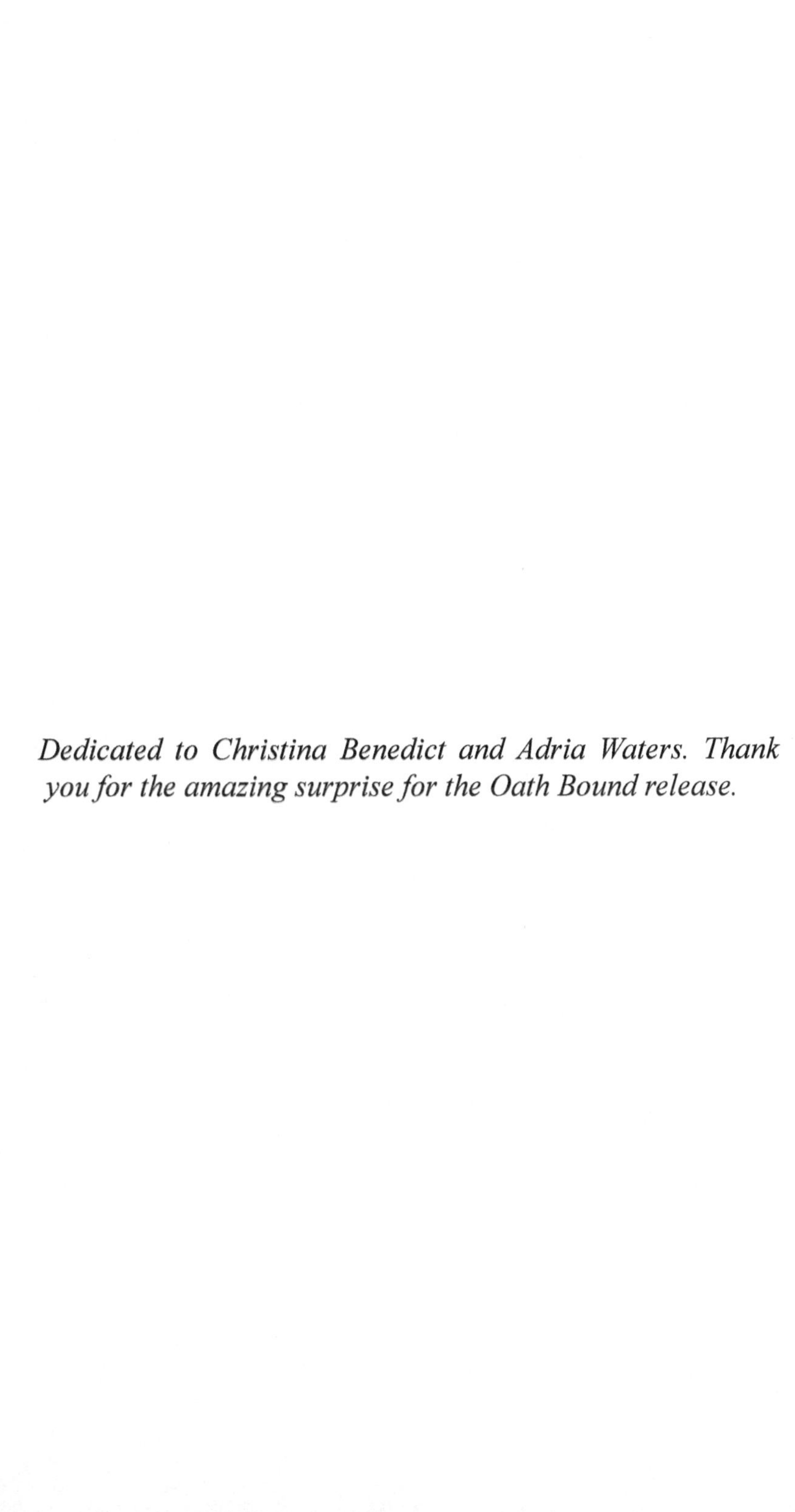

Dedicated to Christina Benedict and Adria Waters. Thank you for the amazing surprise for the Oath Bound release.

CHAPTER 1

RAIN POUNDED AGAINST THE HOOD of the car and Mira shivered. The heat was technically on, but the amount of warmth that spat out couldn't help but be overwhelmed by the cold pressing against the windows.

A flat tire in a storm, is this really my luck now? She knew the answer, but didn't want to admit it. At the moment, karma hated her. The feeling was mutual.

Sighing, Mira snatched her purse and pawed through the contents again. Her cell phone had to be there, right? She never left home without it.

Which naturally meant she'd left her phone at work, or what was left of work.

After the fire, the insurance company had balked on payment, so they'd demanded a walk through to stall for time. Seeing the charred remains of her store had been difficult. She kept reminding herself that at least she hadn't gone up in flames with the merchandise, but the thought didn't help the fact that she had little left.

Mira leaned back against the seat and stared out the window. A few cars zipped past her, apparently in a hurry to get home in case the rain decided to turn to ice, which it threatened to do at any moment.

How far to the nearest... anything? A large stone wall lined the interstate here, keeping people on the road—along with the trash they threw out their windows—and out of the nice clean backyards of the houses that stood not more than a hundred yards away. Only the lights of the houses shone through.

People didn't freeze to death in their cars anymore, right?

Well, probably not when they carry their cell phone. She unzipped her purse again and looked through it. Someone driving by would be bound to call in to report her vehicle. No one would stop in this weather, but surely they would call her stranded car into someone.

The sound of the rain turned sharper. A little more tick to the drops. While she stared, little chips of ice dropped on the roof of her car.

This is ridiculous, she told herself to keep from getting too upset about her predicament. She had faced down monsters and a murderer—she could survive a little rain. Mira worked hard to ignore the fact that she never would have survived any of it if not for an angel.

What spells did she have ready? Shell might keep the rain off if she could boost it somehow, but she felt sure someone would notice if she walked down the road and wasn't getting wet during this mess. Ignite was ready to go, but she didn't feel the need to be in another fire.

Lights flooded her car and she let out a huge breath with relief. Then, realizing she had no idea what kind of person might be in the car behind her, she tensed and started mentally flipping through her spells faster.

Ignite, Shell, Reflect, Sunburst, Twilight—

When someone knocked on the window, she jumped. The man under the umbrella was easily recognizable. She was safe, she knew. Her anxiety ramped up for a whole host of other reasons, none of which she had a spell to cure.

Gabriel waved her out of the car, looking resigned to the fact he was out in this muck.

Mira turned off the car, leaving her hazard lights on, grabbed her purse, and made sure she had everything she needed before jumping out of the car.

She tried to say, 'I'm so glad you're here,' but her voice disappeared in the pounding rain. He gestured rather impatiently, and then led her to the passenger side of his car. Once she was out of the weather, Gabriel took his time walking around to the driver's side. He even paused at his door, standing in the rain.

Blessed warmth washed over her. The heat was cranked up high and Mira pressed her hands to the heater vent.

Gabriel got in, letting in a blast of cold air. He folded up the umbrella and closed his door before tossing the umbrella in the back. He didn't appear to notice the water he slung all over his car.

"Thanks for the ride," Mira said.

Gabriel's only response was a strained grunt.

Mira fell silent. She wanted to tell him this wasn't her fault, but she felt certain that at least some blame fell on her. Gabriel had sworn to protect her while in the Ether. That was all on him. The fact that he was in the other world and had just discovered he was an angel, well... most of that blame fell to her.

The sound of the driving rain kept the silence from becoming awkward. When they entered her neighborhood, the snowplows were hard at work, treating the roads.

"Are you still at Lance's?" Gabriel asked.

"No, I'm back at home." She wanted to add that he would know she had left Lance's if he had bothered to talk to her, but the thought just depressed her. Gabriel had visited twice in the past week, but he hadn't been in the mood to talk either time. At least not to her. He talked at length to Lance on one visit. Gabriel didn't even indicate why he was there, because he'd only said a few words to her.

The other time, he had appeared to move her the two feet she needed to avoid an enormous large icicle from spearing her. Apparently, he had been in the middle of something and didn't appreciate the interruption.

This time, Gabriel pulled into Della's driveway and drove around to the back of the house, stopping at the staircase that led to Mira's apartment.

"Sorry about dragging you out tonight," Mira said, "but thanks for the ride."

Gabriel drummed his fingers on the steering wheel.

"See you around." She left the car, a black depression threatening to drown her faster than the rain.

Halfway up the stairs she heard the car door shut behind her. For a heartbeat, she froze. If Gabriel was following her, was she in danger?

Did it matter either way? Mira had spells at the ready, so she continued up and inside, leaving the door open for Gabriel.

Shivering from the cold, she looked around. Everything appeared normal.

"You didn't have to follow me up," Mira said when Gabriel came in and shut the door.

"We need to talk," Gabriel said.

"Can it wait? I'm soaked and freezing. Aren't you?"

When she asked the question, she took a better look at him. He stood, barely wet.

"I'm fine, and I'll wait."

Alchemy and Oracle, Mira's cats, entered the room—Oracle at a run, and Alchemy at a more sedate saunter. She reached down to scratch Oracle's ears, but the cat didn't pause on his way to visit Gabriel.

"Fine," Mira muttered, watching Gabriel pet the cat. She hung up her coat and hat next to the door and gestured for Gabriel to do the same. "There's tea and water in the kitchen. Help yourself."

On her way to her room, her eyes strayed to the carpet near the kitchen where she had activated a spell using her own blood—and Gabriel's.

Not a trace of the nightmare remained. The Reinfield Concierge Service had taken care of everything. No one would be able to imagine she and Gabriel had helped Emmit kill a monster and stop a dimensional rift in this very room.

Still her eyes always trailed to that spot.

Once she locked herself in her room, she threw off all her clothes and took a fast, but scalding-hot shower in an effort to warm herself up.

Back in her room, she dug out a sweater. She had it halfway on when she heard Gabriel at her door.

"Listen, Mira, this can't keep happening," Gabriel said through behind the door.

"What?" Mira's voice came out muffled while pulling on the sweater.

"This. Me showing up all the time. It has to stop."

Mira felt her blood pressure shoot up. "Do you think I did this on purpose?" A little squeak entered her voice, but she was too outraged to care. She found some wool leggings and tugged them on.

"I know you didn't," Gabriel mumbled behind the closed door. Louder, he added, "You have to put a stop to it."

She grabbed a pair of socks and yanked open her door, glaring at him. "What do you mean I have to put a stop to this? I didn't do this." Well, broadly speaking she hadn't.

"I could have had plans tonight," Gabriel said.

Could have, but didn't? Mira tucked the information away and stalked past him. "What do you want me to do, stay locked up in my apartment forever?"

"What were you even doing out this late? And in this weather?"

Remembering the trip to her damaged teashop drained some of her animosity. "I had to meet an insurance investigator at the store." She dropped onto the couch and put on her socks.

"Oh." Some of the fire went out of Gabriel's eyes, but he pushed on. "Still, there has to be something you can do to put an end to this... arrangement."

"I could ask around to see if anyone else has had any dealings with angels—"

"No!"

Mira sighed and slumped back on the couch. "I don't have any spells on how to break the promise of an angel. You made the pact in the Ether. If it's still active here, there's got to be a way you can stop it."

"I've tried, but I don't know what I'm doing." The last part sounded like it was hard for Gabriel to admit. "Couldn't you just... I don't know. Be more careful?"

"It doesn't work like that." She didn't want to bring up the other option, but she knew she had to. "Maybe if you told Ian—"

"No!" Gabriel was even more emphatic.

"Don't yell at me," Mira snapped. "If you'd talk to him, he might not fight the spell so hard. I'm stacking up more bad karma as we speak."

"No one forced you to bind my partner." He looked like he was trying to keep his temper, but failed miserably.

"You're right! I did that to help the community. That's on me and I accept that, karma and all. But no one is forcing you to come track me down every time you think I need help!"

"You don't understand what it's like!"

Mira glared at him. "Neither do you!"

Seething, Gabriel reined in his voice, although he couldn't manage to drown his anger. "Dammit, Mira, there has to be *something* we can do here."

Mira's lips twitched. ·

"What?" Gabriel appeared bewildered at her sudden change in attitude.

"Nothing." Mira bit her lip. All her fury evaporated with one word.

That didn't appear to help Gabriel's mood. "What's so funny?"

"It's just..." Mira tried to stop the grin, but she was losing the battle. "It's just funny to hear an angel cursing."

Gabriel sighed and closed his eyes. When he opened them again, he glared at her, as she still struggled not to laugh. Shaking his head, Gabriel flopped into a chair.

"This isn't funny." He sounded resigned, so Mira tried her best to stop grinning.

Alchemy and Oracle hopped onto his chair, looking for affection, which Gabriel gave.

"I know it's not funny," Mira said, trying to sound sincere. "You're right, and you're also right about this needing to stop. When you show up I never know if I'm about to die, or stub my toe."

Gabriel smirked, but didn't look at her. "I get the idea I'd need my gun or an ambulance instead of a bandage when I come to find you."

Mira rolled her eyes. "Yeah. That makes me feel a whole lot better."

"Look," he said, "I'm still trying to wrap my head around all this."

"I know."

"Maybe—" Gabriel shook his head. "I can't tell Ian until I understand this better. Is there any way you can... I don't know, forestall karma."

Mira's eyes widened. "No, you're talking about a dark path I refuse to take. I've seen people try to avoid karma and it didn't end well for anyone."

"What happened?"

He could probably use the distraction, so Mira, after some hesitation, filled him in a little on her background. "You saw my file—from when I worked as an occult expert for the FBI."

Gabriel nodded.

"I was in college at the time. There was... Well, I did something that I didn't think was bad at the time. I made a spell called Bliss. It was..." Mira shivered as she remembered. "It was an amazing feeling. I was having a hard time, and Bliss made everything bad evaporate."

"Like a drug?"

"Exactly like a drug. Another witch took the spell, twisted it, and turned it into something much more dangerous. Then he started giving it to other people. Humans, mostly."

Gabriel frowned and sat up straighter.

"You know a little about how karma works. It was my spell, so when something bad happened, everything it touched stacked against me."

"Shouldn't that have been on the other witch?"

"Part of it, yes. He made the spell and manipulated people with it. He used us." Mira gripped her hands together. She hated remembering, but if it would help Gabriel understand, it would be worth it. "But he found a way to escape the karma, at least for a while, by pushing it off on me."

Gabriel's eyebrows knitted together. "How does that happen?"

Mira shook her head. "It shouldn't happen, but it's possible. It nearly killed me, and I didn't even know what was happening. I thought it was all my own karma."

"What was he doing?"

Mira studied her hands. "We think he tried to summon something."

"What, like John did? One of those things from the other side?"

Mira frowned. "I... I don't know *what* he was trying to summon. Thankfully, we didn't find out."

Could he have been trying to summon something from the Ether? Mira's arms broke out in gooseflesh.

"How did the FBI get involved in something like that?" Gabriel asked.

"One of the people involved was the son of an influential politician. I had left the group, but she asked me to help her son out, so I went back. The FBI agreed not to press any charges for my part in the creation of the 'drug'." Mira used her hands to make air quotes.

"Did they think it really was a drug?"

"Not all of them. One or two people knew the score and worked with the local conclave."

Gabriel deflated. "Conclave? I don't even understand what half this crap means."

Mira covered her mouth to stop from grinning again.

Gabriel's eyes narrowed. "Crap is not a curse word."

"Well, no... but still." Seeing Gabriel's look, she hurried to continue. "A conclave is a gathering, in this case, of supernaturals. Um, when you're ready... I mean, if you want... I'd like to take you to one."

"What do you do at these gatherings?"

"Usually the elders of each race meet. They bring up issues or things other people in the community should be aware of. For the rest of us, we get the chance to mingle. It's a place where we can be ourselves. Essentially."

"But not completely?"

"Well, the werewolves aren't going to shift in front of everyone. The elves aren't likely to spar. *Sometimes* the witches share or swap spells and those sorts of things, but we all get the chance to be open about who we are."

"Open?" Gabriel looked morose. "And no angels?"

"Not that I know of."

Gabriel perked up. "But you don't know for sure?"

Mira shook her head. "You don't have to tell people who or what you are. They won't necessarily expect you to tell them, either. And never ask someone else, it's rude. Extremely rude."

He looked confused. "Why is it rude?"

Mira shrugged. "Most of our communities have been massacred at some point. Witches and sorcerers were burned at the stake, werewolves were hunted, and vampires were dragged into the sun and staked. Although, even Lance will admit that many of the vampires deserved it at the time. Some of them got out of control, but almost every race has been feared, hunted, or murdered, even by each other."

"You mean supernaturals killed other supernaturals?" He seemed shocked at the idea.

"Yeah. It was a long time ago, but even in the last century, witch hunters were still hunting witches."

Gabriel rubbed his temple. "Witch hunters?"

"They're human, but with a little extra, like Sally." Mira felt weighted down, thinking of her friend murdered more than a month ago. "She was clairvoyant."

"And John was a psychic, right?"

Mira nodded, and her eyes were drawn once again to the spot where she had written in blood on her carpet to stop John's madness.

When she turned back, she saw Gabriel also staring at the spot where the struggle took place. They sat silently for a while, each lost in their own thoughts. Mira reflected that despite Gabriel's earlier anger, it was a comfortable silence.

"I'm sorry you keep feeling the need to come and help me," Mira said.

There was a knock at the door and they both glanced up.

"It's not your fault," Gabriel sighed.

He looked defeated, and Mira couldn't help but worry about him. Maybe there was something she could do. She had no idea what, but she could at least try.

Remembering the bitter cold and icy rain, Mira hurried to the door. The sight of Emmit on the other side surprised her, and she pulled the door open wider to let him in.

"I am sorry to interrupt your evening," Emmit said before spotting Gabriel. When he recognized the angel, he beamed.

CHAPTER 2

MIRA WAS LESS THAN PLEASED to see Emmit, but felt a treacherous flutter in her stomach when he turned his gaze toward her. His beautiful British accent always made her toes want to curl.

"Come on in," Mira said, gesturing to the coat rack.

"I should have known Gabriel would make sure you were alright," Emmit said, hanging his long coat. "When I couldn't reach you, I was worried."

There were so many questions Mira wanted to ask, starting with 'where have you been', and 'why should you care'. She hadn't seen him for a week, after all.

"Of course I'm alright," Mira said. "Why wouldn't I be?"

"Your car was spotted. Well, what was left of it," Emmit said.

"What do you mean what was left of my car?" Mira asked, confused.

Emmit frowned and turned from Mira to Gabriel. "That was your car on the interstate, correct? On the side of the road?"

"It might have been mine," Mira said. "It died on the way home."

"You weren't in an accident?" Emmit asked.

"No. I was just," Mira waved her hand through the air, "stranded."

"I'm sorry to be the one to tell you this, but your car appears to be wrecked," Emmit said, "or so I'm told."

"What do you mean?" Mira asked. "Who's telling you this stuff?"

"Reinfield employs a great number of people," Emmit said in way of explanation. "Someone drove into your car."

Surprised, Mira turned to Gabriel, who stood and didn't meet her eye.

"I should go," Gabriel said, stiffly.

"Please, do not leave on my account," Emmit said.

Since entering the room, Emmit had gravitated towards Gabriel, though Mira hadn't noticed until he stood only a few feet away.

"You should stay," Mira said, watching to see if he moved closer to the angel. "Maybe Emmit could help us with our situation."

"No," Gabriel said. His words held a finality that made Mira bite back any arguments.

It hadn't sunk in yet that her car was wrecked. Mira persisted on the idea that Emmit's people were mistaken.

"I take it that Ian is still fighting your spell?" Emmit asked.

Mira sighed. "It seems that way."

"But the case is over, isn't it?" Emmit asked.

"No," Gabriel said. "No one will find John. At least not in this world. No one outside of this room is aware of that, though."

"So Ian is still searching," Emmit said, "and unable to discuss things with his partner." The room was silent for a few moments before Emmit continued. "Is that a wise course of action?"

"Leave it, Emmit," Mira said. "It's Gabriel's choice."

"Which is why I am surprised this is the choice he's made," Emmit said. "It puts you at greater risk."

"Don't make a big deal over it. I'm not in any more danger now than I would be otherwise," Mira said.

Emmit appeared to ignore her. "It must be grating with that constant little alert going off inside."

Gabriel glared at him. "What do you know about it?"

"More than I'd care to say," Emmit said.

"Stay out of it," Gabriel snapped. "It's none of your business."

Emmit stiffened and his voice turned cold. "I've made it my concern, where Mira is involved."

"She says nothing is different," Gabriel said.

Mira could feel a cool wash of energy that began to radiate erratically from Gabriel.

Emmit's eyes turned darker and a strange smile appeared. "And doesn't that little lie just irritate you that much more." His words came out as a taunt followed by his own power—more directed and controlled than Gabriel's.

Mira began feeling queasy as she was buffeted from all sides by energy, running hot from Emmit and cold from Gabriel.

"What's your problem?" Gabriel asked.

"I dislike the selfish direction you are taking," Emmit replied.

Gabriel took a step forward.

"That's enough!" Mira put herself between the two men.

They contemplated her in surprise, and the forces building between the two died away.

Mira scowled at Emmit. "Stop pressuring him. I cast the spell binding Ian. It's my responsibility and my karma. Leave Gabriel alone about it."

Emmit's eyes pinched around the edges. Oracle began to growl from his spot in Gabriel's vacated chair.

"Mira—"

"Shut up," Mira said, interrupting Gabriel while keeping her eye on Emmit.

Gabriel grabbed her arm and gently tugged her back. "I'll think about telling Ian," he said reluctantly. "I just need some time."

"Don't let Emmit bully you into anything," Mira said.

"My decision," Gabriel said. "Remember?" To Emmit, he added, "That's as much as I'm willing to say about it now."

Emmit didn't appear happy, but he seemed to relax. "Of course. I'm sure you'll make a logical decision in the end."

Mira took a quick breath, ready to start telling Emmit off.

Gabriel cut in before she had the chance. "It's been a long evening. I think we should go."

Mira deflated.

"I was hoping to get the chance to talk to Mira," Emmit said.

"Not tonight," Gabriel said. Again, he was so adamant about the assertion that Mira couldn't imagine anyone disagreeing with him.

Apparently, Emmit didn't feel the same way.

"I don't think it's up to you," Emmit stated.

"Tonight it is." Gabriel's voice dropped, but kept its edge.

Emmit's entire stance said he wanted to argue, but he glanced at Mira and took a steadying breath. "Perhaps you're right. Before I leave, though, I wanted to ask about Tyler."

Mira's shoulders fell, and any inclination to bicker with the two went out the window. "I still haven't heard from him. Have you?"

Emmit shook his head.

"I'm meeting with Ian again tomorrow about Tyler," Mira said. "It's been more than a week since anyone's seen him."

"I am sorry." This time, Emmit softened. "He's a talented witch. I'm sure he'll turn up soon."

Mira only nodded, not trusting her voice. Sally died a little more than a month ago. Helen had been found dead almost two weeks past and Tyler had been missing for a week. Mira and Helen hadn't been close, but her death hurt all the same.

"A conclave is being called for tomorrow night," Emmit said. "Will I see you there?"

That little internal flutter tried to deceive her again. "I'll be there."

"Any objections, Gabriel?" Emmit asked, his voice somewhat harder when he spoke to the angel.

Gabriel shrugged, looking uncomfortable at being asked.

"I'm sorry I let myself get upset." He held out his hand to Gabriel.

Gabriel looked wary, but shook hands anyway.

"It is good to see you again," Emmit said. "Thank you for looking out for Mira."

Emmit held on for a few seconds longer than a normal handshake required.

"I'll take my leave of you." Emmit walked somewhat rigidly to the door, stopping only to grab his coat. "I'll see you tomorrow, Mira. If you need anything, I'm sure some of Reinfield's staff will be in the area."

Mira wasn't sure what to say, so she kept quiet.

When he left, she and Gabriel stood in silence for a moment before Mira decided she wasn't going to hold her tongue. "Why did you tell him to leave?"

"It was..." Gabriel seemed to struggle to find the right words, "... for the best."

"He wouldn't do anything to me."

Gabriel sighed. "Probably not. He just rubs me the wrong way."

Mira rolled her eyes. "I never would have guessed that."

Gabriel shifted, looking uncomfortable. "Reinfield. Those are the guys who showed up last week, aren't they."

"Yeah."

"I'm not sure I trust them."

"Why not?"

"Are you kidding? They illegally cleaned up, and then staged a crime scene."

Mira frowned at him. "Because we asked them to. We needed them."

"That doesn't make it right. What else are they doing?"

"Mostly giving rides, I think."

"A car service? I get the feeling they're far more than that."

"Maybe," Mira said, not wanting to add anything else she knew about the service.

"Just be careful around them, okay?"

Mira sighed and rubbed her temples. "I don't know if you're saying that because they're going to hurt me or because—"

"Because I'm a cop," Gabriel broke in.

"That's one less worry, at least," Mira mumbled.

"I should go."

"I'm sorry about tonight."

"Don't worry about it. On my way home I'll call the station to see if someone can track down information about your car."

"Um, thank you," Mira said, not expecting the gesture, "but not on your way home, please. The roads have to be awful."

A small grin appeared. "When I get home, then."

"Thanks."

The next day, Mira started to leave the apartment two times before remembering her car was gone. Gabriel had left her a message telling her the vehicle wouldn't be coming back. Whoever ran into it had sent the car far beyond the realms of mechanics and body shops.

Knowing Ian wasn't a morning person, she didn't call until after eight. Ian practically jumped at the chance to meet her at her apartment instead of the office. An hour later, he showed up looking nicer than a normal day at work required.

"Thanks for stopping by," Mira said, letting him in.

"It's no problem," Ian said. He took off his coat and glanced out the window before following her into the kitchen. "Sorry about your car."

Mira took out a mug for Ian and busied herself with making coffee and tea. "In this weather, I probably wouldn't be going anywhere. How were the roads this morning?"

"Your neighborhood isn't bad. The city's mostly cleaned up, but everything in between is awful."

"Did Gabriel make it home okay last night?"

Ian raised an eyebrow at her. "I guess so. I spoke with him this morning and he didn't say anything."

"Oh." Mira felt her face go pink. She hadn't realized that Gabriel hadn't told Ian that he helped her last night.

Ian looked like he was trying out different things to say in his head. Finally, he settled with, "You two getting along better?"

"Not really," Mira said quickly. "He spotted my car on the side of the road last night and took me home. I thought he would have mentioned it."

Ian didn't say anything.

"I'm surprised he bothered to stop," Mira added, trying to make light of it.

Ian chuckled. "I told you he's not a bad guy once you get to know him. He's been preoccupied lately. I think finding John trying to kill you threw him off balance."

Preoccupied was one word to describe it, Mira thought. Gabriel's mood probably had nothing to do with John, though.

Well, less to do with John and more to do with Gabriel discovering he was an angel.

Ian cleared his throat and continued, "Have you given more thought to, um, giving him the same spell you gave me?"

Mira's forehead crinkled in confusion.

She had performed a Bind spell on Ian, forcing him not to tell any of the secrets of the supernatural community and he'd been fighting it ever sense. Then she remembered that Ian had asked her to do the same to his partner before her trip to the Ether with Gabriel and before John tried to kill her.

The request had slipped her mind, which made sense when it came down to it. Gabriel didn't need the spell to keep the secret.

Ian didn't know that, though.

"Sorry," Mira said. "With everything that happened, I wasn't sure if you still wanted that."

"With John gone, the case has grown cold," Ian said.

"But you know John did it," Mira said.

"We don't know if he was working alone, though. There's no clue as to why he did this, and we have no idea what he's planning next."

"Yeah," Mira said. She was having trouble keeping track of the lies. She knew John died. A being from the Ether had possessed John, killing him in the process. Knowing the creature was inside John, Gabriel had shot John in the chest in an effort to kill the monster.

John wasn't coming back, but she couldn't say that. She also knew John hadn't been working alone, but she didn't know what that meant.

Ian was giving her space to consider his request, which was thoughtful. Maybe Gabriel would be willing to pretend he'd been spelled by her?

"It would help if he knew about Tyler as well. His disappearance might not be related, but another person's point of view would be helpful."

"You have—"

"Another *detective's* point of view," Ian corrected.

Mira sank a little in her chair. "You haven't found anything, then?"

"No leads."

Mira wrapped her hands around her mug and stared blankly at it.

"Look," Ian said, in a kinder tone, "Tyler may have just left town unexpectedly. It might have nothing to do with the case."

Mira nodded, not actually believing him.

"Maybe we'll find out more tonight," Ian said. "Although, someone else helping tonight may be useful as well."

"Emmit and I could help," Mira said.

"I don't trust Emmit." Ian was adamant about the statement. He and Emmit had been opposed to each other from the start. "Besides, Gabriel always spots it if someone is lying. It's a useful skill to have available."

"Everyone lies," Mira said.

Ian appeared uncomfortable. "He knows I'm lying to him. He hasn't said anything since John disappeared, but he's been avoiding me."

"I'll think about Gabriel," Mira said, wondering if she could call him today and somehow convince him to come. He'd made it pretty clear that he wanted to avoid other supernaturals for now. "Are you ready for the conclave?"

"Why don't they just say it's a meeting?"

"Because the community has been gathering for more than a century. Are you ready to talk to everyone?"

"As ready as I will be. Will I know anyone?"

"Barney might be there," Mira said. "He usually came with John, though, so it's hard to say."

"I didn't realize he and John were so close," Ian said.

"John was... is a psychic," Mira said, hastily correcting herself. "Barney is a seer. The powers aren't similar, but the effects they have on a person can be the same."

"Do you think Barney had anything to do with this?"

John had mentioned using Barney's blog, postsfromtheether. com to get messages from the Ether. Either way, it didn't bode well for the real world, and certainly not the supernaturals. But, was Barney actually involved?

"You saw him," Mira said. "He rarely leaves the house. Without spells to block the Ether, he'd barely function. I doubt he's been helping John."

"Well, I'll talk to him again tonight," Ian said. "Who else will be there?"

"I'm not sure. Many people aren't keen on a human showing up."

"I'm trying to track a serial killer targeting their—your people, and them hiding out isn't going to help matters."

"Hiding is what we do," Mira reminded him. "Humans have targeted us throughout history."

"It's not likely we'll start burning people at the stake again."
Mira flinched.

"Sorry," Ian said. "I just mean, society has changed."

"People don't change that much," Mira said. "Besides, some of them hold positions where having a cop aware of them isn't going to make their jobs any easier."

"Such as?"

"Take Della, for instance."

She couldn't help but notice Ian smile and sit up a little straighter. "She works for the district attorney's office. I know you would never hold her supernatural status against her or try to leverage the knowledge to your advantage, but other people might."

"She knows I would never... I mean, she doesn't have to worry about... Does she think I'd do that?"

Mira shook her head, trying to hide her own knowing smile. "Della isn't concerned. She never worries about things like that, but others might."

"Will she be there tonight?" Ian asked.

"Yeah, I'm sure she'll be there." Mira knew all too well Della would show up. Her friend stopped by two days ago after work and tried to subtly find out more about Ian, what he thought about their world, and—more importantly—had he said anything about Della. "Remember, she helped me introduce you to our world."

Introduced was a nice word. Della had worked with others to scare the hell out of Ian while, at the same time, proving that the supernatural world existed.

"Having an assistant district attorney there may help the case," Ian said.

Mira shrugged. "We don't talk about what happens at the conclave out in the real world."

"Never?"

"There was a reason I had to bind you. Since Helen and Sally had only ever met at a conclave, there was nothing I could have said about them knowing each other. If I hadn't spelled you, there would have been no connection between any of the victims."

"Except Sally and Tyler," Ian said.

The idea hit Mira like a cast iron cauldron. She'd never thought of Tyler as a victim. Only... missing.

Ian noticed the look on her face and rushed to correct himself. "Not that he's wrapped up in this. We have nothing to tell us there was foul play in his disappearance."

"Have you been to his house?" Mira asked.

"We've stopped by, but that's all."

"You haven't been inside?"

"Only the first day, just to ensure he wasn't injured or something. Like I said, there's no sign of foul play."

"Maybe there's something you didn't recognize," Mira suggested. "Let's go over there."

"We don't have a warrant," Ian said. "It's not even my case."

"I don't need a warrant. I'm his friend."

Ian hesitated. "I'm not sure it's a good idea. Not until I can let Gabriel in on things."

Mira slumped back in her chair. "You really need to talk to him about all this, don't you?"

"I've said that since the beginning."

"What if he just met up with us at Tyler's? We wouldn't have to tell him about any of the supernatural stuff."

"If you find anything... out of the ordinary... he'll know that you're lying about it. He's been suspicious of you before. I'd rather not go down that road again."

CHAPTER 3

A WEEK AGO, MIRA WOULDN'T HAVE suggested Ian's partner join them for anything. Before Gabriel had learned the truth, he'd procured a warrant and searched Mira's apartment, all behind Ian's back. But, things were different now, even if Ian didn't know why the situation had changed.

"I'll risk it," Mira said. "I want to go to Tyler's house and I want you all to go with me."

Ian appeared ready to argue.

"Or, I can go by myself."

"If there's some sort of evidence about Tyler's disappearance, or of the murders, you could contaminate the scene."

Mira's eyes narrowed. She wanted to defend Tyler and insist he couldn't have anything to do with the deaths, but she couldn't be positive. Mira had a bad track record of trusting people who betrayed her—college had become a disaster when she had trusted the wrong person.

Then there was her current life. She had been certain Sally wouldn't harm anyone, but after Sally's murder, it turned out she'd blackmailed a ton of people. Before Mira and Gabriel were pulled into the Ether, she had taken a disturbing peek into John's mind. Thoughts of Tyler had flown through her from John, but she couldn't tell if it was because Tyler helped him or had been hurt by him.

She couldn't be certain. Not one hundred percent, anyway.

"I guess that means you all will be coming with me?" Mira asked.

Ian seemed lost. "Maybe we should leave Gabriel out of this."

The lies were bearing down on Mira and affecting everyone. "If the worst happens, we can consider bringing Gabriel in on everything."

He appeared perked up by the idea. "I'm sold, but I need to make some calls first."

Another department handled Tyler's disappearance. Ian made them aware that he and Gabriel would be entering the house, with permission, due to their case. With a city as large as this, it wasn't surprising that quite a few people went missing, some for a few hours, others never to be found. Ian and Gabriel received the approval they needed without any hassle.

Mira also needed to reach out to a few people. She started with Tyler's sister. As siblings, the pair had never been close, but she was Tyler's only relative in the area, and Mira wanted to make sure his family knew she'd be opening Tyler's house to the detectives. His sister was thrilled about movement on the case. Mira talked longer than intended because of the worry and concern the woman had. She also left a message for Della.

The thought of calling Emmit flashed through her mind, but the previous night had ended on a bad note, so Mira wasn't in a hurry to reach out to him. Besides, she would see him at the conclave later that evening.

Once outside her neighborhood, the roads turned treacherous, especially in the residential areas. Mira was almost happy that her car had been totaled. It gave her a built-in excuse not to drive. By the way the crow flies, Tyler didn't live too far away. By driving, however, the ten miles turned into twenty-five.

Tyler lived in an old brick house with a deep porch. The snow and ice from the past week laid nearly untouched in his yard and driveway. Mira stared at it before getting out of the car.

The house felt empty. Not in a way that indicated Tyler would be returning soon, but a more permanent sense of abandonment.

When Ian got out, Mira was hesitant to follow. It had been her idea, but now she wasn't so sure. She couldn't pinpoint if she was more worried of finding something grim in the house or finding that there was nothing at all.

She heard Ian and noticed that he and Gabriel stood on the sidewalk talking and glancing at her. Mira forced herself out of the car and into the freezing air.

They looked... the best word for it was strained. The two men that walked into her shop a few weeks ago were gone. Those partners had been in sync and comfortable with each other. Now, a palpable disconnect could be felt.

Mira knew she'd caused the rift and the knowledge weighed her down.

Gabriel nodded to her in place of a greeting. She gave a weak smile and returned the gesture.

"Do you have the key?" Gabriel asked Ian.

"I have it," Mira said. She fumbled in her pocket and held the key out.

"Let's get inside, then," Ian said, taking the key. "I hope the heat's still on."

Mira hadn't thought about that. She stared at the house again and wondered if anyone would come by to take care of it. Indentations in the snow indicated someone had been there, but fresh precipitation filled the prints.

Mira followed Ian, trying to step where he stepped, although his stride was longer, so that didn't always work out.

"The concrete is slick," Ian said. He kicked snow off his boots under the protection of the covered front porch.

For four steps, there was no railing, but somehow, despite her bad karma building by the minute, she managed not to fall on her butt. Ian rang the doorbell, waited for a moment, and tried again. Once Gabriel joined them and stamped off the snow, Ian pushed the door open.

Ian called out Tyler's name and scanned the room before stepping inside. Gabriel snapped the door shut behind them.

Stillness greeted them. It was the first time Mira had felt uncomfortable in Tyler's house.

"Let's do a quick walk through," Gabriel said.

Mira started to go with them, but Gabriel caught her eye and shook his head a tiny fraction. It didn't bother Mira to wait behind. She watched the two move from the living room to the dining room, and then disappear into a hall. The only noise in the house was their footsteps on the hardwood floors, until the heat kicked on.

Mira inspected the front room. Tyler's over-stuffed furniture, normally inviting, now felt unused. She began to search for anything that might be in the open that shouldn't be.

"Is there a basement?" Ian called.

She hesitated before raising her voice in reply. "There's a small cellar, but you have to get to it from the outside, I think." Tyler used the space for spells when he needed direct contact with the ground. She fervently hoped he hadn't done magic in there lately.

Tyler's entertainment system and coffee table were as she expected. Nothing appeared out of place, so she wandered into what was technically the dining room. Tyler never saw the point of eating anywhere except the kitchen, so he'd turned the room into a study of sorts. He had bookcases, his desk, a hutch, and an old apothecary cabinet that held a dizzying array of drawers, even if you didn't count the secret spaces that Mira was sure it must contain.

Spotting a battered text on Tyler's desk, she frowned. Someone had thrown it down haphazardly. Mira recognized it as one of Tyler's everyday grimoires—a benign spell book which some witches might keep on a bookshelf.

Tyler wouldn't leave something like that lying around. Like Mira, other witches had burned him in the past, so he always put his spell books away.

It felt invasive, but Mira went through the spells.

"Find something?" Ian asked.

Mira jumped and slammed the book shut guiltily. "Um, no. Nothing."

Ian raised an eyebrow and waited.

"It's... I don't think Tyler would have left this out. That's all."

He held his hand out and Mira recoiled.

"It's not something that he'd want other people to see," Mira said.

"Is it a journal or something?" Ian moved closer to study the cover. "I need to see it."

"Not exactly a journal," Mira said. She let out a sigh and handed the book over.

Ian's forehead wrinkled as he flipped through the pages. Mira began to scan the shelves, something she'd done almost every time she'd gone to Tyler's. The bookcase rose high above her, filled with a vast collection of fiction, non-fiction, and non-fiction hiding out, pretending to be fiction. Tyler always read and studied everything he could.

"I'm not sure what I'm looking at." Ian kept his voice so low that Mira almost missed it.

"It's a grimoire," she said, not keeping her voice as soft as his. Seeing his confusion, she explained, "It's a spell book. All witches have them."

"But, this is all old-fashioned remedies and cures," Ian said. "My great-grandmother had something similar, but I can't read all this."

"You're human. You're not supposed to be able to read it all. You're right, though, this is all basic little stuff. The parts you can't read are mostly code for the magic."

"Mostly?"

Mira sighed. "I can't—"

Gabriel stalked into the room, looking agitated. His eyes darted around, even up to the ceiling, not resting on any one thing too long.

Ian slapped the book shut, with the look of guilt obvious on his face. "Did you find anything?" he asked, far too quickly.

"Nothing," Gabriel said, striding over to Mira. "There's no one here and nothing looks disturbed. Have you seen signs of anyone else?"

"No," Ian said.

The ground began to shake. Looking around wildly, Mira saw that the whole house shook. The ceiling fixture rattled and swayed. Mira grabbed the bookshelf to try to steady herself, which didn't work since the shelf was as unsteady as she was.

More so, even.

When she put pressure on the shelf, it shifted and fell forward. Gabriel crashed into her, and Mira gasped as she slammed into the floor, too startled and confused to cry out. Gabriel's arms wrapped around her head and his chest pressed into her. Books and objects battered her arms and legs, Gabriel covered the rest of her.

The shelf itself collapsed, stopping only when it collided with the desk, crushing Tyler's monitor.

Mira held her breath while the world trembled. The unnatural movement seemed to go on forever, but couldn't have lasted more than a few minutes.

When the ground stilled, no one moved. Something shattered in the kitchen. She let out a shuddering gasp.

"Gabriel?" She couldn't bring herself to speak loudly, almost fearful that something else might fall. When he didn't answer her voice rose in panic. "Gabriel?"

He released a quavering breath of his own. "I'm okay."

His tone pulled at Mira. Trapped beneath him, she saw nothing but books and broken glass.

"Gabriel!" Ian's voice was tight. Mira could hear him trying to shift the bookcase. "Mira!"

Mira pushed some debris away; her arms were sore and her muscles stiff. Some of Gabriel's weight shifted off her and she dragged herself out from under him, turning when he slumped back down on the floor again.

"Ian! Come help me!" Mira moved some books off Gabriel.

"I'm fine," Gabriel snapped in a louder voice.

Ian came around the desk and pulled Mira to her feet. Gabriel kicked stuff away and crawled out from under the remains of the bookcase.

"Good christ," Ian said, looking over Mira and Gabriel, "are you all alright? You could have been killed."

Mira ignored him and watched Gabriel get up. He winced and shifted pressure off one of his legs. Mira felt unsteady, as though ice stabbed through her heart.

"Let's move to the living room," Ian said, "you need to sit down, both of you," he added, sizing up his partner.

He held Mira's arm and guided her to the other room. Gabriel hobbled along behind them.

"Did you..." Mira shook her head and tried to gather her thoughts around the guilt and panic. "Are you okay?" she asked Ian.

"I don't know what the hell just happened," Ian said. "Nothing fell on me, though."

Gabriel took a chair and Mira watched him closely, not sure of what to say.

"You have some quick reflexes," Ian told his partner.

"He does," Mira said in a quiet voice. "Thank you."

"You okay?" Gabriel asked.

"Yeah," Mira said automatically.

He winced.

"I'm not hurt or anything," Mira added. "Just shaken."

"That's one word for it," Ian said. "What was that?"

"An earthquake," Mira said.

"I've never been in an earthquake," Ian said.

"I have," Gabriel said.

"Yeah, but we don't get earthquakes here." Ian reviewed the room covered in contrary evidence. "At least, I didn't think we were supposed to."

"Did we find anything in the house?" Gabriel asked.

"It's going to be impossible to see if anything else is out of place, now," Ian said, avoiding the question.

"We should take another look around," Gabriel said. "One of us should check the cellar to see if it's still standing."

"Good point," Ian said. "I'll go. I'm not sure anyone checked it earlier."

"Don't go in if it doesn't seem safe," Gabriel said. "We'll take a last look around the house."

Ian hesitated, glancing at Mira.

"It's set away from the house," Mira said. "You'll see the mound and a clay pipe sticking out of the ground." When he still didn't move, she added, "I'll finish checking the house. It's no problem."

"I'll be right back," Ian said, leaving from the front door.

Gabriel snorted when he left. "He doesn't want you and me to be alone."

"He's afraid he'll have to explain something," Mira waved a hand around, "unexplainable. He doesn't like lying to you."

Gabriel shrugged. "I'm not ready to say anything."

"You wouldn't have to," Mira said. "We can just tell him I told you the truth."

"I'll think about it."

Mira nodded and didn't push it.

"You're sure you're not hurt?" he asked.

"You were right," Mira said. "You came in from another room to put yourself between me and something ready to pummel me. This can't continue."

"Just answer the question," Gabriel said, not letting her detour him.

"I'm not injured," Mira said, standing up. "I'll go check the rest of the house."

In Tyler's office, she saw that Ian had dropped Tyler's spell book. She picked it up, checked the cover, and riffled through the spells, examining the pages for bends or tears. Seeing it wasn't harmed, she put the book under her arm and went to the kitchen.

It was a mess. A cabinet hung awkwardly on the wall, some doors had jostled themselves open, and debris littered the floor.

Mira explored the disaster, unconsciously straightening things as she went.

Mira didn't immediately notice Gabriel. She found that he watched her while leaning against the doorframe.

"You should stay off your leg if it's hurt," she said.

"I'm fine."

"So *you* can lie, but no one else can?"

Gabriel rolled his eyes and came into the kitchen. "Nothing's broken, anyway. On me, I mean. This place is a mess."

Mira nodded and turned her back, putting on the pretense of checking the contents of a cabinet. Tyler didn't keep anything important inside, but her eyes were starting to water and she didn't want Gabriel to see.

She tried to think of something else. Something besides the fact that she stood in one of her best friend's house, worried she would never see him again. Thinking about Gabriel and Ian sucked as well. She had damaged their relationship and wasn't sure how to fix it.

Then there was Gabriel himself. She was stuck with a guardian angel that shouldn't be guarding her. He was going to get himself hurt and it was her fault.

"It looks like a tornado tore through this place," Ian said. "Not an earthquake."

Mira didn't look up. She only moved to another cabinet, one where Tyler kept a few important—although benign-looking—objects.

"We've been called in," Ian said. "Everyone has. The whole city was hit hard."

"Let's talk in the other room and let her do her thing," Gabriel said. Louder, he added, "If there's anything you need to check, check now."

Mira nodded and they left. Finally alone, Mira gripped the edge of the counter and squeezed her eyes shut. The earthquake had been too reminiscent of the earthquakes that had hit the shadow the city cast in the Ether. One more thing to add to the gaping hole she'd dug for herself. Seeing Gabriel limp out was another source of regret.

One more thing for karma to grab hold of and raise her debt.

She pushed the thought out of her head. Tyler was what mattered here, and stopping Gabriel from throwing himself in front of the karmic bus was more important than earthquakes.

Concentrate on what you can do, Mira told herself. She didn't know how to break Gabriel's promise, but maybe there was some way to lesson his exposure. Her hand strayed to her neck where her pentagram used to lay. The trip to the Ether and the fight with John drained the ward it had contained, which was no small feat. It was reduced to a regular necklace and the memory of the boy who made it for her.

Nevertheless, the protection had helped when it counted. If she made one for Gabriel, it might be possible to reduce his risk. Once she thought that over, she figured making one for Ian couldn't hurt, either. The case was almost as dangerous for him. Once she got home, she would start the process of creating wards for the partners.

She didn't know many of Tyler's secret compartments, but she didn't see any that had popped open under the strain of the earthquake, which was good.

She took one last glance around the room. Mira was fairly certain Tyler didn't keep the important stuff in the kitchen, and there was no way to tell if anything had been moved around before today, because everything had shaken itself up. On her way out, she pressed on molding, tapped the floor with her foot at a few likely spots, and knocked on the doorframe. Everything seemed normal. In the hall, she heard Ian and Gabriel talking from the living room. Knowing they were busy, she slipped into Tyler's spare bedroom and looked around.

There wasn't as much wreckage here. Mira's chest relaxed a little, seeing that not everything of Tyler's was ruined. The hardwood floors squeaked as she moved across the room to the closet to the only private spot Mira was aware of.

Witches rarely shared all their secrets—not even with other witches. Family was the only exception most witches would make. Still, she and Tyler had worked together quite a bit, and they'd each shared some of their spells and hiding places. Inside the closet, Mira shifted some boxes aside and crouched down. She pushed hard on the floorboards until they creaked, and then, while pushing down, she lifted up the wide baseboard.

It was tempting to poke her hand straight in, but after the earthquake, she had no clue what bottles had opened and mixed. For that matter, she also didn't know what Tyler might have stashed in there. She patted her pockets for her phone before realizing she had left it in the ruins of her store.

She went to the kitchen and searched Tyler's junk drawer, coming up with a small flashlight. Ian and Gabriel were still having their hushed discussion, so she went back to the bedroom to check the contents of Tyler's hiding spot.

Everything that she expected to be there was there. She shifted a few packets of ingredients around. A few bottles weren't labeled, which was odd for any witch. It spelled a recipe for disaster if you forgot what you'd stored.

Having blank potions wasn't unheard of, though. Tyler was careful, so if he didn't label something, it was probably for a reason. The labels wouldn't tell most people what was inside the bottle, but families had their own language for labeling. Mira knew many of Tyler's codes and symbols, and noted that the other mixtures were normal stuff.

One of his more important spell books was here as well.

A packet made Mira uncomfortable and she snagged it out, stowing it in her pocket. The seer's potion. Tyler often made it for Barney. She hadn't seen Barney in over a week, and with Tyler gone, wondered if anyone had made sure Barney received everything he needed. Maybe she could get Ian to stop by when he took her home.

Satisfied, Mira slid the baseboard back into place and shifted the boxes back. She closed the door and looked around the room, not sure what to check next.

There probably wouldn't be much of anything in his room. Possibly a grimoire, but everything else, witches tended to keep out of the bedroom. She gave the remaining rooms a quick glance, concentrating more in the laundry room. Tyler had added the room onto the house, so she knew he kept things in there. She just had no idea what or where it might be.

The important thing was, nothing showed. Once she'd satisfied herself that Tyler wouldn't be exposed as a witch, she went back to the living room, finding Gabriel alone there, poking around the stuff on Tyler's entertainment system.

"Where's Ian?" Mira asked.

"He went in to work. I told him I'd catch up with him."

"I'm surprised he agreed to that."

CHAPTER 4

GABRIEL MADE A NONCOMMITTAL GRUNT and continued his search. Mira watched and realized he was doing some of the things she would have done when trying to find a witch's hiding places. He pressed the moldings and anything decorative, he ran his hands along the inside of cubbyholes, and checked above and below drawers.

Mira grinned. "You've learned some bad habits. Stop that."

He turned, looking surprised. "Isn't that what you're doing?"

"No. I'm checking the places I know about already. If I open a concealed compartment that I've never seen before, how am I supposed to know if anything is out of the ordinary inside?"

He shrugged and went back to inspecting the woodwork. "He could be hiding something."

"Of course he's hiding something. He's a witch."

"Do you think he could be keeping things from you?"

"I know he is. That's the way we work."

Gabriel kept prodding. "Did you find anything in the other rooms?"

"Tyler didn't put away a spell book. It's not like him to do that. The spells are basic—ones he might show other witches—but Tyler wouldn't leave it out."

"Mind if I take a look?" Gabriel asked.

Mira hesitated, but realized she had already shown Ian, so she handed it over. "It's not something I would normally share, especially since it isn't mine."

Gabriel flipped through the pages, occasionally stopping to read a few lines. "Find anything else?"

"Not really. It's hard to tell if anything was disturbed in the kitchen."

"Do you want to check anything else?"

Mira glanced around the room. "No. I don't think there's anything further I can do here."

"I'll take you home," Gabriel said, giving her the book back.

"Mind if we make a stop on the way?"

"I think that's going to depend on what it's like outside. I'm not sure what kind of damage the city might have, but I imagine the traffic is going to be bad."

"It's important," Mira said. "I'd like to check on Barney." Mira explained about the seer and the spell she found which had reminded her Barney might need a refill.

"We'll try to get there."

Mira checked the back door, ensuring she'd locked it. On their way out, she made sure the front door was secure as well. The frigid air tried to bite into any exposed skin, but she still took her time on the icy stairs. The last thing she wanted to do was fall in front of Gabriel—especially after he'd stepped between her and a bookshelf.

In the car, she waited patiently for the heat to kick on and her eyes were drawn to Tyler's empty house again and again.

"We'll do all we can to find him," Gabriel said.

"I know," Mira said. She couldn't muster a positive attitude, though.

"You two are pretty close, I take it."

"We are."

"How long have you been seeing him?"

"We never dated. We've been friends for years, though."

"And he usually helps this guy, Barney, with spells?"

"We both have at some point."

Mira stared out the window. Too much seemed to be piling up at once. Tyler was still missing, Ian and Gabriel were at odds, bad karma lurked around every corner, and then there was Gabriel himself. His future held pain and agitation if he kept dragging her out of the way of anything that might harm her in some way.

Karma could wait. Tyler and Gabriel couldn't.

"Ian's going to your meeting tonight, isn't he?" Gabriel asked.

"Um," Mira had to run the question through her mind again, "yeah, if he can get away from work. I guess." After a few heartbeats, she added, "You're invited, too, of course."

"Why's that?"

"You're one of us. All supernaturals are invited, assuming they stick to the rules."

"What rules?"

"Regular ones, really. No fighting or snacking on anyone. No turning inside the house. No spelling or using magic against someone. No magic if it might cause harm, um... there's no threats or vendettas, and killing is prohibited."

Gabriel chuckled. "Those are normal rules?"

"For supernaturals they are."

"Is Ian going to be the only one there without super powers of some sort?"

Mira laughed. "We don't have super powers. And there will be other humans as well."

"How did they get an invite?"

"Only humans with a little extra attend. Like Barney as a seer and John... well, there are lots of different abilities that humans might have that would earn them an invite. Seers, psychics, witch hunters—"

"You mentioned witch hunters before. What are they?" Gabriel broke in.

"They don't hunt witches anymore. William is a witch hunter, and he and Tyler are actually good friends."

"We should talk with William."

"He wouldn't hurt Tyler. He's just talented at spotting witches."

"How does it work?"

"I never wanted to know the details, but you know how you can tell someone is lying?"

"Yeah."

"It's similar. At least that's my understanding. Like I said, I didn't want to know too much about it, and I didn't get the feeling William or his family wanted to share."

Gabriel didn't say anything for a moment, seeming to let that sink in.

"You know," Mira added, bracing herself to dive into the conversation, "if something goes wrong at a meeting, you can't come running in."

"Can't?"

"Absolutely. Can. Not. The rules don't apply if they don't know you."

"And if they know me?"

Mira sighed. "If most of them know you are a supernatural, it won't matter if you barge in. They'll assume there's a reason. That's really not the point I was trying to make, though. You were right last night. I'm not your responsibility."

Gabriel winced.

"I'm not sure if there's anything I can do," Mira continued, "but I'll try."

Silence permeated the car. Mira wondered if she should say anything else, but since she had no idea what that might be, she stayed quiet.

"It feels... important," Gabriel said after a while.

"What do you mean?" Mira asked.

"When something is about to happen, I feel the need to be there."

"So, you don't feel like you *have* to be there, but you feel like you should be?"

Gabriel gripped the steering wheel. "I haven't tried not to go. It just feels wrong if I don't."

"How do you find me?" Mira asked, interested, despite the fact she wanted his compulsion to end.

"I just know where you are."

"Do you see me or something?"

"No. I get in my car and go. It's kind of like driving on auto pilot."

A glimmer of an idea spring up. "That's how we could stop it. I could hide myself from you somehow."

His knuckles went white and he concentrated hard on the road. "I'm not sure I like the sound of that."

"It's worth a try."

"Maybe," Gabriel admitted, and then he grinned. "Don't want me around?"

"It's not that. You can come visit me anytime you want. It's just..." Mira grappled with words to match her feelings on the issue. "You shouldn't be compelled to pick me up beside the road at night or jump in the way of falling bookshelves. It's not right."

"I wouldn't say I'm compelled—"

"Good," Mira interrupted. "That just means it'll be easier for you to stop."

"And if something happens to you?" Gabriel asked.

"I'm not defenseless, but if something happens, it happens. That wouldn't be your fault."

"So I should have let the bookshelf fall on you?"

He had been half grinning when he said it, but Mira's response was adamant. "Yes."

He shook his head, but said nothing.

"I'm surprised the streets aren't worse," Mira said after a while.

"Me too." He sounded relieved in the change in subject. "While you run in and talk with Barney, I'll wait in the car and call Ian to see what's going on."

"I thought you wanted to talk with Barney?"

"Ian should talk with him."

"We need to discuss you and Ian as well. He needs you on the case."

"I'm not ready to start telling people I'm an angel. I don't even believe it. It seems less and less real each day."

"You don't have to tell anyone."

"How does that work?"

"No supernatural is going to ask what you are, or if they do, you can choose to ignore them, because it's extremely rude to ask. If you don't want to tell Ian, we can imply I spelled you, just like I did him."

"Imply?"

She shrugged uncomfortably. "I've caused enough trouble between the two of you. I don't want you both to have to lie to each other anymore."

Thankfully, Gabriel didn't have the chance to reply. He pulled to a stop in front of Barney's building and she hopped out right away.

"I'll be a few minutes," she said before shutting the door on any response.

The sidewalk had been salted, so Mira hurried into the apartment building. The hallway held the same chill as outside. She was grateful to be in the cold for once. She had a feeling warmth would make the smell of rotten eggs stronger.

Mira knocked on the door and waited, bouncing up and down on her toes in an effort to keep warm. There was no sound from the apartment, so she knocked again, louder this time.

"Barney," she called through the door, "it's Mira. I was in the area and wanted to stop by."

"Mira?" Barney said.

Mira jumped, startled to hear him almost directly on the other side of the door. "Yeah. I'm sorry I didn't call first. I don't have my cell phone on me."

Locks began to click, and Barney peeked out. The security chain rattled as he confirmed it was her. He snapped the door shut and dropped the chain.

When he opened the door again, it was barely far enough for her to squeeze in.

As a seer, Barney looked old. Mira didn't know if he aged because he spent time staring into the Ether, or if seers naturally grew old faster. He appeared almost twice her age when he actually wasn't much older than she was.

"I wasn't expecting anyone," Barney remarked. He ran a hand through his hair and refused to look at her.

"Sorry. I figured since Tyler wasn't around—"

"Where did he go?" Barney asked.

"Oh." Mira had expected others to know about Tyler's disappearance. When she thought about it, though, she supposed it might not be common knowledge outside the witches. "He's... he's been gone for about a week now. Did anything break in the earthquake?" She glanced around, trying to find reason to keep the subject changed.

Barney looked around as well. "That was real? It was here?"

"It was," Mira said, carefully, "but you look like you weathered it."

He stared around the room.

Seers didn't always handle their abilities well. It had to be difficult constantly to see things no one else could.

"I brought tea in case you wanted it," Mira said. "Did anyone let you know there's a conclave tonight?"

"John told me yesterday," Barney said, his head bobbing up and down.

Ice struck Mira's heart and began to filter through her veins. "John did?" She couldn't keep her voice steady. "Yesterday?"

"Yes. He usually stops by each week. William called today. He's picking me up."

"Did you... was John here?"

"Are you?"

Mira gave him a smile—which felt as though it trembled— and handed him the tea. "I am."

"That's good. Thank you for the tea. John said I should avoid taking it, but he never really understood."

She nodded, afraid to ask when John had said that. She

struggled to catch her breath without knowing any more. He'd seen John, or thought he saw him, yesterday.

John died. A creature had possessed him, and Gabriel had shot him through the chest. There was no way...

But, Barney was the one saying this. Sure, he's a seer, but maybe he remembered something from a long time ago.

Or something he'd thought would happen, but couldn't now that John was dead.

That must be the case. It was the only thing that made sense.

"I've got someone waiting for me." Mira reached for the doorknob, ready to get away, "but I'll see you again tonight. We should talk."

He smiled. "I'd like that."

As she opened the door, his eyes went blank and he stared at nothing. A coolness began to steal over the room. Mira froze. The Ether closed in on Barney, allowing him to peer into probable futures. She wanted to run and she berated herself for not thinking this through.

Mira had never been comfortable with the wall between the worlds thinning out, but now that she had been to the other side, the experience had become so much worse. Her imagination showed her dark beings stretching out to her. She had been sucked into the other side before. How easy would it be for them to pull her through again if she was around Barney?

"You alright?" Barney asked.

Mira blinked and saw Barney was back to normal. Fear still had a tight grip on her.

"Good," Mira said in a bitterly cheerful voice. "I have to run. See you later!"

She hurried out the door and out of the building. Not caring if karma kicked her on her ass on the icy sidewalks, she rushed to Gabriel's car, desperate to put more space between her and the Ether.

She felt childish when she jumped in the car and pushed the button for the locks. Then she pressed it again, just to be sure, before trying to get her chest to unfreeze.

"What's wrong?" Gabriel asked.

Mira shook her head. "Let's go."

"No. What happened?"

"Please, just go," Mira said.

In the space of a few heartbeats, Mira thought he would argue. He cast a confused glance at the building before putting the car in gear and leaving.

As the distance between her and the apartment grew larger, her lungs began to relax. She slumped back in her seat and closed her eyes.

The spark of adrenaline had gone by unnoticed when the Ether approached, but as she calmed down it left her exhausted.

"You good now?" Gabriel asked.

She nodded automatically. "Fine."

"Don't do that."

"Do what?"

"Lie. It's like a squeaky balloon or fingernails on a chalk board." After a moment, he added, "Plus it aggravates the hell out of me."

She chuckled under her breath. Seeing his point, she opened her eyes and looked around, noting they were well away from the apartment.

"Sorry, it's a habit."

"What happened?"

How did she start? Being close to Barney shouldn't bother her so much, and she didn't want Gabriel to freak out either.

"It shouldn't have upset me. I just didn't think about it."

"Go on," Gabriel prompted when she stopped.

"Did I tell you how seers work?"

"You told me they see a possible future, and it sounds like hell to be one."

"Right! And they get confused sometimes about futures, and what they may have had as a vision about in the past, they sometimes remember in the present."

He thought that over. "It makes sense, I guess. So, what did he see?"

"He told me John talked to him yesterday."

"What? But—"

"It couldn't have happened," Mira jumped in quickly. "And logically, I know that." She gripped her seatbelt. "But, he seemed certain John spoke to him and told him about tonight's conclave."

Gabriel's tensed. She could practically feel his mind racing, trying to figure it out.

"I think," she continued, "that he must have seen a possible future where John was alive, and he's mixed it up with real life."

"How—" He cut off and looked like he struggled with the concept. "How could he confuse the two?"

"I think it would be fairly easy," Mira said. "He sees so much. Some of it happens and some if it doesn't. That can't be... well, it wouldn't keep me stable for long."

"Does he get things mixed up often?"

"I'm not sure, but when I asked him if John had actually been there, he asked me if I was actually there."

Gabriel relaxed. "I get it. I think I do, at least. I can see why it bothered you."

"That was the start of it, anyway."

"What was the rest?"

"Maybe we should wait till we're back at my apartment. I need a few minutes, and telling you while you're driving isn't the best time."

"Now you're scaring me. It's fine, so you can tell me now."

"It wasn't a big deal."

Gabriel frowned and rolled his shoulders.

"Sorry," Mira said, recognizing his discomfort when what she said wasn't exactly truthful. "What I should have said was it *shouldn't* have been a big deal. I overreacted to something completely normal."

"Normal?"

"For supernaturals, anyway."

"Which is a whole new normal for me."

"I know."

"I give. It can wait."

CHAPTER 5

T HE WAIT WASN'T LONG ENOUGH for Mira, mostly because once she was safe back in her apartment, she started to feel foolish for letting herself get so worked up over what had happened.

"This is good tea," Gabriel said.

"Thanks, it's my own blend," Mira responded, looking around the room. The damage to her apartment didn't match the wreckage of Tyler's house, but she definitely had some work in front of her.

She scratched Oracle behind the ears and the cat gave a deep, rumbling purr, which made her relax and feel better overall. Alchemy was sitting stately on the arm of Gabriel's chair, but he leaned into the angel's hand anytime Gabriel stroked his fur.

"I'm embarrassed I let my visit with Barney upset me," Mira said.

"What happened?"

"He had a vision."

Gabriel didn't say anything and looked like he was waiting for the rest.

"I know I mentioned this before, although we were talking about something else at the time." Mira shifted in her seat, uncomfortable with talking about the Ether.

"You'll have to tell me again."

"It's the way seers see things. When a psychic sees things, they see what's really going to happen, but don't see it far into the future. Not usually, anyway. When a seer sees the future, it's a possible future and it could be about anything in the world. It's undirected and uncontrollable."

"So they see things in a different way."

"Right. There used to be oracles as well. They could see far into the future *and* target what they wanted to see. At least that's my understanding. There aren't any oracles left, though, as far as I know."

"And oracles are important because...?"

She shifted in her seat. "They aren't, really. But each of these people see what they see in different ways."

"Makes sense. So, how does Barney see the possible future?"

"He looks into the Ether."

Gabriel eased back in his chair and folded his hands together.

Oracle purred, and then rubbed into Mira's arm once before leaving her for Gabriel. Once Oracle jumped on his lap, the angel appeared to thaw and stroked the cat.

"Are you saying," he said after gathering himself together, "that he has a way to look into the Ether?"

"The Ether kind of... comes to him. It's hard to explain. He had a vision while I was there, and the room chilled and it felt..." Mira remembered the sensation of someone reaching out to her and she shivered. "It felt like the Ether was closing in."

"Does he control it?"

"No," Mira said quickly. "It comes and goes as it pleases. The tea I took to him should reduce its effects, but it can still happen."

"And you let me take you to his house?" Gabriel looked incredulous.

"It's fine. I told you I was over reacting. It's natural for the Ether to come to him like that. I've been around him loads of time when that happened. It's not like I can see the Ether."

"Can those creatures on the other side see him?"

"I have no idea. Until a week ago I didn't even know things lived on the other side."

"You should avoid being around him," Gabriel said.

"That doesn't sound very fair to him. He has a hard enough time the way it is."

Alchemy decided not to vie for attention and joined Mira while Gabriel silently thought over the new information.

"He doesn't control it?" Gabriel asked.

"No."

"What it—" He stopped and shook his head.

"What?"

"Is it possible that he saw John from the Ether?"

"John's dead," Mira said flatly.

"He was pretty lively after he died."

"That sounds awful."

"It does," Gabriel agreed.

Mira let the thought seep in, even though she wanted to avoid the idea completely. "Maybe I can ask Barney a few more questions tonight."

"You're seeing him tonight?"

"At the conclave, yes, and I'm telling you, if you go, you need to go *with* someone. You can't just show up."

"The hell I can't. What if something happens?"

"You said it's important, not imperative. Tonight, you're going to ignore the feeling of wanting to help until it goes away. Besides. Emmit will be there. I'll be fine."

"I don't trust him," Gabriel said.

"Do you trust that he'd help me? Besides, you have two choices. You can come with Ian and me, or stay away. It's time to make a choice."

He made the wrong choice.

Mira didn't think she'd need Gabriel at the conclave, and she didn't anticipate there would be cause for him to come charging in. Ian needed him, though.

Once Gabriel had left the apartment, she started purifying wards for the partners. At the time, it felt like the only thing she could do to support them. She spent the rest of the afternoon straightening up her apartment.

Ian arrived at Mira's dressed nicely in a sweater and slacks, and drove them the short distance to Lance's house.

"Anything I should remember before going in?" Ian asked, holding a few files as though they would shield him.

"Don't ask people what abilities they have unless it is absolutely necessary to the case," Mira reminded him. "There will be werewolves and elves here, so assume anything you say can be heard even when you are nowhere near them."

Ian tugged at the collar of his sweater. "Anything else?"

"Don't worry, either Della or I will be there to help you out."

He stood at the door ready to knock.

"You can go on in," Mira said with a grin. "If everyone knocked when they arrived at a conclave, Lance would need to hire more staff."

Stepping inside, Ian took in the two-story foyer and sweeping staircase of the giant house. He had been here before while taking Mira's statement after the incident with John, but he didn't seem comfortable.

Mira showed him the coatroom and then led him into the parlor. Several rooms flowed together. As they entered, Mira noticed that every werewolf in the room stopped talking and watched him, bringing a hush to the rest of the crowd.

"Did I do something wrong?" Ian asked under his breath.

That earned him a few grins from the wolves, but the others in the room watched stiffly.

"No," Mira said. "They're wondering why a regular human just walked in."

"Didn't someone tell them I was coming?"

"It's not like we have a phone tree, at least not between races. It could be that not everyone heard a detective would be here tonight. Even if they did know, they wouldn't have known it was you."

Before Mira was done, the noise of voices began to resume, but most of the room still kept their gaze on the two. Mira smiled and nodded to a few people when she caught their eye.

"Come on," Mira said, leading him through toward the ballroom. "Let's find—"

"Mira!"

Mira turned, finding her mother coming up behind them.

"Hi," Mira said, suddenly worried about what the older witch might think of Ian being at the meeting.

Her mom embraced her and then let go. She gave Ian a not-so-friendly look before she turned back to Mira.

"How are you doing?" her mom said. "You haven't gotten hold of us all week. Your sister said you ignored two of her calls."

Mira sighed. Robin had this odd little ability that let her know if someone was ignoring her calls or texts or if they were actually busy and couldn't respond. It was an annoying trait that constantly got under Mira's skin.

"Sorry," Mira said. "Between the business being burned down and my apartment getting trashed, I've barely had time to myself."

"Of course not," her mother said. "And this is the detective?"

"Yes," Mira said, "Mom, this is Detective Ian Burke. Ian, this is—"

"Mrs. Clarke," her mother cut in.

"Mrs. Cara Clarke," Mira said. Mira tried to convey 'be nice' with only a glance, but Mira and her mother had never been on the same wavelength.

"It's a pleasure to meet you," Ian said.

"Tell me," Cara continued, "what are you doing to keep my daughter safe?"

Mira felt her cheeks go red. "Mom, I'm helping *him,* not the other way around."

"My partner and I are in close contact," Ian said smoothly. Mira couldn't help but notice that he clutched his files a little more tightly. "By phone and in person. In fact, she's spent most of her days with one or both of us. She's been an amazing help on the case."

That seemed to satisfy Mira's mother to some extent. "As long as that continues until this awful mess is over."

"We'll make sure of it," Ian said.

"We need to go, Mom," Mira said. "Ian has a lot to do tonight."

"Of course he does," Cara said. She leaned over to Ian and stared into his eyes, seeming to see beyond them. "And he could use some Refresh, Mira. If you let him get worn down he won't be able to do his job."

Mira felt the tables had been flipped and now Ian was on her good side. "I'll talk with him about it. Have you seen Della?"

"There were a few sorcerers in the ballroom," Cara said with a dismissive shrug. "Maybe she's with them."

"Great, we'll check it out," Mira said, doubting she would find Della with the other sorcerers.

Older generations of supernaturals tended to stick to small groups—witches with witches, shifters with shifters and so on. Robin melded along those lines as well. Mira and a good deal of the supernaturals under thirty had never seen the point.

"I'm also looking for Barney," Mira said.

"There are a few humans in there as well," Cara said dismissively.

"Great. I'll see you around," Mira said.

Ian stuck to Mira like glue as they entered the ballroom.

"Do you see Della anywhere? Or Barney?" Mira asked.

"Not yet. Hey," Ian dropped his voice to a hiss, "is that Judge Wilt—"

"Stop," Mira said. "Here, she's just one of us."

"Right, of course." Ian's cheeks colored slightly. "I just didn't expect to recognize anyone."

"Ms. Owens," snapped a stern voice from behind them.

Mira stifled a groan and forced her face into a smile before turning around. "Mr. Contrey, it's good to see you. Ian, this is—"

"I would have expected you to take him into the meeting room." Mr. Contrey's face was contorted making it resemble a prune. "He doesn't need to parade around here."

"We're looking for someone before he gets started," Mira said, forcing herself to speak in lighter tones than the old man. "Besides, we need to know who's here to know who to interview."

"We'll send people up as appropriate," Mr. Contrey snapped. "Having a human here is bad enough, but to have him—"

"There should be no issue with Detective Burke being here." Emmit's smooth voice sounded over Mira's shoulder. "He is an invited guest. One that is doing great service for our community."

Despite the fact that Mira was aggravated with Emmit's weeklong absence from her life, the corners of her mouth turned up at the sound of his voice. She could feel the warmth he generated standing so closely behind her.

Mr. Contrey scowled and opened his mouth, then closed it again. He repeated the gesture before clearing his throat. "I'm sure Detective Burke understands the importance of discretion."

"Oh, he does," Emmit said. "Even if he didn't, however, the spell holds."

"We expect him upstairs in five minutes," the old man said with less vigor in the face of Emmit. "There are a lot of people here and he needs to get to work."

He didn't wait for a response, and instead turned and disappeared down the hallway.

Mira tried to remove the smile before she turned, but it didn't work. "Thank you," she said, staring up at Emmit. "I appreciate that."

His gaze softened for a moment when looking at her, but then he took a small step back, inviting Ian into the conversation. Emmit began to scan the room.

"You were looking for Della I take it?" Emmit asked.

"Um, yes," Ian said, stammering slightly. "I—that is, we—thought it might be good for her to sit in on the conversations. Making sure that everyone has someone nearby that knows them."

Emmit grinned knowingly. "Won't Mira be there?"

"Actually, since Mira's been working with us, I wasn't sure how comfortable everyone would be with her in the room," Ian said. "Della hasn't been on the case. I thought people might be more relaxed with her in the room."

"That is very considerate of you," Emmit said.

"I do need to speak with her one more time before we start, though," Ian said.

"She is by the door to the sun room," Emmit said.

Ian peered around, but didn't spot the location until Emmit gestured in the right direction.

"Thanks," Ian said. He took a step towards Della and wavered, taking in the people between the two of them.

Mira took pity on him. "This way." Without thinking, she linked her arm with Emmit's to ensure that he came along.

Emmit stiffened slightly at the unexpected gesture, but when he relaxed, he pulled her closer in a gesture that made Mira's heart beat faster.

There were fewer werewolves in this room to notice the difference in Ian so they managed to go through the crowd with only a few glances.

Della smiled and smoothed out the side of her shirt when she saw them approach—a nervous gesture that Mira hadn't seen in quite a long time. By the time they were within talking distance, though, Della took on her usual self-assured posture.

"Hi," she said when they approached. "You all are causing quite the stir tonight."

"Are we?" Ian asked.

"You are," Della said. "Everyone's wondering what's in store for them this evening."

"That's kind of what I wanted to talk to you about," Ian said.

Della gave him a quizzical look.

"We'll need to talk in private, if you don't mind," Ian said. "Um, the three of us, that is."

"Of course," Della said.

"We're meeting everyone upstairs," Mira said. "There's a study up there that Lance is letting us use. More walls between us and everyone else. Not that it will stop some people from overhearing if they really want to, though."

Mira and Emmit led the way.

"That was some shake up today," Della said. "Did that keep you busy?"

"For a while," Ian said. "It was surprising how little damage it did, though. The power outage was really the worst of it."

"It wasn't what we expected either," Della said. "We didn't even lose power at the office. Traffic was a disaster, however."

"It seems strange that no buildings collapsed or anything—though I'm glad they didn't," Ian rushed to add. "Unfortunately, the hospitals are still full."

"There were that many injuries?" Mira asked as they walked up the stairs.

"You shouldn't be surprised," Ian said. "You were almost one of them." He turned to Della, becoming a bit more animated. "A bookcase started to fall on Mira, but my partner's reflexes are amazing. He ended up taking the brunt of it."

Mira felt her cheeks color.

"Gabriel is exceptional in that area," Emmit said, patting Mira's hand.

Mira couldn't help but feel stilted when Emmit didn't appear the least bit concerned.

"Wow, Mira, are you okay?" Della asked.

"Uh, I ended up with a few bruises," Mira said, "but that's all."

Emmit seemed surprised and gazed at her up and down as though he would be able to see the blotchy marks.

"But like Ian said, the bookcase really fell on Gabriel."

"I tried to get him to go to the hospital to have his leg checked out," Ian said, "but he said it would be a waste of time."

Mira was relieved when they reached the study door. Emmit appeared unexpectedly troubled and she gave him a worried look. He gently squeezed her arm before letting go.

"Is there anything I can do to assist?" Emmit asked as they filed in.

"Actually, there is," Ian said. "Um, people seem to... well... defer to you."

Emmit said nothing.

"We put together a list of names," Ian continued, pulling a piece of paper from a file. "We know the people on the list are familiar with some of the victims. We're looking for more people who knew them. Especially if they knew all of those attacked."

Emmit took the list and read it over. "I think I'll get Lance to help with this. He does know everyone much better than I do."

"Thanks," Ian said.

Ian waited until Emmit was out of sight before turning to Della. "Would you mind sitting in on the interviews today? I think it would make everyone a little more comfortable to know you're here."

"Of course," Della said.

"There may be times, however, that I ask you to leave the room. Both of you, that is, if someone is uncomfortable with you being here."

"Has there been any indication so far that John wasn't working alone?" Della asked.

"Nothing concrete," Ian said. "I need to follow up everywhere I can. Now, how should we get started? Is it okay for me just to call people in?"

"It might be better to go through one of elders," Della said.

Mira nodded in agreement.

"I'll trust your judgment," Ian said. "Also, I do have a few questions for Della before we get started. Mira, would you find one of the elders and give them the list?"

Mira took the list, and with her back to Ian, she waggled her eyebrows at Della. While Ian shifted some files, Della winked at Mira with a confidence that Mira never felt, especially with a guy she liked. That was her friend in a nutshell, though. She was going to make a great prosecuting attorney one day.

She left the others alone and made her way downstairs again. Mrs. Vears was the first elder she saw, which worked out well. She was on the list since she could connect two of the victims in a way that couldn't be exposed before Ian was bound.

"Mrs. Vears," Mira said when she approached.

"Miss Owens, it's good to see you."

Mira couldn't help but smile. Mrs. Vears was in her late sixties or early seventies, but she had a vitality to her that could make a person forget that she was an elder.

"It's good to see you, too," Mira said. "We have a favor to ask you."

"Is it my turn to be interrogated?"

"Um... I..." Mira stuttered, unsure what to say.

Mrs. Vears, on the other hand, laughed.

"Ian... uh, Detective Burke, that is, wanted to speak with you," Mira said, catching her stride. "But that's not the favor."

"Anything for the detective," Mrs. Vears said. "If I was thirty years younger... well, I'd still be too old for him, but we certainly could have loads of fun."

Mira grinned. "We have a list of people that we're starting with. After he's done talking with you, we were hoping you could kind of help things move along and get the next person."

"That's a smart idea." She took the list and reviewed the names. "I can see this is going to be a long night if you're going to fit all these people in. Is he ready for me now?"

"Yeah."

"Good, I'll tell Marvin to start moving that way. He's old and not going to last long tonight. Might as well get him started in that direction or you'll miss him."

"That's a good idea," Mira said.

"This isn't my first stroll through the park," Mrs. Vears said.

Mira wondered what she meant by that, but decided not to ask.

"I'll keep things running smoothly. Does Detective Burke need you?"

"Not really. Della is going to be sitting in tonight."

"Oh good. Mr. Contrey was looking for you. I think I saw him go into the dining room."

Chapter 6

MIRA KNEW THAT WHEN THE conclave met at Lance's house the elders always convened in the dining room.

"We met earlier," Mrs. Vears said. "We were very sorry to hear about what happened to you, but it is a relief to start getting some answers. I just couldn't believe John was involved."

Being reminded of having a loaded shotgun pointed at her didn't do anything good for Mira's nerves. "I'll go find Mr. Contrey. Let me know if you need anything."

It wasn't a smooth escape when Mira hurried away, but no one could know that John had been sucked into the Ether. It felt as though the others could glance at her and jump to the conclusion. Any mention of the Ether would drive the witches into a fervor. If any of the supernaturals found out she had been in the Ether, her own mother would probably disown her.

Mira wondered if her betrayal would kick off a witch burning just for her. Flames danced in her imagination, which distracted her enough to bump into William.

A witch hunter. Would witches use a witch hunter?

She pulled herself back to reality when she realized William had said something. "I'm sorry, my mind was somewhere else."

"No problem," William said, glancing around the room. "I wanted to run into you. Not literally, of course, but it works just as well."

Mira gave a halfhearted laugh.

"I was wondering if you've seen Barney."

"Yeah, I stopped by earlier today. Is he around? I wanted to ask him something."

"That's the problem," William said. "When I went to pick him up, he didn't answer the door."

A wash of guilt fell on her. "Barney was having a rough time, I think. With Tyler gone, he ran out of anything spelled to help lessen the visions. That's why I went to see him."

"I didn't think about that. Is he set now? Sucks that he gets overwhelmed like that."

"Yeah, we'll make sure you're able to keep him stocked up."

William looked troubled. "Is there any news on Tyler?"

"No, I went by his house today with the detectives, but I have no clue where he might have gone."

"You don't think he—" William caught the look on Mira's face. "I'm sure he's fine," he said, the words jumping out. "Tyler's always prepared for anything."

"Yeah." Mira's heart weighed her down, so she tried to bring some levity to the conversation. "He may not be ready for the mess his house is in when he comes home though. We were there for the earthquake and it looks like someone locked a raging minotaur inside."

William grinned. "We can help him out when he gets back."

"You bet." Mira sniffed and stared around the room, trying to hide her misery. "I need to go find Mr. Contrey. I'll see you around."

"Yeah," he said as she whirled away, "see you later."

Weaving in and out of the small crowd of people wasn't hard. For some reason, people seemed to step out of the way and avoided her gaze when they saw her coming. At the double doors to the dining room, she stopped for a moment and squeezed her eyes shut so tears wouldn't have a place to build up.

When she entered, she saw that others were with Mr. Contrey. Five of the twelve elders—thirteen, if you counted Emmit—

were present. She never thought of Emmit as an elder. They didn't have to be old, but they were usually the oldest of their race in the area. As a Harker, Emmit was the only one of his race around, but even a race of one got a seat on the council.

"Shut the door behind you," Mr. Contrey snapped.

Off to a great start, Mira thought as she closed the door.

Lance's dining room was large enough to hold thirty people at the table, but the council members present were bunched up together at one end—much unlike the actual council meetings where they spread out, each race trying to distance themselves from the others.

Not for the first time, Mira wished that the older generations got along better. Although, these five appeared to be cozy.

"You wanted to see me?" Mira asked.

"Tell us what is going on with the case," Mr. Contrey said.

Mira glanced at the others, feeling uncomfortable with the abruptness, but they seemed content to let Mr. Contrey take the lead.

"You know everything I do," Mira said. "We went to Tyler's today, but didn't find anything."

"And the rest of the week?"

"Ian—I mean, Detectives Burke and Flint worked on the case. They took all the evidence from my apartment." She tried not to think about the fact that most of that evidence had been falsified to keep the truth hidden. As far as everyone except her, Gabriel, and Emmit knew, John was alive, but on the run.

"Detective Flint is working with Detective Burke?"

"Yeah, they're partners."

"Why isn't he here tonight?"

"I'm not sure he would come. He doesn't... I mean, he hasn't been spelled." Mira knew Gabriel would keep the secret, but they didn't.

"You haven't bound him?"

"No. We discussed this at the last conclave. I'm working with Detective Burke."

Mr. Contrey's face, already pinched, contorted and his voice grew louder. "That was more than a week ago. You need to move this forward."

Mira didn't know what to say to the scandalous nature of the request, so she stuck with what they had discussed at the last conclave. "A witch can't go around binding people on the spur of the moment. There are consequences. I thought you knew that." In fact, she was positive they knew. Mr. Singer had mentioned the implications, and they all knew how karma worked when dealing with anything supernatural.

"We don't care about that—"

Mr. Bartels put a cautioning arm out, and Mr. Contrey broke off and changed tactics.

"We want John caught." Mr. Contrey's harsh tone didn't change. "Tyler is missing, and now no one has heard from the Hendersons. Whatever you did with one detective is working. Now bind the other. More, if necessary!"

"The Hendersons?" Mira asked. This was the first she had heard of anything new happening.

"Yes! They—"

The door popped open and Mira's relief took place of the confusion and embarrassment Mr. Contrey caused, when Mr. Singer and Noah entered. Mr. Singer glowed with fury, and Noah took his aggravation out on the door by slamming it shut.

"What are you doing?" Mr. Singer asked, glaring at the council members.

Mira had expected him to yell, but he held back.

"I'm not sure I know what you mean?" Mr. Contrey said, his voice losing all hints of malice, although his face was crimson.

"Noah has just informed me about what is going on," Mr. Singer hissed. "You're in here bullying one of our witches into something more dangerous than she's already done."

Mr. Contrey slapped his hand on the table. "Listening in on council meetings is prohibited. Anyone caught—"

"You dare threaten to throw me out!" Noah yelled.

No one wanted to be near a pissed-off werewolf. Not if they were sane.

"This isn't a council meeting!" Noah continued. "If it was, we would be in here!"

Mr. Contrey's nose wrinkled. "I would have thought you of all people would want this over with. Helen was one of yours."

"One of ours, you mean," Mr. Singer spat.

"And we do want this over with," Noah exclaimed, "but not at the cost of someone else!"

"That's ridiculous!" Mr. Contrey's face turned redder until he was flushed all the way down his neck. "Another binding or two isn't going to make a difference. Besides, it's..." He waved a hand at Mira in disgust.

Mira went cold. People knew that she had made some mistakes in previous years.

Mr. Singer sneered at those at the table, and all but Mr. Contrey turned away. "Mira is a very helpful witch doing every one of us a great service, at her own expense."

"She's done worse for her own gain," Mr. Contrey said.

It was true. In her college days, she had strayed so far into the darker sides of magic that it had almost killed her, and she had barely noticed. Addicted to her own creation, the spell Bliss, meant that she hadn't cared until another witch had made her see the effects.

However, that was witch's business. That should only mean the witches didn't like her, didn't it?

"This is helping everyone," Mr. Bartles said in a calming voice. "The karma will balance out."

Getting upset won't help anything, Mira told herself. *What would Della do if she were here?*

"Mira," Mr. Singer said, not looking at her, "it's time for you to go. Noah, please let the other elders know we are reconvening now."

Della would keep her head tall and own the room. The best Mira could do was stand up straight and refrain from running to the door.

When she touched the handle, the ground beneath her began to shake.

The whole room appeared to convulse. A few yells came from the other rooms. Noah ripped open the door and dragged himself and Mira to stand in the more stable doorway.

Mira could hear the chink of glass and worried that the chandeliers might fall. Within seconds, however, the shaking stopped. Several of the council members hadn't even made it under the table.

Mr. Singer stood stock still in the middle of the room, not bothering to go for cover. Instead, he gazed around, as though searching for something. Mira had no idea what he was looking for, but it ended with a look at Mira that made her feel like she was being inspected for defects.

When his glare resumed, it turned on the council again, allowing Mira to let out a deep breath. Once again, all kinds of scenarios about the witches discovering that she had gone to the Ether filled her mind. She had been in the other world during her first earthquake.

In the Ether, the world had shaken, and now... Mira didn't get the chance to finish the thought. Emmit appeared at her side as though he morphed into existence instead of walking across the house.

"Is everything okay?" Emmit asked, addressing his question to her.

"Um, yeah," Mira said, feeling unsteady, "we're all fine here."

Emmit nodded and inspected her before turning his attention to the others.

"If you would join us, Mr. Harker, we are reconvening the elders," Mr. Singer said, not willing to be derailed.

Emmit nodded. "Thank you, but I'll decline at this time."

Mr. Singer turned, his eyes darting to Mira and back to Emmit pointedly. "This one I think you will want to be a part of."

Emmit frowned. "In that case, how can I object?"

"I'm sure the detective still has a while to go," Mr. Singer said, addressing Mira. "But you may want to check on him before asking your mother to take you home."

"Oh." Mira wrung her hands, feeling as though she'd been dismissed for bad behavior.

"I'll call you tomorrow," Mr. Singer added.

"Right," Mira said.

She turned to Emmit, but he watched the elders, trying to search for meaning in the chaos.

"I guess I'll see you around?" She hadn't meant it to be a question, but it came out as one.

"That is a certainty," he said, still not looking at her.

She let her hands drop and turned her back on everyone.

Despite being ousted, she checked on Ian. Walking mutely through the house, she ignored others who practically bristled with energy after the tremors. Their activity seemed to suck more life out of Mira and she was thankful to make her way upstairs to the empty landing.

They had tried to guilt her into binding yet another person. More, even. The first time around, she had volunteered. It had even been her idea. Now the entire plan felt off kilter. What had she been thinking, binding someone against their will? A part of her tried to remind herself that she had started this for Sally. Mira wanted to find her friend's murderer. The fact that Sally had been abusing her own power, hurting other people, made Mira feel lost when trying to decide if she had done the right thing.

"Everyone okay downstairs?"

"What?" Mira asked.

Ian looked worn around the edges. He hadn't even been at it for that long. Or had he? So much had happened that it seemed like an eternity had passed.

"I asked if everyone is okay. You know, after the quake," Ian said.

"Oh. Yeah." Mira glanced down the stairs to the still excited voices. "I think everyone's okay."

"Are you?"

"Sure," Mira said, but she shook her head and scanned the foyer below. "Where's Della?"

"She ran downstairs to check on things."

"Do you still have more interviews to do?" Mira asked.

"Too many." Ian looked as though a weight were pressing down on him.

He is bearing a heavy load, Mira thought. *And I put it there. Now they want me to do this to more people.*

Not that she would need to. It was past time for her to bring Gabriel in. He would hate it, possibly hate her for putting him in that position, but maybe there was a way she could make that up to him, or at least make it a little easier.

Mira felt life flow back into her. She would get Gabriel to help Ian, and at the same time, she'd shield Gabriel from having to worry about her. He'd be helping his partner and wouldn't have to worry about being dragged out of bed in the middle of the night because Mira was doing something stupid that might get her hurt.

She couldn't fix things, but she could make them better. The elders would be happy because they'd assume she did what they wanted her to do. Ian would be happy because he'd have his partner back, and Gabriel would be able to trade helping her for helping his partner.

Everyone wins.

Ian didn't seem to notice her attention wandering. "I hoped to talk to everyone here, but that's not going to happen. I'm getting addresses and phone numbers for everyone on our list and the few names that Emmit and Lance added. We'll have to schedule different times to meet with everyone."

"We can do that," Mira said, feeling slightly more cheerful. "Do you need me anymore tonight?"

"I can't leave for a while—"

"I'm getting a ride," Mira cut in. "If you're done with me, that is."

"Sure. It sounded like Della was going to stick around." Ian's lips twitched up as he mentioned her friend.

"Excellent," Mira said, moving back downstairs. "Call me if you need anything."

"When do you want to get started on these interviews?" Ian asked.

"Tomorrow works for me," Mira said, raising her voice slightly to be heard over the sounds echoing up from the entryway.

People were lined up at the coatroom, waiting for their turn and getting in each other's way.

"What's going on?" Mira asked when she found her mother in the queue.

"There's no cell service," her mother said. "Can you believe that? The ground rumbles a few times and now we can't even call to check on people. Your sister's already gone. Worried about the kids, of course."

Mira moved forward as her mother did. "Would you mind giving me a ride home?"

"Of course I don't mind, but I'm surprised your young detective isn't taking you."

"Della's working with him tonight. I'm off the hook."

Her mom leaned in and lowered her voice. "Has the spell settled yet?"

Mira shrugged. "Mostly, but he's still fighting it."

"Your father was like that. Stubborn as hell."

"Ian's just frustrated." Mira stopped talking when they were able to slip through into the coatroom. They grabbed what they needed and got out of the way.

Cold air punched through her clothes as soon as they neared the door. Mira and her mother hurried down the driveway and jumped into the car, hoping against hope that being out of the fresh air would cut the chill. It didn't. They both waited impatiently for the car to produce something that came close to warmth.

"How are you doing with the spell?" her mother asked as she drove out onto the street.

Mira shrugged, mostly because she had no idea how to answer that. "I'm still here and still helping."

"Nothing bad?"

"John tried to kill me."

"Don't say that," her mother said.

"Well, he did."

"I need to meet Ian's partner and thank him for helping you that day."

"I'm sure you'll get the chance at some point."

"Maybe that was all the pent-up karma? Maybe John finding you was all that negativity dropped at once, but Gabriel was your guardian angel."

Mira wanted to steer clear of that territory. "It could be. It's only little stuff now."

Her mother turned into Della's driveway. "I'd love to stay, but I need to check on the house. Do you have everything you need?"

"Sure, I'm good."

"Where's your car?"

CHAPTER 7

MIRA FELT BETTER ABOUT HAVING a direction to move toward, but trying to convince her mother that everything was fine had dragged Mira's mood down into the mud. It felt like a relief when she finally wished her mother a good night.

A small part of Mira... no, that was a lie even to herself. A large part of Mira thought Emmit would come over. She thought for sure he would want to speak with her after the council meeting. In the prospect of seeing Emmit, Mira stayed up late, but as the time dwindled by, she gave up hope.

In the morning, though, Mira bounced back. Helping Gabriel would solve so many problems all in one go. Convincing him to talk to Ian might be difficult, but she was determined to make it work.

First, however, she needed to make the potion. Luckily, she didn't need to get someone else to take it—it was for her.

How do you hide from an angel, and not just any angel, but one forced to help you? Mira knew her books well and knew they didn't hold any information about guardian angels. Kindling a small dream that she had overlooked something, she pored over the books anyway, pausing only to check on the progress of the wards. They sat in water mixed with some special ingredients to purify the metal and to help amplify the spell.

It was late in the morning when she conceded that she had no specialized information on angels or any other winged supernatural.

Witches were known for being resourceful and inventive, so Mira began to gather known spells to cobble together something new. Several other supernatural races made pacts and promises that were far deeper than the mundane human versions, which gave her a place to start.

When a knock came at the door, Mira glanced at the clock, surprised that it was almost noon and the morning had slipped away without her notice.

The stacks of books might be a problem. She thought of taking a few moments to stash at least a few of them, but dismissed the idea when the knock came again.

After reminding herself that she could use the excuse she was an occult specialist, she went to answer the door. Relief filled her when she opened the door to Gabriel, but it quickly turned to anxiety. Her eyes immediately began to dart around, trying to find anything that might fall on her or that she might trip over.

Gabriel's worn face broke into a small, sad smile and he shook his head. "I'm here to talk, nothing else."

The muscles in Mira's shoulders unwound themselves from the knots that had threatened to form. "Come in. You look like you could use some coffee or something else highly caffeinated."

"I wouldn't say no to coffee," Gabriel said, taking off his jacket.

Mira took it to hang it up and frowned. "How are you staying warm in this?"

"You haven't been outside today, I take it," Gabriel said.

"No." Mira hung the coat and led him to the kitchen. "I've been working on some things."

"The temperature's up today," he said.

"That's good. Take a seat and I'll make some coffee. Sorry for the mess."

"You've had a busy morning." Gabriel sat down and pulled a random book towards him.

"I'm coming up with a new spell."

"Can you do that? Just come up with something new?" Gabriel asked.

Mira glanced at him surprised to find that she didn't care he was inspecting one of her books. "Of course I can. That's what witches do."

"I thought you used old spells. I pictured old spell books passed down for hundreds of years." Catching her eye, he shrugged. "Or something like that."

"There's some of that. My parents gave me spells and I've shared some with a few other witches, but spells need to adapt and change with the times."

"That makes sense, I guess," Gabriel said, flipping through a few pages without really seeing them.

Mira freshened her tea. When the coffee was ready, she poured some for Gabriel and joined him. "You didn't come here to talk spells, did you?"

Gabriel shook his head and mutely flipped a few pages.

Her heart felt squeezed, and she tried to ignore the fact that the amount of concern she felt delved much deeper than she anticipated. "What's up?" The comment came off as off-handed and she inwardly cringed at the overcompensation.

"How did things go last night?"

"Oh, yeah. Not bad, I guess. "Della ended up sitting in on the interviews. I..." As she thought about the pseudo meeting with the elders, the weariness she felt last night threatened to overwhelm her again. "I just chatted with some people."

Gabriel looked concerned and Mira had to stomp down butterflies that threatened to flutter around in her stomach. "What—" He broke off and shook his head, looking back down at the book. "How did Ian do?"

Gabriel had obviously caught the lie, and she felt as though she should be relieved he hadn't pried further—and she was in a way—but a flicker of disappointment was there as well.

"He... well, there was a lot for him to do. He didn't get very far, but he has a list of names that we're following up with." Mira glanced at the clock again. "I'm kind of surprised he hasn't called yet."

"I'm sure he will soon." He didn't sound happy about the fact. "He tried to talk to me, but got ticked off and gave up. We were busy this morning at the office and he left a while ago without a word."

Mira bit her limp and wrung her hands together. "I'm so sorry."

"For what?" Gabriel asked without looking up from his study of the book.

"Because it sucks and it's my fault for putting you both in this situation."

Gabriel shook his head and pushed the book away. "Last week, maybe, but now? No, this is on me. I'm telling Ian this afternoon. If I can find him, that is."

"You can tell him I spelled you if you want," Mira said uncertainly. That had been her plan anyway.

"No. I'm telling him the truth. The whole thing."

"Everything? Even about the Ether?"

"Everything," he said more adamantly. "I should have done this a week ago. It's relevant to the case and he needs to know."

Mira wasn't exactly thrilled about Gabriel telling Ian about their trip to another world. "My spell doesn't cover the Ether."

"What do you mean?"

"He'll be able to tell other supernaturals about the Ether, or ask questions about it if you tell him."

"With John working alongside those things in the Ether, that might not be a bad idea."

Mira felt as though the world around her might crumble. "It would be really bad if people found out we went to the Ether."

Gabriel shrugged. "They only need to know that John was in contact with the Ether. Ian's going to have a lot on his mind. No need to overload him."

"Yeah," Mira said, trying to relax. "I guess you're right. Do you know what you're going to say?"

"Not a clue."

"Is there anything I can do?"

"I doubt it. He's not going to be happy with either of us."

Mira tried to force a smile. "I'm used to him not being happy with me. I'm sure he'll get over it, though."

"Maybe." Gabriel morosely gazed around the room, and then dragged another book over. "What kind of spell are you making?"

Mira could tell he really wanted to change the subject. "One for us."

"Us?"

"You and me."

Gabriel gave her an uneasy look.

"I'll be the one taking it," she assured him. "I'm trying to give you your evenings back."

"You've lost me again."

Mira laughed. "I'm making a spell so you don't feel the need to rush over here just because I trip over my own feet or something."

"How does it work?"

"It doesn't yet," Mira admitted. "When I'm done, though, I think it will hide me from you. Not physically, of course, but from whatever it is that makes you feel you need to rush out and find me."

Gabriel sat quietly for few moments. Mira got back to work, giving him time to think through whatever was on his mind.

"Do you think it's a good idea?" Gabriel asked at last.

"What? Of course it is," Mira said. "Like you said, this can't go on."

"But if something bad happens..." He frowned and trailed off.

"Gabriel, I'm not your responsibility. Not that I don't appreciate everything. I really do." Mira blinked as she mentally added up all that he had done.

"I didn't do much."

"You've saved my life. I probably haven't even thanked you properly." Mira looked down, feeling her face grow hot. "I'm not sure *how* to thank you, but maybe this will help some."

"Maybe—" Gabriel stopped short.

"Maybe what?"

"I don't know."

"What don't you know?"

"Everything." He crossed his arms and leaned back in his seat, watching her.

Mira rolled her eyes and went back to her notes. "That narrows it down."

"There's just too much I don't know. I'm not sure whatever you're doing is a good idea."

"You may be an angel, Gabriel, but you shouldn't be stuck being *my* guardian angel."

He sighed. "I wouldn't say I'm stuck."

"Now who's lying?" Mira asked.

"I'm just not sure how I feel about this. I know what I said the other night, but Emmit was right. I made a promise."

"You didn't know what you were doing. Neither of us did." Mira dropped her pen and leaned onto her elbows, looking at him across the table. "Why are you against this?"

Gabriel shifted in his seat. "It just doesn't feel right."

Mira stared, waiting for more.

"Give me a way to break it," Gabriel said.

"What?"

"I'll feel better if I have a way to break the spell."

"I'm not your responsibility." It came out louder than she'd intended, so she tried again in a more normal voice. "You didn't know what you were doing when you made that promise."

"Give *me* a way to break it," Gabriel repeated. "If I break it, then it's my choice."

Mira wasn't sure what to say to that. It was true. If he broke it, he would know what it meant, but did she want him to have that type of control?

And why would he want it?

The thoughts rolled around in her mind, but they were cut short when someone knocked on the door.

"Alright," she said, standing. "I'll give you a way to break it."

He seemed to relax some, but she still wasn't sure what she thought about it.

Ian waited on her doorstep, but he showed none of the tension that Gabriel had described, seeming energetic and ready to face the interviews.

"I saw Gabriel's car here," he said softly as he came into her apartment. "Do you have good news for me?"

Oh, Mira thought. *That's why he looks excited.*

"Um," Mira said, glancing toward the kitchen. "Yes and no, I guess."

He was crestfallen. "No spell, then."

"Not exactly." Mira bit her lip.

"This is never going to get easier, is it?" Ian tossed his jacket on a peg.

Mira winced. She could feel Ian unconsciously pounding against her spell.

"Hey," Gabriel said.

Mira glanced up and saw him leaning against the wall by the kitchen. Ian nodded to his partner.

"I think it will," Mira said. "Do you want me here?" she asked Gabriel.

He shook his head.

"I'll be in the kitchen, then. I've got some work to do."

"Wait," Ian said, "we have some things to go over today."

"We can shortly." Mira hurried into the kitchen before Ian could say anything else.

There was silence in the other room for a short time. Ian broke the silence by asking 'what's up,' but she couldn't distinctly hear Gabriel's response.

Once she knew they were talking, she tried to block them out. She had a spell to concentrate on, and Gabriel had given her an added element that she hadn't been expecting.

Mira assumed that a spell for an angel needed to be stronger than for a human.

Ian's voice sped up and sounded excited. Grabbing a book, Mira noisily flipped pages to block out as much a she could. Still, it was impossible not to sense Ian's agitation when Gabriel's words started to sink in.

She reminded herself that it was none of her business, but felt guilty all the same.

The spell, Mira thought fiercely. Gabriel was an angel, yes, but nothing of his true nature seemed to pass through into this world. In the Ether, he was a powerful winged fighter. Here, he was a detective. Still powerful, but not really on par with what you would expect from an angel.

Except when Emmit riled him up. Mira stared into nothing and contemplated the few times Gabriel and Emmit had clashed. A cool power had poured out of him. It was undirected and unsophisticated in comparison to the focused heat that had emanated from Emmit, but their strength was on par with each other.

Did that mean Emmit could be an angel?

No, she scoffed at the thought. Emmit and Gabriel were nothing alike. She got the sense they were on different wavelengths.

After casting the spell for Emmit, she had a good feel for him. Similar in power they might be, but they weren't the same race. Emmit was a Harker, anyway. If the secret the Harkers had been hiding was that they were angels, she was pretty sure that would have come out ages ago.

An argument broke out in the other room. Mira sighed and rubbed her temples, wondering what, if anything, she should be doing.

Tea. A nice calming pot of tea. Mira busied herself by filling the kettle and then going through her meager supplies of loose-leaf ingredients.

Meager for her, anyway. Since her store had burned down, she didn't have a varied and readily available supply of tea or spell ingredients.

She put together a calming mixture, momentarily considered a little spell work to go with it before dismissing the idea, and grabbed mugs.

Mixing the tea and filling the tea balls was therapeutic in some odd way. Even when the kettle whistled, the shrill noise didn't bother her. She turned down the stove and reached for the kettle. Gabriel's arm grabbed hers and yanked it back.

"What the—"

She cut off when the gas flames under the kettle stuttered, then shot up.

The flare had been momentary and probably would have done no more than scorch her hand, but fire was fire.

"And what the hell is that about?" Ian snapped from the kitchen entryway.

Gabriel seemed troubled and still had a grip on her arm.

"Thank you," Mira said quietly.

"I said—"

"It's nothing." Gabriel dropped Mira's arm and moved away.

"That's a load of crap," Ian said. "I thought we were being honest here."

Gabriel's jaws clinched. "You're right. It's just that I did something really stupid and don't want to admit it."

Ian snorted out a hollow laugh.

Mira turned away from them and shut off the stove. Gabriel's words, 'really stupid' stung more than she had expected they would.

"But I'm fixing it," Mira said, trying not to sound stiff. She poured the hot water into mugs. "Have a seat. I made tea."

"What's in it?" Ian asked.

Even though she couldn't see him, she could hear the sneer in his voice.

She set down both cups with more force than necessary. "It's herbal tea. There's herbs in it."

Ian looked like he was going to say something, but stared her in the face and swallowed his words. He still made no move to drink the tea.

Gabriel drank, but it seemed more out of the need to do something than anything else. Mira joined them at the table, feeling uneasy about being around either of them.

Mira thought it better to steer things in a different direction.

"Did you hear anything about the Hendersons last night?" Mira asked.

"Who are they?" Gabriel asked. He also seemed ready to change the topic.

"Supernatural family," Mira said. "Someone last night mentioned they were missing."

Ian looked reluctantly from one to the other, and then sighed. "I only heard that someone's been trying to reach them and they haven't been around."

"That doesn't sound too ominous," Mira said.

"Agreed," Ian said, "but going to their house is on my list of things to do today."

"That reminds me," Gabriel said. "Did you talk with Barney last night?"

"He wasn't there," Mira said. "William said he didn't answer the door when he went to pick him up."

"Why are you two looking for Barney?" Ian asked.

Mira tried to word her answer in a way that wouldn't make Ian more upset. "Gabriel took me over there yesterday. With Tyler gone, I realized Barney didn't have anyone bringing him the seer's spell."

"And he wasn't there?" Ian asked.

"He was there, but when we talked, he mentioned he spoke with John the day before," Mira said. "I wanted to ask him more questions about it."

Ian glared at his partner. "Why didn't you ask questions there? We need to find this guy."

"I didn't go in with her," Gabriel said. "No one else knows about me. Only you, her, and—for some ungodly reason—Emmit."

"So, I'm not the last to know?" Ian asked.

"I'd rather not tell anyone," Gabriel said. "I'm certainly not going to parade around announcing it to strangers."

Ian seemed slightly mollified since he found out before others, so he turned to Mira. "I'm surprised you didn't ask any more questions while you were there."

"He also asked me if I was really there," Mira said. "You know Barney. Besides, it's not like John could have *actually* been there."

"I didn't get to that part," Gabriel muttered.

"Oh," Mira said, staring at Ian.

"What am I missing?" Ian asked.

"Actually," Mira said, slumping back in her chair, "you're both missing so much I don't know where to start."

"Start with John," Gabriel said. "Chasing after him is wasting time."

"You want me to tell him?" Mira squeaked. The two men watched her expectantly. "I'm going to need something stronger than tea."

CHAPTER 8

DISCUSSING THE REAL STORY ABOUT how John had attacked her was more unsettling than Mira had anticipated: remembering the shotgun blast, seeing Emmit on the floor, John pointing the gun at her, and Gabriel shooting him.

Cross didn't even begin to describe Ian. Each time he tried to interrupt, however, Gabriel gave him a warning look and Ian would reluctantly listen.

"So he's dead?" Ian asked at the end. "And there's no body because he's been sucked into another world?"

"Yeah," Mira said.

"I can't tell if you all are screwing with me or if all of this is real," Ian said. "I can't see how any of this is possible, but—"

"It's the truth," Mira said.

"I've relied on him for the truth for too long," Ian said, taking another jab at his partner. "I'm not sure I know what it looks like anymore."

Gabriel pushed his chair away from the table, scraping it across the floor, and stood. "I should go."

"No," Mira said. Then—looking from one man to the other—she became more forceful. "No! Gabriel, sit down. Neither of you are going anywhere."

"Let him—" Ian started.

"No!" Mira glared at them. "I get that you're angry, but you're both going to have to suck it up and get over it."

They stared at her in surprise.

"Look, I'm sorry I did this to you two," Mira said. "I really am, but the fact of the matter is, we—the supernatural community, that is—still needs help. Another family may be missing and we need to check on Barney."

"I can—" Ian started again.

"No!" Mira snapped. "It's we. All three of us. If it's not, then both of you can get out and I'll do this on my own until I find someone else."

Mira took a moment to catch her breath. Realizing that she had essentially just yelled at both of them, she felt her face turn red, but she wasn't about to back down now.

"Ian," she said when she had more control over herself. "I know you're upset that Gabriel didn't tell you right away. I get it. I'm sure we both do," Mira added, glancing at Gabriel. "But put yourself in his shoes. Gabriel is hard-pressed to believe this himself. Seven days ago, he found out that he's an angel. Think about that for a moment."

Ian seemed bothered and looked his partner up and down. "You seriously didn't know?"

"No," Gabriel said. "I seriously didn't know."

"How can you tell?" Ian asked.

Mira hesitated. She hadn't thought this part through yet.

"I just can," Gabriel said. He seemed to be much more prepared to answer. "The fact I can tell when people are lying should have tipped me off that something was wrong with me."

"Nothing is *wrong* with you," Mira said.

Gabriel leaned on the back of the chair, gripping it.

"She's right, you know," Ian said when his partner didn't agree. "I've been working with everyone for the past week and there's nothing wrong with any of the community. Okay, there's something wrong with John, obviously, but nothing more than what could be wrong with any other human."

"It sure as hell feels like there's something wrong," Gabriel said.

Mira slapped her hand over her mouth to hide her grin.

"Oh, for christ's sake," Gabriel said, plopping back down in his chair again.

Stifling the laugh was difficult, but she managed to cut it off.

"What is it?" Ian asked, looking quizzically from one to another.

"Apparently, I can't curse anymore." Despite his words, his demeanor lightened when he glanced at Mira trying to hide her laugh.

"You can," Mira said, "it's just, I keep picturing you with wings, along with a sword and shield and stuff. You know, being all angelic. It just amuses me when I hear an angel saying hell."

"Why the sword and shield?" Ian asked.

Mira felt ready for this one. "The arch angel Gabriel was a warrior. It just seems to fit."

"I see what you mean," Ian said, finally cracking a smile. "I just can't really imagine you with those weapons."

"Good," Gabriel said. "Let's keep it that way."

"Seems kind of cruel for your parents to name you Gabriel, though," Ian said. "Especially since they didn't tell you."

"They still won't tell me anything," Gabriel said. "I'm on my own."

Mira reached out and patted Gabriel's arm sympathetically. "You're not alone."

He put his hand over hers for a moment before they both drew away.

Ian cleared his throat again, this time with a small grin. "At least we'll be able to work together again. We know John is out of the picture, but he mentioned the fact that there were others."

"And they were using Barney's blog to get messages," Mira added. "But I don't know how. I read the posts and I can't find anything that looks like it might be a message from evil creatures from the Ether."

"I'm not sure what those messages would look like, but I'd have to agree," Ian said. "I read his notebooks and blog and I wouldn't say any of his visions are messages."

"Maybe they aren't" Gabriel said. "Maybe John and his pals are just crazy—or brain washed or something."

"You think they've deluded themselves into thinking there are coded messages in Barney's visions?" Mira asked.

Gabriel shrugged. "I haven't read them, but I don't think we can rule anything out. You say you have his notebooks?"

"I have copies of some of them," Ian said. "Anything that Barney might have seen around the time of the murders."

"Good thinking," Gabriel said.

"But I couldn't find anything," Ian said.

"Mind if I take a look?" Gabriel asked.

"Sure," Ian said. "I'll bring them tomorrow. Today, we need to check on Barney and the Hendersons. Are there going to be any issues with Gabriel joining us?"

"Parts of the council were pressing me pretty hard last night to bring more detectives in on the case." Mira curled her nose up at the memory. "I should make a call or two, but I don't think anyone will mind."

"Is that what the fight last night was about?" Ian asked.

"What fight?" Mira asked.

Ian shrugged. "Most people were gone by the time things got heated up, but there were still a lot of people upset."

"What happened?" Mira asked.

"I'm not altogether sure what went wrong, but a bunch of people were in a room arguing."

"The elders?" Mira asked.

"I don't know who they were. That woman helping out, Mrs. Vears, she was with them," Ian said.

Mira nodded. "She's one of the elders. Go on."

"The only thing I know for sure is that one of the werewolves shifted in the room," Ian said. "Someone said an elf goaded him on, and someone else said magic was used first. It was a mess. The werewolf attacked someone, and Lance had it out with the werewolf."

Mira's mind filled with the horror of it. Imagining Noah attacking someone was bad enough, but Noah and Lance fighting? She covered her mouth with her hand and her eyes began to sting.

"It sounded like Mr. Contrey would have been dog food if it wasn't for Mr. Singer in the room."

"Emmit was there," Mira said quickly. It felt as though a draft of winter was winding its way around her. "Was he okay? I thought he'd stop by last night, but he didn't."

Ian cast a quick glance at Gabriel before continuing. "I didn't see him. Someone ordered Della to get me out of there. I've seen a werewolf before, but he was in control when I saw him that first night. There was no restraint last night, so I wasn't about to stick around."

"I can't believe this," Mira said.

"Della was pretty upset by it. She said she was going to call you."

"I don't have my cell phone," Mira said. "I need to call her, and I also need to check on Emmit."

"She's in court today," Ian said, " but she said she'd be home tonight."

"Do you have Emmit's number?" Mira asked, looking from one to the other.

They shook their heads.

Mira stood up and started to search for her car keys before remembering that they would do her no good. "I left my phone at the store. Can one of you take me there?"

"I'm sure he's fine," Gabriel said.

"You don't know that," Mira said.

"Take a breath," he said. "Calm down. Do you have Reinfield's number?"

"Yes! They can give me a ride," Mira rushed into the living room and grabbed her purse.

Distantly, she heard Gabriel and Ian exchange a few words before Gabriel followed her.

"I didn't mean you should get them to give you a ride," Gabriel said. "*We* can give you a ride. They probably know how to reach him, though."

"You're right," Mira said.

Gabriel passed her his phone. Mira snatched it and hurriedly dialed the number on the business card. The phone rang twice and then there was silence.

"It's Mira, uh, Miranda Owens." She always felt put off by Reinfield Concierge Services. They would do almost anything for a client, including stage a fake crime scene.

"Ms. Owens, how can we help you today?"

"I'm looking for Emmit."

"I'm afraid we cannot disclose his location."

"I just need him to call me. Can you ask him to do that?"

"Certainly. If this is an emergency, can you tell us the nature of the emergency?"

"It's not really an emergency," Mira said. "I just... I haven't heard from him and I..." She looked around the room, suddenly embarrassed, but she saw that Gabriel had left her alone. Still, she lowered her voice. "I was just worried that something happened to him last night."

It sounded as though the speaker covered the phone with his hand, which was unusual because they generally put her on hold if necessary.

The phone went silent for a few moments, and then he was back. "We can pass a message on to Mr. Harker."

"Thank you," Mira said, feeling slightly disappointed.

The man cleared his throat and dropped his voice, not whispering, but not projecting the clear tone that Reinfield employees usually maintained. "It may take a while to reach him. He was dropped off this morning and has not requested pickup for another hour." Using the clear voice again, he continued, "Should he return the call to this number?"

"Yes," Mira said, letting out a steadying breath, "I'd appreciate that."

When she hung up the phone, Mira had fewer misgivings about the concierge service.

"Everything okay?" Gabriel asked, poking his head out from the kitchen.

Mira beamed a smile at him. "I think so. They're going to have him call me back, but they, uh, let slip, that they had seen him today."

"That was nice of them," Gabriel said with no real feeling.

"I hope you don't mind, but I think he'll call back on your number."

"No problem." Again, a leaden monotony.

"Everything okay?" Mira asked, nodding toward the kitchen.

"It will be," Gabriel said, beginning to loosen up. "We're going to see Barney and the Hendersons. Coming with us?"

"She has to," Ian called before coming out of the kitchen to join them. "No one's going to talk to us without her being there."

"I thought you knew Barney?" Gabriel said.

"Even him." Ian said. "When I dropped off his notebooks after making copies, he wouldn't discuss anything. Della would talk to me, and maybe a few others, but not many. And you said no one else knows who you are."

"Emmit would talk to you as well," Mira pointed out.

"Lucky me," Ian said. "There's something wrong with that guy."

Mira put her hands on her hips and glared at him. "There's nothing wrong with Emmit."

Ian shrugged, but she was happy to see that he appeared slightly abashed.

"He's okay some of the time," Gabriel said.

Mira stopped glaring, happy to see Gabriel giving Emmit a break.

"Anyway," Gabriel said, "we should go."

"Let me grab my stuff," Mira said.

She wanted to bring so many things that she could have filled a duffel bag. Instead, she grabbed her notes before kicking the men out to give her the chance to hide her books.

Outside, Mira was struck with how warm it was. Remnants of snow clung on in shaded areas, but the rest was gone.

"I thought it was supposed to snow again tonight," Mira said, taking in the bright day. By the time she reached the bottom of the stairs, she shrugged off her jacket.

"Yeah," Ian said, "the forecasters are trying to make heads or tails of the weather, but that's almost always the case. Traffic was worse on the way over here than it was after the first earthquake. Everyone's playing hooky to enjoy the weather."

"I can see why," Mira said.

"We'll go to your store first," Gabriel said.

"Thanks," Mira said.

Ian watched his partner for a few moments, but Mira had a hard time placing the look. Now that the truth was out, though, things were bound to settle down between the two.

"You can sit up front," Ian said when they reached Gabriel's car.

"No," Mira said quickly. She wanted things as much back to normal between the two as possible. "I'll be working on my notes anyway."

Mira settled into the back seat and had a flashback of her first ride Gabriel and Ian in Gabriel's car. They'd just met her, and Gabriel had insisted on taking her to the police station for further questioning in Sally's death.

"What are you grinning about?" Ian asked, looking back at her.

"Just thinking about the last time I was back here," she said.

She couldn't help but notice Gabriel's eyes flash back to her in the rear-view mirror before he drove around Della's big house.

Ian chuckled. "It's hard to believe it wasn't that long ago. What are you working on?"

Mira tapped her notebook, while looking over the short list of information she had. "A spell."

"Is it for the case?" Ian asked.

"Only tangentially," she said without thinking. Realizing Gabriel wouldn't want Ian to know about the spell, she tried to switch the subject. "I'm not sure what I can do to help the case. I've tried searching for Tyler, but I haven't had any luck."

"Does that mean he's not in the area?" Ian asked.

"Not really," Mira said. "If he had a ward of any sort, a locater spell wouldn't work."

"Is there any kind of spell that could find out who John was working with?" Gabriel asked.

"Not that I know of," Mira said. "If we had a suspect, maybe Truth would help us, but it depends on who it is."

"You have a truth spell?" Ian asked. "That would be really useful."

"You can't force people to confess." Mira remembered that Gabriel had done just that in the Ether. He had told her to confess and she had gibbered non-stop every thought that had been in her head. "Besides, you have Gabriel, which is much better than a Truth spell. He doesn't force you to tell the truth."

"Not normally, anyway," Gabriel muttered.

Mira grinned. "Normally, he only knows if a person is lying. Knowing that already gives you all the advantage. Besides, Truth takes away someone's free will. That's super bad for your karma."

"Bad karma doesn't seem like a high price to pay," Ian said.

"It's *far* too high a price," Gabriel said.

"You must understand it more than I do," Ian said, sounding defensive. "I thought bad karma just caused little accidents. A few bumps and bruises."

"It varies," Mira said, cutting off whatever Gabriel had been going to say. "Anyway, spells and law enforcement don't mix well. There's always a more powerful witch that can cheat the spell."

"Is there a spell that would narrow down our other suspects?" Ian asked.

"I haven't been able to think of one. There's a reason we need you two," Mira said. "Magic may be able to help things along, but this needs professionals."

Ian seemed to be thinking hard on something. "If we find someone else involved, what happens if that person is a supernatural?"

"That's going to depend on who is involved," Mira said.

"Let's say it was a witch," Ian said, "what would happen? I mean, can we put a witch in jail?"

"Plenty of witches are in jail," Mira said. "We're just like any other person. We make mistakes, we pay the price."

"But a witch could do something to get out," Ian said. "Couldn't they?"

"Most witches wouldn't take the risk of being discovered," Mira said. "They'd have to be crazy to do something obviously arcane."

"Whoever is doing this isn't exactly the poster boy for sanity," Gabriel said.

For the first time, Mira realized that Gabriel was as interested in the answer as Ian was.

Mira twisted in her seat and frowned. "There are a few different options. The community of witches could bind the person, which would work for many of the supernatural races."

"But you said there's always a more powerful witch," Ian reminded her.

"Yes, but in this case, it wouldn't just be one witch. There would be thirteen working together, all convinced that binding is the correct action, and with the backing of the community. There's not much that could break that kind of spell."

"What's the other option?" Gabriel asked when she didn't continue.

Mira hesitated. This was bringing in more about the supernatural world than the community itself knew. The only reason she knew was because of her experience in college.

"There are... people that could be called in," Mira said. "Specialists, I guess you could say that deal with this sort of thing. If magic could be exposed, people will show up and make the situation go away."

"Go away how?" Ian asked.

"Look," Mira said, "it's not something that we talk about. You shouldn't even know about it. Hell, I shouldn't even know about it."

"How do you know, then?" Ian asked.

Mira bit her lip. "College," she said after a few awkward moments.

"What—" Ian started.

"Drop it," Gabriel said.

Ian shrugged. "I guess even supernaturals have their boogie men."

"Oh," Mira said, "a boogie wouldn't be involved."

Ian frowned and turned back at her. "You mean boogie men—"

"We're here," Gabriel said. "Damn, this place looks bad."

"I see what you mean," Ian said.

Gabriel noticed that Ian wasn't looking at the remains of Mira's store. Ian was looking at Mira and both of them grinned.

"Dammit," Gabriel snapped. "I'm just going to stop talking all together."

CHAPTER 9

"YOU SHOULDN'T STOP TALKING," MIRA said with a hint of laughter in her voice. "It lifts the mood." Ian nudged his partner on the arm, but Gabriel only rolled his eyes.

"I'll go in with you," Gabriel said, snapping off his seatbelt. "This place looks like it's going to fall down on its own. I'd hate to see what another earthquake would do to it."

"It's not that bad," Mira said, getting out of the car and looking at the boarded-up windows. "The fire department said the structure is stable."

"I'll wait here," Ian said, getting out of the car and leaning against it. "You two take all the time you need."

The keys jingled in Mira's hand as she nervously unlocked the door. A soot-stained mess greeted them. There hadn't been as much damage in the front room, but it was bad enough for Mira to look around glumly and curse her previous landlord.

Gabriel followed Mira into the back, which held a great deal more damage. He and Mira exited the Ether during the fire, so Gabriel had his own memories to reflect on.

Trying not to touch the stove, Mira picked up her cell phone where she had mistakenly laid it. Naturally, it was dead, but she was sure Gabriel's car had a charger.

"I guess this is all I needed," Mira said, looking around the room.

"I can't tell which version of this place is worse, here or in the Ether," Gabriel said.

"Well, the Ether had monsters chasing us," Mira said.

"And here we chase the monsters," Gabriel said.

Mira gave him a halfhearted grin. "That's the plan anyway."

"Do you have all of your—you know, stuff—out of here?" Gabriel asked.

"My stuff?"

"The witchy stuff?"

That pulled a chuckle. "My business partner and I cleared out the witchy stuff."

"What did you do with the mirror?" Gabriel asked.

She didn't need to be told which mirror. "I didn't feel good about having it around, so I destroyed it."

"I don't blame you for that."

"I never thanked you for taking care of things that night. I should have."

"Don't," Gabriel said.

"Why not?"

"I sent you out into the night alone with nothing, after just having faced monsters. It was freezing and you didn't even have a coat. I still feel bad about that. Besides, bigger things came up."

"I had a ride," Mira reminded him.

"Reinfield. I don't trust those people."

"I'd trust them for a ride, at least," Mira said. "And I trust they wouldn't let the wrong thing slip in public."

"They're discreet. I'll give them that."

"Come on," Mira said, "let's go see Barney."

Emmit called on the way to the seer's house. Mira's stomach tumbled with butterflies when Gabriel passed her the phone.

"Hello," Emmit said, "I understand that you were looking for me."

Mira closed her eyes and smiled at the sound of his accent. "Yeah, um, Ian said he didn't see you last night and I heard there was a fight."

"I understand," Emmit said, "I'm sorry that I worried you."

She waited for more, but after a moment, she realized that there was nothing else coming. "So, you were okay? Nothing happened?"

"It was a regrettable incident, but I assure you I am fine. Will you be at home tomorrow evening?"

"Yes." Mira cringed at the eagerness in her tone. "I should be home by six or so."

"Would you mind if I called on you tomorrow evening?"

"I'd like that."

"I'll see you around six, then. Please ask Gabriel if he'd be there as well."

Emmit hung up and Mira's mouth fell open. That hadn't ended as she had intended. It couldn't be a date if he asked for someone else to tag along, could it?

Mira passed Gabriel's phone back, her mind lost in thought. Did she want a date with Emmit?

Well, yes. That was a stupid question. She still remembered the heat between them when they'd kissed. It was a kiss that would have ended up being so much more if it hadn't been for other interruptions.

Then she'd almost been killed and he had disappeared for a week.

"How am I supposed to know?" Gabriel's sharp voice brought Mira out of her reverie. "Drop it."

"We're partners. I should at least know what it is you can do." If anything, Ian sounded more cross than Gabriel did.

"Nothing, okay?" Gabriel snapped. "Nothing that you don't already know."

"There's no superpower, then?" Ian asked.

"Ian," Mira broke in, "they're not super powers and you know you can't ask that."

"The hell I can't," Ian said. "I'm his partner. I need to know."

"Enough." Gabriel's voice was tinged with fire, although the energy swirling around the car held a cool note to it. "We can talk about this later."

A note of command in Gabriel's voice made Mira take note. Gabriel didn't think he had power in this world, but Mira was beginning to suspect otherwise.

The static between the partners was almost palpable. Mira took out her notebook and turned her mind to the spell in order to ignore the angst the men radiated.

She made a few more notes for the spell before Gabriel parked in front of Barney's apartment building.

"I'll stay here," Gabriel muttered. "Gotta make sure no one steals the tires."

"The neighborhood isn't *that* bad," Mira said.

Gabriel only shrugged and rolled down his window.

"Come on," Ian said, "let's see what Barney can tell us."

"I guess two people might be more comfortable for Barney," Mira said, not liking the fact that the partners were intent on not getting along.

Windows were open in one of the apartments, allowing music to spill out into a day, which seemed even warmer than a few hours ago. Someone had also propped the door open to allow the dim hallway to air out, which it desperately needed.

Ian stood aside and let Mira knock on the door.

"Barney," Mira called, "it's me again, Mira." She listened intently for any sound coming from Barney's apartment before knocking again. "I just wanted to stop by and talk and see if you needed any other supplies."

She frowned at Ian when there was still no noise from inside. Mira banged louder on the door. "Barney. If you're in, just let me know, okay? I'll go away if you want, but I need to know that you're alright." Mira bit her lip and without catching Ian's eye, she turned the doorknob.

The door swung open.

"Uh, um... Barney?" Mira called into the apartment. "It's not like him to have his door unlocked," she whispered to Ian. "He usually has several locks, the deadbolt, and the security chain on."

"Barney," Ian called, "we just stopped by.... I feel stupid calling to no one. He's not here."

"Should we check inside?" Mira asked.

Ian hesitated. "Yeah, but I'll grab Gabe first. Wait here."

When Ian went outside, Mira stepped into the apartment. Thoughts of Barney lying somewhere inside injured or worse filled her head.

She scanned the living room and kitchen, but hesitated before going any further. For some reason, his apartment, empty of everyone but her, felt creepy. It was only yesterday that she was here and felt the Ether reach out.

Still, if Barney was in there.... She took a few hurried steps, enough to look down the short hall, and saw nothing. The bedroom door was closed.

When she heard Ian and Gabriel's voice nearby, she jumped.

Glad they couldn't see her, she took a hurried step toward the door and tried to make it look as though she hadn't been looking around.

"Did you find anything?" Gabriel asked.

"I just poked my head in to make sure he wasn't lying hurt on the floor," Mira said.

"Uh, huh," Gabriel said, giving her an annoying little grin. "Well, he's your friend, so lead the way."

Mira rolled her eyes and went through the living room, inspecting things more closely as she passed in case some information could be gleaned from the room.

She stopped at the bedroom door. Opening the door seemed invasive, and she'd be horribly embarrassed if Barney was asleep inside, so she knocked.

When there was no answer, she moved to open the door.

"Don't," Gabriel said.

Mira froze, unsure what Gabriel might have sensed.

"Let me," he said. "Just in case."

She didn't want to think what it might be in case of, but since he wasn't jumping in her way, he must not have been too worried. Mira stood back as Gabriel poked his head into the room. Ian was doing the same with the spare bedroom that Barney used as an office.

"Nothing here," Gabriel said.

"Nothing here, either," Ian said, in a tone that seemed to indicate the opposite of what he said.

When Ian walked into the room, Mira followed behind him. There was no body on the floor, no blood, and nothing to indicate that something might have gone wrong.

The room felt empty, but wasn't. Barney's desk and a tiny spare bed were here. Her eyes roamed over the room to see what had Ian upset when it hit her. No boxes.

"Oh crap," Mira said.

"What is it?" Gabriel asked.

"He had boxes in here," Ian said. "Lots of boxes. He wrote down every prediction, back to when he was younger."

Mira went to the closet and held her breath, hoping that maybe Barney had just rearranged things.

There were boxes inside, but she knew right away that they were the wrong ones. Barney's cryptic filing system wasn't written on the boxes. She opened one and found notebooks. Unfortunately, they were the blank ones. She pulled one out and flipped through it, just in case.

Ian grabbed one and handed it over to Gabriel. "Barney had hundreds of notebooks, all exactly like this. We need to search the house to see if Barney stashed them anywhere." Ian's voice held a professional edge. He was a detective and this was his job.

Gabriel did the same thing. They spoke as they moved through the apartment, though Mira stayed put. She flipped through a few more blank notebooks in a fruitless effort to find anything of use.

Looking around the room, she wasn't sure what she should do next. Should she help search? Was this a crime scene now? Should she call someone? Mira was at a loss.

She gravitated towards Barney's desk. Barney updated his website, postsfromtheether.com, regularly, so he probably spent a lot of time at that desk.

After moving the mouse around, the screen came alive, but it looked as though a password was needed to access it. Nothing near the computer had the password written down.

"You okay?" Gabriel asked from the door.

"Yeah," Mira said with a dullness to her voice that made the lie obvious, even without Gabriel's skill.

For once, though, he didn't say anything.

"Do you know if anyone has a key to his house?" Gabriel asked.

"I'm not sure. William might know," Mira said.

"Would you mind giving him a call? I don't want to leave this place open."

"Is this a crime scene?"

"There are no signs of foul play here. From what you and Ian have told me, it could be that Barney went away on his own."

"He's not crazy," Mira emphasized.

"I get that, but he does seem to have a hard time with things. Maybe the community can find out for us."

"Maybe. I think I have William's number in my phone."

"Ian and I will finish up here before long." Gabriel passed Mira his car keys. He looked at a loss for what to say.

Mira wasn't much better. Neither of them wanted to admit that Barney could have met with a bad end, but the thought lurked on the fringes of Mira's mind.

Outside, Mira found she wasn't comfortable standing around and talking on the street, so she got in Gabriel's car, rolled all the windows down, and then made her call.

"Hey, William," Mira said when he answered.

"Hi, I was going to call you today."

"Really? What's up?"

"I wanted to know if you'd heard anything about Tyler."

Mira's heart sunk at the reminder. "Nothing yet."

"Oh, I was hoping that with the earthquakes and the freaky weather, he might have reached out to someone."

"Not yet. Um, I was actually calling to ask you about Barney."

"I'm afraid I haven't heard from him."

"When you came over last night to pick him up, was his door unlocked?"

"He never leaves his door unlocked. There was no answer, and I couldn't hear him, so I left."

"Do you have the keys to his place?"

"I think I have two out of three of the locks. Why? Is he home?"

Mira hesitated, unsure of what she should say, but Gabriel asked her to check with the community. "He's not and his door is unlocked." There was silence on the other end of the phone. "William?"

"That doesn't sound good," William said eventually.

"Ian and Gabriel are taking a look, but they said his place isn't a crime scene or anything. But they did want to make sure the doors were locked."

"I'll come over," William said.

"Do you know of anywhere Barney might have gone?"

"His parent's house," William said. "He goes there every now and again. If he's feeling... you know, up to it, he'll visit people."

"Do you have his parent's number?" Mira asked.

"I'll call them. I'll make some other calls as well. Have you let the elders know?"

"Not yet, but I will." She wasn't looking forward to speaking with the elders. After hearing about what happened last night, she wasn't sure whom to turn to.

"It should only take me fifteen minutes or so to get over there."

Mira laid her head back on the seat. It was Mr. Singer she had to call. He had been planning on talking to Mira today anyway, but she had no idea what to say.

She took a deep breath while looking up his number and held it through the first two rings.

"Good afternoon, Mira," he said when answering.

"Hello, Mr. Singer," she said.

Mr. Singer paused. "Is this about Sybil?"

"Sybil? Um, no," Mira said, her heart freezing. "She's from Robin's coven, right?"

"We're having trouble finding her," Mr. Singer said.

"How long has she been gone?" Mira asked.

"She was at the conclave last night, but there was a coven meeting this morning and she wasn't there. She's also not at home. We've called almost everyone."

"I haven't seen her," Mira said. "Any word on the Hendersons?"

"No." His voice sounded dull.

"I was actually calling about Barney." Mira's kept her voice low, her normal voice sounding suddenly too loud for her. "No one has seen him since yesterday. He was supposed to be there last night. William is reaching out to his parents."

"We'll wait until we hear more before incorporating him into our calls. About last night..."

Mr. Singer seemed hesitant to go on, so Mira stepped in. "I'm sorry for all the trouble at the meeting. I'm not sure exactly what happened after I left, but I didn't intend—"

"Never mind that," Mr. Singer cut in. "It's what I walked in on that I wanted to discuss."

"Oh." Mira had no idea what to say. She knew she hadn't done anything wrong, but it still felt like she was being called into the principal's office.

"The way Mr. Contrey went about things shouldn't have happened."

The way he went about things? "It wasn't something I expected," Mira said carefully.

"I think everyone has started getting more anxious. There have been several disappearances this week. People are... concerned that Detective Burke alone may not be enough assistance."

"Yeah," Mira said, allowing a trace of the bitterness she felt mar her words, "I got that last night."

"The witches are meeting later today." Mr. Singer spoke more slowly, as though considering every word before speaking them. "We may discuss finding a volunteer to bind—"

"Detective Flint is helping now," Mira interrupted. "Don't ask anyone else."

"Two is more than any one person—I mean, one is more than any one person should consider, but two." He didn't sound upset by the fact, though, Mira noted. If anything, he sounded relieved.

"I didn't," Mira said.

"You didn't bind him?" Mr. Singer's voice rose an octave. "Telling a human without council approval is not a rule that can be broken. Not for this. Not for anything."

CHAPTER 10

MIRA WAITED FOR MR. SINGER'S short tirade to be over. "But killing myself is okay?" She hadn't intended to say it, but there it was.

Mr. Singer didn't say anything for a few moments. "I understand that you've been put in a difficult position."

"Right," Mira said hotly, "I didn't need to break any rules to tell him."

"I'm not sure I understand," he said, slowly.

Telling him that Gabriel was an angel was out of the question. Even telling Mr. Singer that Gabriel was supernatural went against protocol, but it was either that or risk them trying to bind her power and banish her from the community.

Having to say anything about what she was doing ticked her off, though. "Well, I wouldn't want to say anything I'm not supposed to." She noticed tears falling and she wiped them away. They only fueled her frustration.

"He's one of us?" Mr. Singer asked.

"It's a breach of protocol to ask such a thing," Mira said.

"If you can't be certain—"

"I'm positive," Mira snapped. "He didn't know, and now that he does, he's not interested in letting anyone else know."

Mr. Singer let out a slow breath of air, audible through the phone. "People will assume he's bound. At this point, I don't think anyone will ask, so let them believe what they want."

"I'm sure he'll appreciate that," Mira said tightly.

"You may want to let your mother know. She thinks—I mean she's worried things might get bad," Mr. Singer said.

"They already are," Mira all but yelled, then took a steadying breath, realizing that she was the one that had signed up for this. "She doesn't need to know that."

"If there's something we can do, I mean, there are ways to deflect—"

"You know as well as I do that would only makes things worse in the end."

"That is true. You are a strong witch, though. I'm sure you'll be okay."

"Sure enough that you were going to ask me to do it again," Mira muttered.

"With Tyler gone, you may be one of the few outside of a coven—"

"It's a moot point now," Mira said, trying to get a grip on herself.

"Well, let us know if there's anything we can do." Mr. Singer sounded lost.

"Right, I'll let the others know about Sybil. One of them will call you."

"It might be better for you—"

Mira sighed. "Goodbye, Mr. Singer."

She ended the call, not waiting for a reply.

They had been going to ask her to do it again. Sure, he said that they were going to meet about it, but she could tell by the tone of his voice that they wanted her to volunteer.

She closed her eyes and laid her head back against the seat. She felt as though she'd been shunted away. They'd probably figured she was already a lost cause, so they might as well have her go all out.

They probably thought it would kill two birds with one stone. Get what they needed by having more officers involved, and get what they wanted: a powerful witch that they thought had strayed too far off the beaten path out of their way. Eventually, anyway.

You did volunteer for this, Mira told herself. *This is on you.*

Maybe they just thought she was strong enough to manage binding two people. She'd like to think so, but she really didn't think that was the case.

"You okay?" Gabriel asked, leaning into the passenger window.

Mira jumped and quickly wiped her face of any dampness she may have missed. "Sure."

Gabriel opened the door and got inside. "Want to talk about it?"

"God, no. William is on his way over and I let the elder witch know about Barney. They are going to wait until they hear more from his parents or William before adding him to their phone tree."

"Phone tree?" Gabriel asked, raising an eyebrow.

"Witches won't use a computer. They contact each other by phone, each person calling two others down the line, making sure everyone gets the news they need."

"Sounds sensible, I guess."

"Mr. Singer will tell the other elders. I have no idea how they pass information around. Um, I also told them that you were involved in the case now." Mira braced herself for Gabriel's disapproval.

"Better you than me," he said.

Mira frowned, but relaxed some. "I thought you'd be upset."

Gabriel shrugged. "I'm going to have to take your lead here. I'll need to talk to people at some point. Do they know what I am?"

"No," Mira rushed to fill in the details of her conversation with Mr. Singer.

"So, no one but Mr. Singer knows I'm supernatural?"

"Not unless you tell them or if you start showing up at meetings or something."

Gabriel nodded. "And he's the one that has you so upset? It's not me, is it?"

"No," Mira said, "it's about me. Me and the witches, that is."

"The other witches are upset about something?"

"I don't want to talk about it. I did find out that Sybil, one of the coven witches, has gone missing."

"No wonder you're upset." Gabriel sat up straighter. "Why didn't they call us?"

"They're still checking with everyone. They'll let us know later today."

A car pulled off the side of the road a little ways up the street and William got out. Mira pulled down the visor to check for a mirror and found it covered with papers clipped to the visor. It looked like takeout menus. She snapped the visor up and used the rear-view mirror to check and make sure her eyes weren't puffy or anything.

"On the way home, Ian and I grab lunch and food a lot," Gabriel said, gesturing at the hidden menus, "when we carpool."

Mira smiled and nodded to the man approaching the building. "William's here."

"He's the witch hunter, right?" Gabriel asked.

"Yes, but he's also a friend," Mira said. "Don't let his title sway your judgment."

Mira got out of the car and called to William who stopped before entering the building. She hurried around the car up the path, Gabriel trailing behind.

"Thanks for coming on such short notice," Mira said.

William looked troubled and didn't wait for any niceties. "His parents haven't seen him."

"I see," she said, more to stall for time than anything else.

"Who's this guy?" William asked.

"This is Detective Flint," Mira said, then introduced the two. "It's okay to talk in front of him."

"Mr. Contrey is going to get an earful when people find out," William said.

"What do you mean?"

"My dad was still ranting about Mr. Contrey when I spoke with him this morning. Dad was in the elders' meeting for the humans yesterday."

"I didn't know he was an elder," Mira said.

"Sometimes he is, sometimes he's not," William said. "We're not quite as put together as some of the other races. Still, it's not fair what he did." William glanced at Gabriel and back to Mira again. "You're going to be okay, right?"

"Don't worry," Mira said, "this may even help things."

"I can't see how," William said, "but I'll take your word for it. Right now, we need all the help we can get, though that doesn't make it right."

"Finding everyone is what's important now," Mira said. "Did Barney's parents call one of the elders?"

"No," William said, "they won't have anything to do with the community, but I'll call."

"Let's make sure the detectives have all they need," Mira said.

"William, do you mind if I talk to you for a few minutes?" Gabriel asked. "Alone."

"Is that okay?" William asked Mira.

"It's up to you," Mira said, "but it's okay to talk to him."

"If it helps, I'm game," William said. "Here are the keys."

Mira took the keys and left the two men alone on the front lawn. Inside, Ian was poking his head into cabinets.

"Find anything?" Mira asked.

"Nothing," Ian said. "He has fruit and some milk in the refrigerator. Most people would toss that out if they had planned on going away, but I'm not sure if Barney would or not."

"I'm no help there."

"Do you want to take another look around? See if anything is out of place?"

"Sure." It wasn't something she was thrilled about doing—it felt intrusive. She couldn't get over the fact that Barney could walk in at any minute and freak out because people had gone through his stuff.

This time through, she tried not to touch anything, but took a close look at everything.

It wasn't a large space, so it didn't take much time. "Nothing seems out of place," Mira said after finishing the circuit of the apartment. A coolness washed over her and she froze on the spot.

The feeling of people watching her—of standing next to her—was so real that she jerked her head from right to left, expecting to see people. She closed her eyes and took a steadying breath. It had to be her imagination. Barney wasn't here. There was no one to receive a vision, so it couldn't be the Ether pushing into the world. It wasn't possible.

When she opened her eyes, she half expected to see the leathery creature from the Ether. There was nothing to see, but she didn't need her eyes to know that the Ether pressed in.

"What the hell is that?" Gabriel asked.

Mira turned around, afraid of what might be creeping up behind her.

"It's not..." Gabriel started. "Come on, let's get out of here."

Mira wasn't sure which direction to move. It felt as though the Ether surrounded her. If she lifted her feet off the ground, would she be able to stay in their world?

Her eyes darted from left to right, and she began to ready one of her spells carefully. She pulled an old iron coin from her pocket. Holding it, she said a few words. Not enough to trigger the spell, but enough that she could throw it at any moment.

Gabriel appeared in front of her, seemingly from nowhere. It startled her enough that she almost released the spell.

"Come on," he said.

She could tell he felt something as well. He tried to take in everything at once and had his hand on his holster.

"Take my arm and don't let go," Gabriel said.

Mira nodded and gripped his arm tightly. His muscles were taut like a tight wire.

Was the room dimming? No, it couldn't be. Mira whipped her head around, intent on watching their back. That's when she really noticed Gabriel. At his back, almost completely transparent, Mira saw the outline of wings.

Dreading what seeing Gabriel's wings might mean, she tried to watch every shadow as Gabriel guided her out of the apartment.

The feeling of the Ether lifted the moment they reached the hall. When she studied Gabriel, any trace of his angelic qualities was gone.

Mira's breath was shallow and she watched the apartment, wondering what might be lurking in there.

"Was that—"

"Yes," Mira said, cutting Gabriel off.

"Did you expect—"

"Shouldn't happen. Shouldn't be possible. Not without Barney around."

He stood in the doorway and watched the room, much like she did. After a few moments, he reached in, grabbed the door, and slammed it shut.

"You have the keys?" he asked.

Mira dug into her pocket and pulled out the keys William had given her. Gabriel took them from her unsteady hand.

"I think it's okay, now," Gabriel said while locking the door.

"Right," Mira said, "you're right."

It wasn't until Gabriel rubbed his hand over hers that she realized she still clutched his arm.

"Sorry," she said, letting go as though she had grabbed something hot.

"It's okay," Gabriel said.

"It just took me by surprise," Mira said, trying to get a grip on her racing heart. "Where's Ian and William?"

"Outside and thank god for that."

"They may not have noticed," Mira waved her hand at the locked door, "whatever that was."

"No, but I feel like a real idiot for being so freaked out just walking across a room," Gabriel said.

Mira cracked a smile, but glanced nervously at the door. "I imagine we looked a little weird." It didn't sound as though

Gabriel had noticed that his angelic side had surfaced, so she didn't mention it.

"Hard to explain something like that," Gabriel said.

"It shouldn't have happened," Mira said.

"But it happens when Barney is here?"

"Sometimes."

Gabriel watched the door as though he could see through it. "Let's get out of here," he said after a few moments. "This place gives me the creeps."

"Yeah," Mira said, following Gabriel. She took one last look back at the apartment before stepping out in the sunlight. The sun scoured away the coolness the Ether had left on her skin.

"Hey, Mira," William lifted a hand as a wave, "I've gotta run. I'm playing intermediary between Barney's parents and my dad."

"Let us know if you hear anything," Mira said.

"Same," William said. He turned to go, and then stopped. "Is there something we should be doing?"

"You're doing it," Ian said. "Keep us informed. The moment you hear anything, give one of us a call."

William nodded, but didn't seem happy with the response. "I'll see you around."

"Time to visit the Hendersons," Ian said as they got into the car.

Mira sat in the back seat and flipped open her notebook.

"What can you tell us about the Hendersons?" Ian asked.

"Not much," Mira said. "They don't come around often."

"Are they witches?" Ian asked.

"Not exactly," Mira said.

"What's that mean, not exactly?"

Mira twisted in her seat. "They're... well, we call them hedge witches."

"What's the difference?" Ian asked.

"They use magic, but they aren't witches."

"Sorcerers?" Ian asked.

"No," Mira said. "They aren't warlocks, either. As far as we know, they're human magic users."

"I didn't know humans could use magic," Ian said, twisting around in his seat. "Is it something anyone can learn?"

"No, you'd have to be a hedge witch, and their magic isn't the same as ours. It's... I don't know how to put it. Not as powerful, maybe? Although, that's not quite it, either."

"Is it kind of like sorcerers and witches?" Ian asked. "You're both powerful, but in your own way?"

Mira beamed at Ian. "Kind of like that. You've learned a lot in the past week."

"Not enough," Ian said.

"I know the feeling," Gabriel added.

Ian grinned at Gabriel before he appeared to remember that he was upset with the angel.

"What are we doing at the Hendersons?" Mira asked.

"Hopefully we're finding them at home," Ian said.

"And if we don't?" Mira asked.

"We'll generally poke around," Ian said. "Though we can't enter without a reason unless someone lets us in."

"Are we going to Sybil's house afterwards?" Mira asked.

"Sybil?" Ian asked.

"Sorry," Mira said. "While I was speaking with Mr. Singer, he let me know that Sybil hasn't been seen today. It's unlike her, but she hasn't been gone long."

"That's three groups—two people and one family—gone in three days," Ian said, "and Tyler's been gone for a week."

Mira noticed the tense look he gave Gabriel.

"Things are escalating fast," Ian continued. "We need a better plan and more officers."

"We don't have any supernaturals on the force," Gabriel reminded him. "At least none that we know about."

Ian nodded and was quiet for a while. "Mira," he said after a lengthy pause, "could you—"

"No," Gabriel said.

"But even one more person—"

"No," Gabriel was more forceful this time.

Mira fiddled with her notebook while a part of her shriveled up inside. *Just one more.*

"William told me what he knew about it and I've seen some of the results myself," Gabriel said, watching her in the rearview mirror. "You're lucky to have survived karma this long with only Ian involved. Add someone else and it will likely kill us both."

"You make it sound like she's on the edge of death," Ian said. "She's fine, and what does it have to do with you?"

"We can talk later," Gabriel said. "But Mira *isn't* binding anyone else. We need to come up with another idea."

Ian didn't argue. Maybe he sensed something in Gabriel's mood, or perhaps he trusted Gabriel enough to know he had his reasons.

Mira couldn't help but think that it wouldn't have an effect on Gabriel if she finished her spell.

"The only way to get more people is going to be to recruit some of the members of the community," Gabriel said after a while. "Do you know anyone else that you know for certain isn't involved?"

"Della," Ian said, "and there's some others that I don't think were involved in any way, but no one that could be useful."

"Emmit," Mira said from the backseat.

"I don't trust that guy," Ian said.

"Would you trust that he would help with the case?" Mira asked.

"I have zero confidence that he'd stay within the confines of the law," Gabriel said. "In fact, I know he won't."

Mira shook her head and watched out the window.

"But there might be something he can help with at some point," Gabriel said reluctantly.

"We could ask around and see if there's anyone that has any military experience, or even some sort of law-enforcement background," Ian said.

"I'm pretty sure Noah does," Mira said. "I'm sure there are others."

"Noah's a werewolf," Ian said.

Mira narrowed her eyes. "And?"

"No," Ian said quickly, "I didn't mean that in a bad way. He has a really good sense of smell, right?"

"Yeah," Mira said.

"How good?" Gabriel asked.

"I don't know," Mira said. "It's really good, but I don't know exactly what he can do."

"He might be able to help us track similarities between the missing," Ian said.

"Do you think we can rely on him?" Gabriel asked.

"Well, we might want to ask him a few questions together," Ian said, "but I think he's a good place to start."

CHAPTER 11

L ET'S SEE IF YOU CAN get Noah to meet with us
today," Ian said.

"I have a spell to perform tonight," Mira said.

"Tonight?" Gabriel asked.

"I think so, yeah. I'm not sure it should wait."

"Tomorrow morning?" Ian asked.

"We have to report in tomorrow morning," Gabriel said.

"Right," Ian said. "We're going to want to talk about that. Tomorrow afternoon or evening should be okay, right?"

"I guess that depends on Noah," Mira said. "There has to be something else we can suggest to the community."

"They should start sticking together," Gabriel said, "and check often to make sure everyone is accounted for. Maybe set something up like the phone tree thing you have."

"And they should be on guard, even at home," Ian said.

"Okay." Mira started jotting down notes.

"What about wards?" Gabriel asked. "Do a lot of people have those?"

"Some will," Mira said, "but maybe the witches can come up with some other protections as well."

Mira didn't wait for a response. As Gabriel approached the Hendersons' house, Mira pulled out her phone and called Mr. Singer again.

"We haven't heard from Sybil yet," Mr. Singer said when he picked up. He sounded tired.

"We're going by her house shortly," Mira said. "We'll let you know if we find anything."

"Her brother is over there now, in case she comes home. I'll make sure he knows you're coming."

Mira got out of the car with the other two, but lagged behind to talk with Mr. Singer. "We've been chatting and the detectives have some ideas."

Mira filled Mr. Singer in while she watched Gabriel and Ian spy through the windows when no one answered the door. She even saw Ian check the doorknob in case they could get lucky twice in one day.

"I think the detectives might be looking for some people in the community with a law-enforcement background as well," Mira told Mr. Singer.

"We've already checked. Thoroughly," Mr. Singer said. "Do you have any contacts from college that could come in from out of town?"

College rears its ugly head again. "No," Mira said after quickly thinking through possibilities. "Well, maybe one. I'll see if I can reach him. A military background might also be useful. Wasn't Noah in the military?"

"Yes, and we have several others as well."

"Can you get us a list? The detectives also want to meet up with Noah tomorrow afternoon."

"I'll ask him to call tonight," Mr. Singer said.

"I think that's it," Mira said.

"We'll start letting everyone know, and the witches can start putting together some spells that will be useful. I know some of them are already using some sort of protection, but if we work together, we can help a lot more people."

"That's good to hear," Mira said.

"Is everything okay on your end? I could send something your way as well," Mr. Singer said.

"I'm covered," Mira said, following Gabriel and Ian back to the car. "Do you have any ideas for what I could do for the detectives?"

"Wards are your best bet for when you're not around. Maybe get them something they can use to put together a circle."

"I've started on wards. Do you think something like a premade circle would hold for long?" Mira asked, getting back into the car.

"That is going to depend on what they're up against."

"I guess so," Mira said, "and we have no idea what that might be."

"Some Clarity wouldn't hurt," Mr. Singer said.

"I think I'll do that. Thanks."

"Be careful and let us know if you need anything."

Mira hung up and saw that they had already left the Hendersons place, and could tell by the mood in the car that they hadn't found anything.

"Someone is at Sybil's house," Mira said. "Her brother. He can let us in."

"Do you know anyone who could let us into the Hendersons house?" Ian asked.

"No, but I'll ask around," Mira said.

"We're going to call in the Hendersons to the local law enforcement. Someone needs to be a contact for the officers to reach out to."

"Any information you can get on them and Sybil is going to help," Ian said. "Anyone who knew them, what their schedules were like, everything. We also need to ask for another meeting."

"How soon?" Mira asked.

"Day after tomorrow?" Ian asked, looking to Gabriel. "That gives us tomorrow and the next to track down everything we know we need to work on."

"Seems like an awfully long time out," Gabriel said, "but I don't think we can do anything sooner. Tonight, we need to get caught up on everything."

At Sybil's house, Mira introduced the detectives to Sybil's brother, and then stepped back outside to call Mr. Singer again. While she passed information on, she watched the sun sink behind the clouds and marveled at the fact it was still warm outside. It felt like an evening late in the spring, which was out of place making an appearance in the dead of winter.

She was wrapping up her call when two cars drove up. One of them was a typical police car and the other was plainer. Mira hurried to the door and rapped twice before poking her head in.

"Guys, the police just pulled up," she said, interrupting their conversation.

Gabriel smiled at her, but he looked as tired as Mr. Singer had sounded. "We called them. It's okay." Turning to Ian, he added, "I'll go meet with them. I think it's best our consultant comes with me."

Gabriel joined her and closed the door behind them. "Don't say anything unless they ask you a direct question. If I don't want you to answer, I'll interrupt." He gazed down at her. "Don't worry. It's a good thing they're here."

Mira nodded mutely and waited until the newcomers came to the porch and Gabriel introduced himself. He didn't give Mira's name, but mentioned her as a consultant.

Gabriel told the officers they were here for a case and found that Sybil's brother was worried because she hadn't come home. Due to the nature of the case, Gabriel and Ian had called them in, since it was outside their jurisdiction.

In the end, it made perfect sense to Mira, but she still gritted her teeth and prayed they didn't ask her anything. The local police would search for Sybil and give any pertinent information over to Ian and Gabriel. Several times, Gabriel assured the officers that neither Sybil nor her brother was strong suspects in the case and that he and Ian were only there for information.

It was another thirty minutes before they left, but Mira knew Sybil's brother would be at the house for a while. She felt sorry for him, but knew that he—like all the other supernaturals in the area—could keep the secret.

Gabriel and Ian fell into conversations on the case as soon as they drove away. It didn't take long for Mira to realize that today hadn't given them much in the way of insight.

No one had any idea what they were dealing with. Probably more than one person, Mira mused, because that was what John had suggested, but even he may have been boasting. Somehow, she doubted he was, though. Remembering the chanting on the wind, Mira figured there must be quite a few other people involved.

Mr. Singer had suggested wards and a circle for the Ian and Gabriel. A spell they could use in case of emergency would be tricky, but Mira considered trying one anyway. The detectives couldn't cast, so the spells would need to be different from those she herself carried around. Hers weren't fully cast, so the effects weren't ready to go and didn't have to be renewed as much as anything she would give Ian and Gabriel.

The wards she could possibly finish tonight, although it would take all night. There was also the other spell she needed for Gabriel, but she thought about combining the two.

The circles and other spells would wait. It wasn't likely they were going to walk straight into a group of people trying to kill them in the next day.

"Mira?" Ian said, shifting around from the front seat.

"Yeah?" she said, her mind still on magic circles.

"Barney's site," Ian said. "Was there anything new this week?"

From the sound of his voice, she could tell he'd asked her once already and she had missed it.

"I haven't checked," she said, "but I imagine there is. He added to his online predictions almost every day."

"Well," he said, addressing Gabriel again, "you can go through what I have, and I'll search the site for anything new."

"Your house or mine?" Gabriel asked.

"You all can work from my apartment if you want," Mira said.

"We won't be in your way?" Gabriel asked.

"No, I have a lot to do tonight." Looking around, she saw that they were in her neighborhood already. "I can order dinner for us first, though."

"Thanks," Ian said.

Mira noticed that when they pulled into the driveway Ian took particular interest in the illuminated windows of the big house. Smiling to herself, Mira took out her phone and texted Della.

A certain detective is working from my apartment. We're ordering dinner first. Want to come over?

I was told today that we needed to check up on each other, Della texted. *I think I should visit my best friend. I'll order for us and be over.*

Mira grinned and gathered her stuff together, throwing it in her bag.

The detectives were standing next to the car when she got out, though neither of them seemed to be in a hurry to go inside.

"It's hard to believe it's this warm," Ian said. "With the earthquakes and the weather, I'm surprised the city isn't on edge."

"They're enjoying the heat wave," Mira said.

"I think once the new disappearances hit the news, people are going to be sticking indoors more, no matter how warm it is," Gabriel said.

"Sybil and the Hendersons are outside the city," Mira said, finally digging for her keys and heading toward the stairs.

"That only makes it worse. It's in the metro area, so no one will feel comfortable." Ian sighed. "We've got a lot of work to do. I'll grab the files."

Gabriel followed Mira up the stairs to her apartment.

"I'm going to open the windows," Mira said as she entered. "Alchemy and Oracle need a chance to enjoy the weather." As though summoned, the two ran into the room and wound themselves around Mira's legs before doing the same to Gabriel. "They really like you—even Alchemy, and he doesn't like much of anyone."

"I'm good with animals," he said, and then his face soured. "It's probably an angel thing."

"It could be just a Gabriel thing," Mira said, sensing his mood.

He looked slightly cheered by that. "I can hope."

"You haven't changed, you know," Mira said. "You're still you."

"Am I? It doesn't feel like it anymore."

Mira rubbed his arm, trying to convey some sort of empathy, but jumped when Ian knocked on the door.

She gave Gabriel a quick smile before pushing the door open for Ian so he could lug in the box he had.

"All of that isn't Barney's notebooks," she said, "unless you went back for more."

"No," Ian said, "these are extra copies of the case files with... well, with other notes on them. I never know where to keep them."

"Other notes?" Mira asked, raising an eyebrow and frantically thinking through her binding spell to see if she had missed something.

"I had to make sure I remembered everything," Ian said. The look he gave Mira wasn't too friendly. "I couldn't even write what I wanted, but I made do with shorthand."

No wonder he fought the spell so much, Mira thought. *He's probably still fighting.*

"Sorry," Mira said, feeling once again like she was the bad guy in the situation. She was, when it came down to it, so there was nothing else she could add to the sentiment.

"You have me now," Gabriel said, trying to lighten the mood. "You'll miss keeping it to yourself before long."

"That'll never happen," Ian said, not pacified. "Where should we work?"

"The kitchen or living room, wherever you all want. Um, I thought Della might be of some use," she added, not liking how the evening was getting started. "She's ordering dinner for us and will be over before long."

That did the trick. Ian's frown disappeared on his way to the kitchen. Mira watched him go and sighed. When she glanced around, she noticed Gabriel watching her.

Before he could say anything, she stepped in. "Do you all need anything?"

"Coffee," Ian called from the kitchen.

Gabriel frowned toward his partner, but Mira smiled.

"Coming up," she said, gliding past Gabriel and not giving him a chance to talk. "I've got spell work to do, so I'll show you where everything is in case you want it again later."

"Are you going to use the kitchen for that?" Gabriel asked at the kitchen entry.

"No, I'm going to need the circles downstairs tonight, and some Awake added to my tea since it'll be a long night. If you all want any—"

"No thanks," Ian said quickly.

"Maybe later," Gabriel said. "I didn't know there was a downstairs to the apartment."

"There's not, really," Mira said. "Della walled off part of the garage for me so I could keep more permanent magic circles and ones that were closer to the ground."

"Is that important?" Gabriel asked.

"Not for everything," Mira admitted, "but for the big stuff, it is. *On* the ground is even better, but hard to do anymore."

"Can I see it?" Gabriel asked. Quickly, he added, "If it's private, of course, you don't have to. I was just..."

Mira smiled, feeling somewhat relieved that he didn't want to treat her as a pariah. "Sure, I'll show you." Once the coffee was brewing, she led Gabriel downstairs and was pleasantly surprised to see Ian following behind.

"This reminds me of your shop," Ian said.

Both men wandered around the room, looking at the jars, tiny bottles, and various plants.

"It has a lot of the same stuff," Mira admitted. "I've been sending some things to previous customers."

"Mail-order spells?" Ian asked.

"Something like that," Mira said. She found it interesting that Ian would walk through the magic circles on the ground, but Gabriel walked around them. Neither of the men could see the circles and they weren't active, so either could walk through without an issue. She wondered if Gabriel somehow sensed the repeated laying of the magic.

"What are you working on tonight?" Ian asked.

Gabriel gave her a tense glance that she barely caught—and Ian missed completely.

"A few things, actually," Mira said.

"For the case?" Ian asked.

Mira wrung her hands, uncertain how Ian would take the idea of wearing a ward. He seemed to be of two minds when it came to magic, depending on how aggravated he was with the binding spell and how frustrated he was with the case.

"I'm putting together something to keep you all safe," Mira said. "Wards, for now. It'll block magic, at least to some extent, along with some other things that might come up if supernaturals are involved."

"That's really nice of you," Gabriel said quickly, before his partner could talk. "I'm sure they'll be really useful."

"Yeah," Ian said, not sounding as convinced, "thank you."

The doorbell upstairs rang. "That'll be Della," Mira said.

"Can I talk to you a minute first?" Gabriel asked. "Ian, do you mind helping Della?"

"Sure thing," Ian said. He was out of the room and up the stairs before Mira could say anything.

When he was gone, Gabriel continued looking over one of her workbenches. They could hear voices upstairs, and Mira couldn't help but smile at the thought of giving the pair time to talk alone.

Looking back to Gabriel, she saw that while he was looking at the plants, he was also pushing on spots here and there on the sides of the workbench. Her smile widened and she giggled.

"You better be careful," she said. "You might not like what you find if you open one of my many witch panels."

His fingers froze for a moment, but then continued. "Am I going to get zapped by something?"

"Doubtful at my house."

"You didn't seem the type to set some sort of horrible trap."

She felt her face go pink. "Nothing that would hurt someone, no, but you may not like what's inside."

"Eyes of newt? Frog legs?"

Mira laughed. "You can buy frog legs at one of the grocery stores in the city, and I don't think I've ever used eyes. Some of the ingredients can be pretty gross, though. You might feel the urge to arrest me for a few."

Gabriel stopped and raised an eyebrow at her. "Illegal?"

"You'd have to find them and tell me."

He stopped searching and leaned his back against the workbench, crossing his arms. "I don't like the sound of that."

There was something in the way he leaned so casually against the table that made her heart beat faster. Maybe it was the way he looked at her.

Maybe it was the way his biceps tensed.

Her face went redder and she tried to tear her mind away from that train of thought.

"Let's just say that if anyone who didn't know I was a witch found some of the items I store here, they'd think I was a giant freak."

He relaxed. "I know you're not that."

Damn, Mira thought, *why did he have to be so cute?*

"What are you really working on tonight?" Gabriel asked.

CHAPTER 12

I TOLD YOU," MIRA SAID, "I'M working on wards for the two of you. Yours will just have a little something extra with it."

"Something I'll be able to break, right?" Gabriel asked.

Mira rolled her eyes. "The ward part, no. The rest? I'll attach my spell to the necklace. Once it's broken, the spell will be as well."

"Could I just take the necklace off for it to stop working?"

"That will stop the ward, not permanently, but it only works if the medallion is against your skin. It won't do anything for the other spell, because that one isn't on the necklace. It's on me."

"So you're hiding yourself from me, not stopping me from seeing you?"

"Something like that," Mira said. "I can adapt things a little easier if the spell is on me. I'm not sure what type of adjustments I'd need to make on you. Even on me, I might need your help. I've never done anything like this before."

"I'm still not sure it's a good idea," Gabriel said.

"This," Mira waved back and forth between the two of them, "isn't fair for either of us. It was an accident."

He didn't say anything.

Mira could think of nothing to convince him further. She felt if she told him that she would do the spell with him or without him, it would be seen as a challenge more than anything else.

"Let's go get dinner," Mira said. She took a final look around the room before leading the way upstairs.

"We were just about to call down for you," Della said when they came into the kitchen.

Mira gave her friend a knowing glance, silently conveying, *Sure you were.*

Della grinned. "Anyway, let's eat— you all have a busy night."

"It looks that way," Gabriel said.

"Is there anything I can help you with?" Della asked.

"It wouldn't hurt to have another set of eyes on the case," Ian said. "Maybe your legal expertise will come in handy. Not to mention the supernatural side of things."

"I'd be happy to help," Della said. "Mira, I think this occasion calls for some Awake for everyone."

"I'll get you some," Mira said.

"You'll love this," Della said to the others. "It's better than coffee and Mira makes it better than anyone I know."

Ian twisted uncomfortably in his seat.

"I'm not sure the detectives want spells in their drinks," Mira said.

"I'll give it a try," Gabriel said. "It will be a long night, after all. Ian?"

Mira noticed the mischievous look Gabriel gave his partner.

"Sure," Ian said, "anything to help, I guess."

"Some Clarity wouldn't go amiss, either," Della said.

Ian shifted in his chair.

"Good idea," Mira said, "but maybe tomorrow. I don't have any made up."

Della checked her phone. "There's probably time."

"I'm making wards tonight," Mira said, "for Ian and Gabriel."

Della gave her friend a softened smile. "All in one night?"

Mira shrugged.

"It sounds like you need more help than they do," Della said, "and something a lot stronger than Awake."

"Is making them that hard?" Gabriel asked.

Della raised an eyebrow at him. "Something that lasts virtually forever and is strong enough to repel magic? Very few witches anywhere could manage them in one night, but if anyone can do it, Mira can. I can still help things along."

"You know," Mira said, catching her friend's eye before glancing meaningfully at Ian. "I think helping with one of them would really help give it a boost."

Wards were always best when they came from someone that really cared about the person receiving the ward. The higher the emotion and attachment, the more powerful the ward.

Much to Mira's surprise, Della actually blushed.

"I'll get things started and call you down when I need you," Mira said.

"After dinner," Della said.

The four chatted—mostly about the case—throughout dinner and Mira excused herself afterward.

Because of the destruction of her store, she'd been getting stock delivered to her house. Witches wanting mail-ordered materials didn't stop when the store had burned down. This meant she had pendants on hand that could be used for wards.

Mira left the necklaces in their herb and spring water bath, while she started to put together her other spell. The wards were all about power—raw strength channeled into the specific purpose of protection. There was a spell to trap the power, but that complexity was mild in comparison to the one she had planned for herself.

The biggest problem in the spell she wanted to cast was that she had *no idea* what she was doing. Usually for something like this, she would have asked Tyler to go over everything with her. The more complex the spell grew, the more likely ingredients could clash or cancel each other out.

Mira took out each ingredient and inspected it before she compared it to the other ingredients on her list. Even with extra measures, it was possible that the spell would fall flat. Better the spell fail than go in the opposite direction, though. If she ended up magnifying the bond between herself and Gabriel, she wouldn't be able to forgive herself. He really would be running over here every time she stubbed her toe or brushed through a tangle in her hair.

She cringed at the thought and was pleased that Gabriel came up with the idea of being able to break the spell. If she did screw it up, she could break the chain as easily as he could.

When she had all her ingredients lined up, she went over the list again. Who knew what it would take to hide from an angel? Remembering the strength of Gabriel's voice in the Ether, she adjusted the amounts of a few items.

A part of her said she should finish the wards first, but another small voice agonized over the new spell, prodding her to go over the ingredients again.

The new spell was as good as she was going to get. Instead of checking everything another time, she took a deep breath and dove in. Once she started mixing, there was no going back.

It all began with her anchor spell. That was her sure-fire shortcut to getting things started. Without it, any spell would take much longer than she wanted.

In three separate cups, she mixed ingredients, a little anchor in each, and then she took out a silver chain and placed all four items in the center of her circle.

It had been a while since she'd used her circles. They were so used to her, though, that it only took the smallest spark of power to energize the largest one. She shivered a little as the power, more strength than she had anticipated, jumped from her.

She was out of practice. She had only performed one real spell since she'd come back from the Ether. After Mira had helped Emmit, mixing both her and Gabriel's blood to get the job done, she had been left with a hollow feeling and she had avoided magic for longer than necessary.

Mira rolled her shoulders before sitting down cross-legged on the floor in front of her materials. She closed her eyes, meditated for a few minutes to make sure her magic flowed freely, and then she got started.

Using pure water, she wrote symbols onto the concrete while starting to speak the spell. She began blending the ingredients, pausing before each combination to add another layer to the spell and another row of symbols onto the floor. Water would normally have evaporated from the concrete, but with magic flowing through the letters, each drop stayed firmly where it was drawn.

She closed her eyes, falling deep into the magic, swirls of energy drawing colored sparks across her mind. Power rose to fill her circle and her skin began to tingle.

Mira allowed a moment of exploration before adding the final ingredient, three drops of her own blood. Her skin tingled often when doing magic, but it usually meant she was straining herself and she didn't feel like that was the case. Once she was secure in the knowledge that her magic was holding, she moved on.

Without opening her eyes, she pulled out a pen and added three drops of blood.

Mira heard Della's voice and figured her friend could sense the magic and knew it was time to help. Mira went through the last phases as quickly as she dared. She dropped the chain into her spell, said the final words, and drank her creation, making sure not to swallow the chain with it.

Once she felt the spell settle into both herself and the jewelry, she pulled the silver from her mouth.

The magic didn't immediately cut off. Instead, Mira let it ebb away before opening her eyes.

Della stood at the edge of her circle with arms crossed and foot tapping.

Mira stared around, wondering what had gotten her friend so riled up, but they were alone.

"What's wrong?" Mira asked, letting her circle fall.

"What the hell was that?" Della asked.

"A spell. What did you think it was?"

"I know it was a spell, but I also know your power, and that wasn't it."

The accusation brought Mira to her feet. "What are you talking about? Of course, it was mine. Whose else would it be?"

"What are you using to amplify your magic? You know shit like that goes wrong fast."

"I'm not doing anything." Mira felt a little lightheaded, but nothing had seemed out of the ordinary to her.

"It's addictive, Mira. Power boosts may feel great in the short term, but it will leave you worse off than the Bliss."

Mira glared at her friend and dropped her voice. "That's a low blow. The only spell I've used in over a week was the Awake we drank upstairs. And that was stale."

Della's arms dropped, looking unsure of herself—which was a rare sight. "You didn't take anything?"

"No," Mira said, adding some force to her voice, "and it's a shitty thing to suggest."

"What spell were you doing?" Della asked.

"None of your business," Mira snapped.

"Listen, whatever you did, it was stronger than I've seen from you. From anyone," she stressed, "and that includes my father, which you know is saying something."

Mira shrugged. "I used some strong ingredients."

"And you haven't worked magic in a while," Della said, more to herself than Mira. "You haven't built some sort of magic battery, have you?"

"That would be just as bad as something boosting my power."

"No, that energy would be yours, only stored."

"That—" Mira thought about it for a moment. "That's actually not a bad idea."

They stood in awkward silence for a while before Della spoke. "I'm sorry I accused you."

"You should be," Mira said, not willing to let go of her frustration.

"I was just worried about you," Della said. "I know you've been under a lot of stress. From the elders, the case, and Tyler going missing. It's enough for anyone to search for an edge."

Knowing that Mira's own bad history with addiction fueled Della's concern didn't make Mira any happier with the situation.

"I assure you," Mira said, trying to take the bite out of her voice, "I'm not doing anything to alter my magic."

Della nodded and stared around the room, still looking uncomfortable.

"Are you taking an inventory?" Della asked, motioning to her workbench lined with ingredients.

"Something like that," Mira said, not admitting anything. "How's it going upstairs?"

"They're reading Barney's blog. Need any help down here?"

"The pendants should be ready soon."

"What did you use?"

"I didn't have much of a selection, but I found a very nice protection rune and a small fox spirit."

"Fox spirit? I like that."

"I thought it would be a good choice for Ian." Seeing Della's secretive grin at the mention of Ian and the fox made Mira finally let go of her frustrations. "I thought you'd like that."

Della's confidence seemed to grow now that Mira wasn't upset. "Are you doing both pendants together?"

"No, I think they'll work better if we focus on them one at a time. I could use your help with Ian's." Mira used a glass rod to stir the pendants, checking them. "In fact, why don't you pull out the fox—he's on the left—and keep hold of it."

Della did so and automatically moved to the circle. "This isn't silver."

Mira set the necklace she had just worked on carefully to the side before joining Della. "Platinum, actually."

Della whistled. "You went all out."

"They deserve something that will last," Mira said, trying not to blush, "and like I said, my stock is short and I wasn't about to use gold. Twenty-four carat gold wears down eventually."

"This is really great of you," Della said, turning the fox over and over in her hand.

"You know the drill," Mira said, forcing them back on task. "Just concentrate on keeping Ian safe and aim your energy. Once the fox is charged, I seal it in." Mira once again added a touch of power to activate her circle. "Ready?"

"Let's do it." Della closed her eyes and raised her power.

Della's power as a sorcerer ran strong, raw, and fast. She didn't need magical words—at least not many. What she did need was magical movement along with willpower and force, which Della had in spades. Especially, it seemed where Ian was involved.

Mira did her part to perform the actual spell, but it was her turn to worry as Della kept going. She was on the verge of warning Della to pull back, when Della gave the signal. Mira fixed the charge into the fox and sealed it.

After the spell was over, Mira noticed her friend sway.

"Della?" Mira said, steadying her. "You okay?"

Della blinked a few times before nodding her head.

"Here," Mira said, leading her over to a chair, "sit down before you fall."

Once Della sat, Mira put her hands on her hips and glared. "Weren't you just lecturing me?"

Della sighed. "Yeah, I know, but like you said, it's important. You going to be okay doing Gabriel's on your own?"

Mira glanced back at her workbench. "I was planning on it."

"I see," Della said with a smirk.

"Don't look at me like that," Mira said. "I'm going to get Ian to take you home."

"I can go on my own," Della said.

Mira laughed. "Of course you can, but that's really not the point, is it?"

"Give me a minute first. I don't want him to see me all... blah. He'll think I can't handle my magic."

"He'll want to help take care of you," Mira said.

"That'll turn out well," Della said, her voice dripping in sarcasm. "Unless I'm on death's door, I don't want anyone around who's going to try to hover over me."

"Well, tonight's a good trial run for Ian. Go easy on him, though. He might not actually know that you just need sleep."

"Sleeping definitely wasn't what I had in mind. Maybe I should have thought this through better."

Mira laughed again. "Wait here."

When she entered the kitchen, the two men glanced up.

"How is everything going?" Mira asked.

"Slowly," Gabriel said, flipping to another page. "How's the magic?"

"It's great," Mira said. "Della put everything she had into the last spell. Ian, would you mind making sure she gets home okay? I still have more work to do."

Ian glanced at his partner. "It might be a good idea to get up and move around some."

"Go help her out," Gabriel said. "A break isn't going to hurt."

After Ian started down the stairs, Gabriel relocated Oracle from his lap to the table before he stood and stretched. "Della seemed pretty ticked off when she headed downstairs. Everything okay?"

Mira rolled her eyes. "She was worked up over nothing."

"We can clear out whenever you need," Gabriel said.

"Don't worry about it," Mira said. "I still have a lot to get done tonight."

"Anything I can help with?" Gabriel asked.

"No, I really need to handle the rest. Besides, you've got more than enough to do."

Gabriel rolled his shoulders. "I feel like I'm missing something. Maybe if I had met Barney, I'd understand his predictions better."

"What are you having trouble with?"

"Nothing's connected. He's all over the board with random stuff." Gabriel picked up a file and flipped through it. "Like this, 'accident involving a red car and green truck on the corner of 12th and Main. City unknown.' I can't believe the Ether reflects this kind of uselessness."

"It may not be useless for someone that drives those streets."

"But John was getting messages out of this?"

Mira curled up her nose at the memory and her eyes strayed to the spot where her blood had marred the floors. "That's what he said, but can we believe him? He was crazy."

"We don't have to believe him, but we can't disregard it either."

"Maybe it's in code," Mira said.

"You think Barney was sending encrypted messages?"

"I think Barney was writing what he saw. But who's to say those things on the other side weren't directing the visions."

Gabriel flipped through a few pages and sat back down. "I don't like the idea of people communicating with those creatures."

"Me neither," Mira said. "What kind of person does that?"

CHAPTER 13

"Z EALOTS?" WHEN MIRA STARED AT him blankly, Gabriel continued. "Remember the chanting that seemed to flow through the house when Leatherface took over John's body?"

"I remember."

"And John mentioned gods."

Emmit mentioned them as well, but Mira wasn't about to bring that up.

"History is filled with people doing horrific things for their god," Gabriel said.

"Those monsters on the other side were definitely not gods," Mira said.

"No, but they talked about gods as well."

Mira rubbed her forehead. "And these people are killing supernaturals for their gods?"

"Maybe. It's only a theory. We don't have enough to go on yet."

"I think you might be right about the religion stuff, though. Crazy people talking about gods all of a sudden can't be a coincidence. When you go through Barney's predictions, keep that in mind."

"Like, the gods are telling their followers to avoid 12th and Main?" Gabriel asked.

"No, but colors and numbers can have significance in religion. Look for patterns or repeats of the same thing. Certain words could even be a clue."

"It's worth a try," Gabriel said. "Thanks."

Mira covered her mouth to stifle a yawn.

"It's late," Gabriel said, "you should get some rest."

"After I finish my spells."

There was a knock on the door and Mira poked her head into the living room as Ian came in wearing a very big smile.

Mira grinned, but turned her head before Ian noticed. "Help yourselves to anything. If you leave, lock up behind you."

"Thanks," Gabriel said.

"I'm back to work," Mira said before yawning again. "Good luck."

Downstairs, Mira went straight for the doors to make sure Della and Ian locked up on their way out. With that done, she felt more comfortable fishing the pendant meant for Gabriel out of the purification bath.

It seemed right that it had spent extra time purifying. If she'd had the time, she would have preferred for it to sit even longer in the concoction. She wanted to make something fit for an angel.

On reflection, the protection rune may have been a bad idea when mixed with the chain of her other spell, but it would work for now.

Holding the platinum tightly in her hand, she went to the circle and let her power charge it once again. With Della helping, things went fast. They always went fast with a sorcerer involved.

This time she made herself comfortable on the floor, cupped her hands around the pentagram, and began to pour all of her focus into keeping Gabriel safe. He'd saved her countless times, even before he accidentally made himself her guardian angel. Sure, he'd almost killed her once or twice as well, but no one was perfect.

Going through all the dangers Gabriel could face—magic, psychics, guns and knives, werewolves, vampires, and fiends from the Ether, maybe even gods—she felt a little overwhelmed. Mira fixated on her ward blocking everything possible. Concentrating hard, her magic poured in, turning her focus into a reality.

With her magic running high, Mira felt that prickly sensation on her skin again. This time, it seemed possible she was pushing herself too hard.

She ignored it and continued. If she could save Gabriel even once, the extra effort would be worth it.

He deserved the protection and the peace of mind, along with much, much more.

When the prickling feeling on her skin relocated to her mind, Mira began to seal off her ward. There was no way to add any more, so what she put into the spell would have to work.

Once her magic was securely sealed away, Mira opened her eyes. She couldn't tell if she was moving or the room was, but she could tell she'd overdone it. Even the tiny bit of magic feeding her circle was too much to bear, so she dropped it quickly.

More than anything else, she wanted to curl up and go to sleep. Her head pounded, and her brain felt fuzzy.

Maybe she already was asleep. When she turned her head, vertigo kicked in and she felt as though she were drifting on the ocean.

Stupid, stupid, stupid, Mira thought. She should have saved at least a little bit of her strength in reserve.

Lying on the floor until the room stopped moving sounded divine, but instead, she closed her eyes and meditated, focusing on the flow of energy in her body. Time ticked by and Mira started to feel more like normal. Not wanting to chance things, she meditated a little longer before scooting to her workbench and leveraging her tired body off the floor.

She turned the pendant over and over in her hand. It was a good ward. Without trying, she could feel the strength. That, at least would settle down and become unnoticeable after a while.

Taking her earlier creation, she unclasped the necklace and worked the pendant on before closing it again. The two spells hummed together. Proud of her work, she felt a flutter in her chest at the idea of giving it to Gabriel. It was enough to lend her a boost long enough to get upstairs.

Gabriel was alone in the kitchen, stacking files neatly on her table. Mira almost groaned when she saw the clock. Three AM wasn't a time she wanted to see.

"Oh, hey," Gabriel said, "I wasn't sure what to do with these." He waved at the files.

"Leave them there," Mira said, "you're the only company I'm expecting."

Gabriel raised an eyebrow. "Aren't you seeing Emmit tomorrow night?"

"Later today," Mira said. "You'll be here, though, right? Did I ask you earlier?" Mira tiredly rubbed her eyes, trying to remember, but it seemed forever ago.

"Why would I be here?" Gabriel asked.

"Emmit asked me to ask you. Sorry," Mira said. "I must have forgotten."

"I don't intend on being a third wheel," Gabriel said, a bit more forcefully than Mira had expected.

She blinked at him in confusion. "Emmit wanted to see both of us, not just me."

It was Gabriel's turn to look perplexed. "It's not a date?"

"Not that I'm aware of." Although Mira really didn't appreciate the reminder.

He appeared uncomfortable. "My mistake."

Mira only nodded before stifling another yawn.

"I should get out of here and let you get to sleep," Gabriel said.

"Are you okay to drive?" Mira asked.

"I'm fine."

"I have something for you before you go." She held out the necklace.

Gabriel took it carefully and studied the pendant. "This is nice. You really didn't have to do this."

"Of course I did," Mira said, smiling broadly.

"This is the ward?"

"The pendant is the ward. The chain is for the spell that hides me. You can take the chain on and off, but if you break it, it breaks the spell."

"So you've already cast it."

"Yes."

"So if something happens to you?"

"You won't know, and you won't have to worry about stopping it."

"And the ward still works, even if I break the chain?"

"Yes, but there's no reason to break the chain. Neither of us wants that."

Gabriel nodded and eyed the chain, not looking at Mira.

"Remember, the ward needs contact with your skin to work. The chain will bond with my spell no matter what."

"Got it." Gabriel went into the living room for his jacket. "I should go. Ian will call you tomorrow about meeting Noah, but it won't be until the afternoon."

"Good," Mira said. "I'll probably sleep until then."

Gabriel hesitated at the door, looking at Mira for the first time since she'd handed him the necklace. He seemed as though he were going to say something, but then changed his mind.

"Drive safe," Mira said.

"Call us if you need anything."

Mira didn't intend on sleeping into the afternoon, but she did want to sleep late. Instead, it was nine when she woke. Alchemy lay on the bed next to her, whipping his tail in her face. Mira sighed and rolled over, only to come face to face with Oracle, who purred before head butting her.

"I see how it is," Mira mumbled. "You two are ganging up on me this morning."

In answer, Alchemy jumped over her to join Oracle and they both stared at her.

"Fine, I'm up."

It wasn't until she'd pried herself out of bed that she noticed that she was worn. Not exactly surprising. Making a ward was enough to exhaust anyone.

After she'd fed Alchemy and Oracle and freshened their water, she got ready to face her day. When she was dressed, she realized she didn't have much of a day to face. Magic was out of the question. Just the thought of doing an easy spell made her bones ache. Most of what needed to be done required a car—including going car shopping, which didn't appeal to Mira in the least.

Making use of the time, she returned a few phone calls that had come in when she hadn't had her cell phone. Then she cleaned up a little before becoming at a loss for what to do.

The files were waiting for her. Ian and Gabriel hadn't said she couldn't go through them, right? They had been comfortable enough leaving them there with her, so they wouldn't mind her going through them.

Besides, she might be able to help.

Taking the top file, she opened it to find printouts of Barney's blog. Mira smiled when she read the notes off to the side. Gabriel had taken her advice and made note of numbers and colors.

Mira took out her ever-present notebook and copied Gabriel's notes while jotting down her own. She copied the numbers and colors and wrote down the dates each of them had been written in case the order would be important. A few other words caught her eye as well. Broken, crashed, wrecked—they all went down in her notebook.

An hour went by. Mira rubbed her eyes and got up to make tea and move around. She took a chance and opened the window, finding another warm day. Much warmer than any winter day should be, but Alchemy and Oracle immediately jumped onto the windowsill to soak up the sun.

Mira returned to her task, feeling refreshed. It wasn't long before she reached the end of Gabriel's notes. From that point, she wrote notes following Gabriel's pattern before making her own.

When she came to the word bluebell, she stopped.

It had to be a coincidence; she knew that. Her parents had decided to name her Miranda Bluebell Owens when she was born, and it had been a thorn in her side from her first day of school. She never used the name now.

Did Barney even know her name?

She read the message again; *bluebells north of Short Park find sun and then die when summer kills winter.*

Mira glanced outside. Summer kills winter. Could that be what was happening now? It would be one way to describe it. Frowning, Mira grabbed her laptop and searched for Short Park.

Vancouver?

She shook her head. There was no way she was going to Vancouver.

She wrote 'blue' off to the side for Gabriel and then took her own notes. Die and kill were probably important words though, so she added those along with bluebell and the date.

The date. 39/28/00.

Mira looked at the previous message. March 18. She read the one before that and found the same date. The one after the message had March 19, written out.

Mira tapped her pen on the table and stared at the note. Barney did use his own codes, but he knew no one else knew them. Besides, the ones she had seen used symbols, letters, and numbers, not just numbers and slashes on their own.

It was probably an accident. Mira flipped through a bunch of pages of Barney's notebook, each showing the month and day written out. She opened another file, and then flipped through a few pages at random before closing the file and looking over the bluebell passage again.

There was nothing odd about it apart from the date. All of Barney's predictions were random things that didn't make too much sense. Once again, Mira searched the internet for Short Park, and this time added the name of the city.

Street names popped up. *Well*, she thought, *every city in the country probably had streets named Short and Park.* She pulled up the city map for more detail.

Every city probably has a street with the name short and park in it, but how many of those cities had those streets crossing each other?

Once again, probably quite a few. But how many had someone named Bluebell that might be reading this?

Should she tell Ian and Gabriel?

It was a stupid thought and she felt ridiculous. Barney had written this ages ago. They would tell her she was seeing something there because she wanted to, and they'd be right.

The passage ingrained itself into her mind. Mira tried to move on, but she came back again and again to bluebell.

Glancing at the clock showed what she already knew—it was early afternoon, however, Ian wasn't planning on meeting with Noah until later in the afternoon. Maybe if she went down there and saw for herself, she could get the idea out of her head.

Her car was gone, so that was a problem. Calling Reinfield Concierge Service meant Emmit would immediately know, so that was out of the question.

Did she want to waste the money on a cab?

What had the passage meant when it said find the sun? The sun was out, bright, and shining away.

Mira packed up her notebook, put the file folders back in order, and made sure her phone was charged before she called the cab.

As soon as the taxi showed up, Mira locked up and rushed down the stairs, feeling ridiculous about the whole thing. There were too many coincidences for her to dismiss the idea, though.

"Can you take me to the corner of Short Street and Park?" she asked.

The driver punched the address into his GPS. "That should take about twenty minutes."

"Excellent," she said.

"Although," the driver added as he drove away, "with so many people around, it's hard to tell for sure."

"Why are there extra people?" Mira asked, figuring she must have missed an event.

"It's the weather," the man said. "The forecasters and news people are in town because no one knows what's going on. People in the surrounding areas are mostly looking for a bit of a break from the winter."

"Is it warmer here than the surrounding area?"

"Ha! Go too far out of the metro area and snow is still on the ground. Meanwhile, we can put on our shorts here."

"I hadn't realized," Mira said.

"Ah, it's good for business, though. The shops are full, the museums are full, and every taxi driver in the city is busy busy."

Mira felt a momentary pang for the fact that her shop wouldn't see any of the benefit. "No one knows what's causing it?"

"Everyone has a theory, but no one knows. Personally, I think it's one of them sun spots."

"Sun spots?"

"Yep. Radiation from the sun is heating us up."

"Interesting," Mira said, not believing a word of it.

"Yeah, and it messes up radio signals, which would explain the cell phone outages the other day."

"I thought the earthquakes caused that."

"Well, they thought it was the earthquakes, but it warmed up right after."

"Interesting." She said it because she had nothing else to say. Mira was pretty sure the meteorologists would know about a sun spot, though. And she didn't think for a moment that one could heat the city.

"We're almost there. No trouble at all," the driver said. "Will you be needing a ride back?"

"No," Mira said quickly, "I'm visiting someone down the street."

The car pulled to a stop and Mira passed up her debit card. The driver swiped it and handed her a small tablet for her to sign.

Seeing the tip when she passed it back, the man smiled. "Well, be careful out there and call us again if you need anything."

"Thanks for the ride," Mira said, jumping out of the car.

As the cab drove off, Mira looked around. On the map, she had been looking at the area from above and assumed it was a neighborhood. Instead, it was more of a business district. She turned north and crossed the street.

These businesses weren't the ones that people went in to buy something from. These were the places people went to build things or store them.

She passed a small metal building with a few cars parked out front. It read, Perkins Wood Works, and gave a website. Across the street was a gated storage place that took up half the block.

Not a lot of cars were on the streets. She heard noises from some of the buildings, but she felt alone and isolated walking through this part of town.

She tucked her purse tighter to her and cursed herself for being here in the first place. When her phone rang, she jumped at the sound and scrambled to get it, just at the chance to talk to someone.

"It's Ian," he said when she picked up. "Noah wanted to meet over in Aken. Are you free?"

"Um," she glanced around and continued to walk, "yeah, I'm free. I'm not at home, though." She stopped and stared at the wooden building next to her. The street address caught her eye. 3929 Short Street.

"Where are you? I'll come by and pick you up," Ian said.

Mira was barely paying attention. Across the street was an old brick building with the numbers 3928 in black fixed to the side.

CHAPTER 14

"THIRTY-NINE TWENTY-EIGHT," Mira murmured.
"Thirty-nine twenty-eight, what," he said.

The building was two story, but it had some sort of addition off to the side that was a single story. It must have been added much later than the rest of the building, because the brick didn't quite match up. Curtained windows lined the addition.

"What?" Mira asked.

"Where are you?" Ian asked again.

"Oh," Mira said coming back to herself. She kept an eye out to see if anyone was watching her. "I'm at thirty-nine twenty-eight Short Street."

"What are you doing over there?"

"It was something..." she trailed off, looking more closely at a curtained window that fluttered open.

"Well, Gabriel is meeting with one of the officers from last night to get an update," Ian went on, "but I'm on my over to pick you up."

"It's Barney," Mira said as the curtain twitched back shut again. She was imagining things, but just for an instant, she could have sworn she saw Barney's face.

"What's Barney?" Ian asked.

"Oh," Mira said, not trusting herself, "it's nothing."

"Are you okay?"

"Yeah." She checked for traffic and scampered across the street.

"Will you be ready when I get there?"

"Yep," she said. "I'll see you soon." She hung up and muted the phone.

There were no cars in the gravel parking lot, but a small alley wrapped around the building and it was possible someone had parked back there. She went up to the front door and hesitated. The sign said New Horizons, but below it, someone had affixed another sign that said *Members Only* in black letters.

If Barney were kidnapped, this would be dangerous, right? Mira thought through the various spells and grabbed a silver coin and silk thread out of her pocket, holding them tightly in her hand, ready to cast if needed.

If he had been kidnapped, she reasoned, it wasn't likely that he'd be poking his head out the window.

Crap, she thought. He hadn't been taken, he ran away.

She grabbed hold of the indignation she felt and let it push some of the raw terror away, which made a sudden appearance when she thought about kidnappers.

When she cracked opened the door, she did so as quietly as possible. She held her breath and listened for any sound in the building, but only heard her heart trying to break out of her chest.

She slid inside and made sure she was alone before softly closing the door behind her. She was in a small foyer. A wooden staircase—painted white—was there, but the rest of the space sat empty. She ignored the two hallways leading off the room and padded over to the double doors that must have led to the new addition. They were stained dark wood and shone as though someone routinely polished them.

Mira tried one of the knobs and found it locked. The other yielded the same result. She had Push ready to go, but blowing open doors would be really loud, and more importantly, it would be obvious witchcraft, which was a no no in public. Although, it might be easy to explain away. A gust of wind in the freak weather, maybe?

She glanced around the foyer. There were a few decorations, but her gaze landed on a frame next to the door. A big old key hung from a pretty ribbon inside the frame. That wasn't even what she'd call hiding in plain sight. It was just *in* plain sight.

She took the key out of its frame and tried it on the door, jiggling it a few times before she heard a click. There was still no one around, but if anyone came in, they'd probably notice the missing key, so she put it back on its nail in the frame.

After spending a few moments listening at one of the doors, she slowly pushed it open.

The room appeared empty. Slipping inside, she closed the door before taking a good look around. Rows of seating were to the left and right of a wide carpeted walkway that ended at a wooden podium at the front of the room.

The carpet hid her footfalls as she slipped silently between the rows of benches.

Pews, she thought. *These are pews.*

The place didn't seem much like a church, but someone was definitely trying hard with the pews and aisle.

Mira froze at the sound of someone moving. Frantically trying to find the source, she found nothing, so she crept forward, a little faster, intent on checking the room quickly. As she neared the first row, however, a head came into view.

She edged slowly closer. The person sat on the floor in front of the pew, not on the seat.

When the head turned her direction, her heart leapt into her throat. The fear that froze her quickly melted away.

"Barney!"

He jumped to his feet. "Shh," he hissed. "Real or not, you need to be quiet or they'll come again."

Mira glanced nervously around the room and closed the space between them. "I'm real. Who are they?"

Barney's eyes darted around the room. "They are the voices in the air." He giggled.

Somehow that strangled little laugh made Mira even more afraid. "Have you been here all this time?"

"What time?"

"Barney, no one has seen you in two days. People are really worried."

"The voices find me when I go outside," Barney said.

It seemed as though she should have felt sorry for him, but unease insinuated itself deeply and wasn't going away. "I'll protect you from the voices. I'll get you some tea. You'd like that, right?"

"John says you feed me tea to poison me and keep my gifts locked away."

"Tyler and I would never do anything to hurt you," Mira said. "You don't have to drink it. We only want to help."

"John says he wants to help, too. He brought me here."

"To hide you from the voices?"

"They come when I try to leave and they say terrible things. The voices John brings say nicer things." He stared around, turning in a full circle before leaning to her and whispering, "I think they are the same."

Mira had a hard time keeping up with his delusions. "The voices are the same?"

"They say they aren't. John says they aren't." Once again, he leaned forward, eyes constantly looking fearfully into shadows, and he whispered, "But they are the same."

She couldn't help but stare into the shadows as Barney did. "Let's go. You can fill me in on the way back to my place."

"They won't let you leave," Barney said.

"They won't be able to stop us."

Barney stepped back and his eyes sought after something on the floor. Mira followed his gaze and found a line of silver glinting in the weak light. She followed the line as it went around them and disappeared under the pews.

The doorknob rattled, and Mira frantically searched for somewhere to hide.

"Too late," Barney said, his voice tinged with regret.

Both doors opened wide and six people entered wearing shiny mustard-colored robes edged in deep red. They wore hoods pulled low, so their faces couldn't be seen. All six people lined up silently at the back of the room. Mira gripped the coin in her hand and grabbed Barney's arm with her other, trying to drag him behind her.

Two more people entered. They also wore robes, but theirs were a shimmer of maroon, lined with black. They walked forward and knelt on the floor, causing Mira to lose sight of them.

The two hidden men spoke together in unison, but Mira didn't understand the words.

Power flared, and the silver line behind and around her erupted with energy.

A final person entered, in all black.

The robed figures had their heads bowed, causing their faces to be completely indistinguishable.

"Barney," Mira said in a voice as quiet as she could make it, "are these people holding you against your will?"

"John brought me here," Barney said. "It hurts when I try to leave."

"Stop saying that," Mira said. "John is dead."

Barney looked at her as though *she* was the one who was mad and pointed at the figure in black. "He's right there."

"Possibly both are correct," came the response from the hooded man.

Mira shivered. The voice was almost John's, but a slithery sound was there, which belonged to the leathery creature that had repeatedly tried to kill her in the Ether.

"Who are you people?" Mira knew the answer really didn't matter, but her brain seemed to be stuck on the voice.

The man with John's voice raised his hand and the six robed people lifted their heads and began to chant.

When the chanting started, it too sounded frighteningly familiar. The last time she heard the noise it was on the wind, whirling around her apartment. Emmit had put a stop to it when they sent the possessed John back to the other world.

Mira gripped Barney's hand and stepped back. She felt... something. The chanting wasn't only reaching her ears. It snuck inside and tried to latch itself to her bones.

A jolt of electricity seared her back and tossed her forward onto the ground. It took a few moments for the static pop to work itself out of her. Panting, she pushed herself unsteadily up to a sitting position.

From under the dark hood, laughter rang out. It seemed as though the chanting dropped just enough to allow the malevolent chuckle to sound more formidable. When she squeezed her hands into fists, she realized she wasn't holding onto Barney anymore. Looking around, she saw that he sat back on the floor in front of the pews.

Probably for the best, she thought.

Her knees quivered and threatened to buckle when she stood.

"You cannot step out of the circle," the voice under the black robe wheezed. "Not one created by nine. As a witch, you should know better."

It may have been built by nine, but only two held it, she thought. Or maybe those chanting were helping, bringing the total to eight. But unless someone hid in the shadows, Mira was sure there weren't nine.

"It will allow me to enter, however." The black hood was pushed back and Mira saw the face she feared.

"You're dead," Mira said.

What had been John chuckled. "Would that make things any better for you?"

Mira glanced around the enclosure, seeing power rise from the silvery circle, but she never let her eyes stray completely from John.

She had a few spells, but they'd never make it out of the circle. If he stepped in, though, maybe she could put an end to him.

How do you kill a dead man? Emmit hadn't managed to slay the thing. Mira wasn't sure what Emmit had done, but the thing inside John was certainly still alive.

She glanced at the cowering Barney and around at the circle once again.

"What should we do with you?" John asked in a taunting voice. "We had such plans back home."

Mira shuddered, remembering a few of those and clutched for the ward that was no longer there. Death would be better.

"Although, there are plenty of things I wouldn't mind trying here. But," John mockingly sighed, "the others would appreciate the amusement of a witch. For one as powerful as you, we could develop unique torments. I think we should send you back."

Mira noticed John glance down, perhaps at the two men holding the circle.

The circle belonged to them, her thoughts whizzed by, frantic in her own mind. John put his arm into the circle.

Mira would die before letting that thing get near her. She plunged her hand into her pocket and grabbed the crystal.

John glanced down once again and hissed something at the two men. Mira saw the circle shudder slightly to allow John to come all the way through.

One thing stopping her. Barney. There was a good chance that they could both die here. She knew that. The vague idea of what they had in store for her made her want to cast the spell anyway. When she glanced at Barney, he nodded sadly at her.

It was all Mira needed. She had no idea if Barney knew what was coming or not. When she muttered a few words, heat began to build around her as power gathered.

A part of Mira noted that John didn't seem to notice, at least not immediately. Someone chanting broke rank, however.

There was a witch there.

John did notice that. He turned and spat orders at the person and they fell back into line. With an irate glint in his eye, John smiled at Mira again before putting his arm through once again.

Mira gripped the stone's sharp corners hard enough to cut into her hand. A small part of her thought blood added to the spell might be a mistake, but the idea was drowned by a keening terror that tried to encompass the rest of her brain.

As John began to step through, Mira released the fire.

Flames erupted along the circle. Mira and Barney were inside the circle, true, but fire flowed along the wall of their enclosure, rubbing up against the silver one as though they were longtime friends sharing a greeting.

John screeched. He tried to pull back, but the flames grabbed at least part of him, greedily eating his robe, and Mira fervently hoped, some of his skin.

Their own circles stripped the fire from John's arm as he exited the barrier, but John was pissed.

Mira gave him her own derisive smile.

"Keep the circle going!" His glare told her he was going to try to make her pay. He studied her for a moment before turning. "Lock her in!"

When he stepped out of the door, he turned to glower at her a moment longer before disappearing.

Mira had been giving John all of her attention. It wasn't until he was gone that she noticed the chanting had grown louder. If the others were meaning to lock her and Barney inside the room, though, they seemed in no hurry to do so.

Barney began to cough.

They might not have been in a hurry to leave, but chanters also weren't trying to reach the pair.

Not that they had to. Unable to move out of their circle, the fire began to move inward, and even the smoke wasn't finding an escape.

The melody that dipped inside her seemed to solidify.

Mira went to Barney and knelt down with him. He covered his face with his shirt as best he could and she copied him, although the material of her shirt was much thinner for such a warm day.

"We need to move toward the center of the circle," Mira said. "I can make a new one to keep out the worst of this until they drop theirs." Seeing their circle tremble, she thought that might not even be necessary. If they dropped theirs, she could use Push to get her and Barney out.

Her arms began to tingle and she rubbed them distractedly.

It took tugging on Barney's arm a few times before he began to move with her. The magic surrounding them trembled and dropped away. Some of the trapped smoke began to billow out.

When she crawled to the aisle, keeping low to the ground, she saw the robed figures walking out of the room. They were still chanting, but they were leaving, which was the important part.

"Come on, Barney." She moved unsteadily to her feet and would have fallen, but for Barney holding her up. Mira had no idea how the spell had taken so much out of her, but she *had* turned it into a blood spell at the end. It was sometimes tricky how much power those spells used.

"Once we get close to the doors, I'll push away the fire. It will—" a hacking cough struck her.

Barney got the gist, however, and helped them both get as close as they could. Mira almost fumbled the coin, but when she gripped it firmly in her hand, she closed her eyes and began to trigger the awaiting spell.

Push was intended for people, or—as Mira's mother once taught her— furniture. It was defensive magic intended to clear the witch's path. A clear path was what they needed now.

Mira tried to fling up her arm to better direct the spell, but her hand flopped up and back down again. Sheer willpower drove the enchantment forward. Out in the hall, they managed to get almost to the door before Mira's spell dropped. For the first time since moving through the flames, Mira realized that she wasn't walking so much as being dragged along by Barney.

The seer fumbled with the door. Mira tried to help, but found that she couldn't move her arms any more.

"What the hell?" Mira tried to say. It came out as 'wha te hey,' and panic gripped her again.

Barney finally leveraged the door open without dropping her and staggered outside.

"Mira!"

She tried to look up at the sound of Ian's voice, but she was having trouble moving her head.

"Oh crap," he said. "I've got her, Barney. There's an ambulance on its way, but we need to move across the street."

"No ambulance," Barney said, "they can't help her."

"What do you mean?" Ian said. "Where's she hurt?"

Mira's legs gave out and he was forced to pick her up. She tried to say something, but nothing came out.

"Magic did this," Barney said.

It wasn't until then that Mira felt the chanting stop. She wasn't sure how long she hadn't physically been hearing it, but she felt it the moment they actually stopped.

"They are back," Barney said, his voice quavering.

"Barney," Ian said, "what's wrong, what happened?"

"So loud. They crawl under your skin and get you." This was emphasized as Barney began to scratch. "They got her."

Mira felt herself being lowered to the ground.

"Barney!" Frustration rang out of Ian's voice. "A lot of people are going to be here very soon. What happened to Mira?"

"They locked her in," Barney said, then whimpered and dug his nails into his arm scratching fiercely.

"I don't know what that means," Ian said.

"She's there. All there. But trapped inside. She's not hurt. Not in a way that any doctor can help with."

"Stop!" Ian yelled. "You're going to scratch your skin off."

"Because they live in there," Barney said, and then giggled before wailing. "They won't let me go!"

"Listen," Ian said, taking hold of Barney, "you are going to help me get her into the car. Then you are going to sit in the front seat and not move. Do you understand me?"

"Hmm," Barney whined.

"Do you understand me?"

Barney nodded.

Ian picked up Mira and laid her out across the back seat. He took a moment to stare into her bright eyes.

She felt alert as well. Mira tried to talk, to move her arms and legs, to scream—anything. When nothing got out, the screaming went on in her mind.

Barney got into the front seat and put his seatbelt on before staring straight forward.

A fire truck arrived. Moments later, an ambulance along with the police came on the scene.

It didn't take Barney long to start talking to himself. First, he muttered about the creatures living in him, and then he moved on to the voices. Mira wanted to comfort him or at least to shut her ears when he started talking about the voices.

After what seemed like a lifetime later, Ian got into the car. "Say nothing until we've passed all the emergency vehicles," Ian said. He waved at a few people as he slowly pulled away.

Mira assumed Ian must have been talking to Barney, because she was mute and getting more pissed off about it by the second.

Ian took out his cell phone and called his partner.

The car speakers made Gabriel's voice fill the air. "I'm on my way back—"

Ian cut Gabriel off, "Meet me at Mira's house now."

CHAPTER 15

"WHAT HAPPENED?" Gabriel asked quickly.

"I have Barney. It's not good," Ian said.

Since he didn't mention her, Mira knew Ian was trying to save his partner at least some worry.

"I'll be there shortly," Gabriel said before hanging up.

"Okay," Ian said, turning to Barney, "talk."

Barney opened up like an overripe melon, but it was all ramblings.

"Okay, stop," Ian said, rubbing his forehead.

Barney didn't stop. "They want to know things. They get into your head and make you talk. John made it better, but only after he made it worse."

"Enough," Ian said, not unkindly. "You're away from there now. Whatever happened, you're with us. We'll get this sorted out."

Barney didn't stop talking, but he kept his mutterings to himself.

"Is there anyone you know who can help with this kind of thing?" Ian asked him. "Barney, this is important. It's for Mira. Is there anyone you can think of—"

"Tyler," Barney said.

"How is she doing back there?" Ian asked, checking his rearview mirror again. "Is she asleep?"

Barney twisted in his seat. "Not asleep. Just trapped." He

stared at her for a few moments. "I wonder what they are making her hear."

Gooseflesh broke out on Ian's arms.

The strange thing to Mira was that she could hear something. Like a voice carried on a nonexistent wind. She couldn't quite make it out, but after hearing Barney's words, she didn't dare try to make sense of it. She focused on the sounds around her.

Once Ian was quiet again, Barney took to talking to himself once more.

"Can she hear us?" Ian asked.

Barney glanced at Mira again and shrugged. "Who can say?"

"We're almost there," Ian said. "Is there anything else you can tell me?"

"They tell me a lot. Too much. Magic is all I know. Magic against magic. Nine against one. They talk all the time. But when I leave, it hurts. It's like needles in the brain. Like now. Sharp little needles. Poke poke poking. I wanted to go, but I want to go back now."

"Don't worry," Ian said. "We're going to Mira's house. We'll find a way to make you safe."

Barney let out a chuckle. Then the floodgates opened up and he laughed. "Safe? Safe from words? Safe from dreams?" He choked and coughed a little. "Safe from the voices?" He laughed again.

Ian looked at him from the corner of his eyes. "Thank god," Ian said when he pulled into the driveway.

"Stay!" Ian barked the command at Barney when the seer yanked off his seatbelt.

Barney looked at him reproachfully.

"I mean, wait here," Ian corrected. "Please. Keep an eye on Mira."

When Ian was convinced Barney would stay put, the detective jumped out of the car and met his partner.

The voices were muffled through the car glass, but Mira was glad to hear Gabriel's voice. Between Ian's frustrated panic and

Barney's insane ramblings, she wanted to pull her hair out. But Gabriel could sort things out.

Gabriel yanked the back door open and leaned over Mira, brushing the hair out of her eyes. Her eyes were the only thing she could move. Despite what people may read, it's hard to will someone to do something using only your eyes. Muscles in the face need to move to create meaning.

Mira couldn't help but try.

"Let's get her inside," Gabriel said.

He sounded calm, but Mira could feel the storm of energy begin to rise around him when he pulled her out of the car.

Gabriel carried Mira upstairs, and she could hear Ian going back and forth with Barney.

"Do you have a key?" Gabriel hollered down to Ian.

"No. If she had her purse she must have lost it in the fire," Ian called.

"Fire," Gabriel muttered. "Great." He did his best to hold Mira and check her pockets. Mira figured the two of them looked ridiculous, but the important part was, he found the key.

While holding Mira upright, he shoved the door open, then picked her up and took her to the couch. There, he felt for a pulse in her neck and made sure she was breathing. He was taking off her jacket when the other two arrived.

"What happened?" Gabriel asked without looking at them.

"I've been trying to piece that together," Ian said. "I only know magic was involved. Barney said the doctors wouldn't be able to help her."

"Tell me," Gabriel said, looking at Barney.

"They're everywhere," Barney said. "With me all the time. Needles in my brain, voices on the air. The voices got her. Locked her up inside herself."

Gabriel glared at his partner.

Ian told him everything he knew, which wasn't much.

"Can Della fix this?" Gabriel asked when Ian was done.

"I tried to call," Ian said. "No answer."

Gabriel pulled up one of Mira's sleeves and started to check for injuries. "Do you know any other witches to contact?"

"Ones that I know we can trust? No. I'm not even sure a witch can undo it. Barney said nine against one. It doesn't sound like something that just anyone can do."

Gabriel sighed and pulled out his phone. He scrolled through the numbers and brought one up before handing the phone over to Ian. "Tell them we need Emmit."

"Are you sure you want him over here?" Ian asked.

"No," Gabriel snapped, and then paused for a moment, "but I know we need help."

Ian clicked the button and started to pace. "Hello?" he said after a few moments. "This is Ian Burke. I need someone to get hold of Emmit Harker." There was a pause. "I don't give a damn if you know me or not, you need to let him kn—a" Ian paused again. "Just get him a message."

Ian covered the phone. "They won't even admit they know Emmit, since they don't know me."

Gabriel stalked over to Ian and grabbed the phone. "This is Detective Gabriel Flint, and I sure as hell know that at least some of you assholes know who I am. Tell Emmit that Mira needs him. Now." Gabriel moved back to the couch and sat next to Mira. "We don't know, but he might be able to help. Get him here now." He clicked off the phone and dropped it.

"Barney," Gabriel said, "is there anything else... Barney?" He looked around the room until he spotted that Barney had sat down out of the way in the corner.

"I don't think he's able to help much. He hasn't been able to pull himself together," Ian said.

"Mira's tea might help," Gabriel said. "The special one she makes for him."

"I'll check the kitchen," Ian said.

Magic doesn't have to leave a mark, but Mira couldn't pass this information on to Gabriel. He checked her arms, legs, and even her head as though to check for damage.

"I can't tell what's what," Ian said. "I'll run to his apartment."

Gabriel nodded.

"You going to be okay here?"

Gabriel glanced at Barney. "He seems pretty settled in over there."

"I meant... Look, she's going to be okay."

"Yeah," Gabriel said.

"I'll be back."

When Ian left, Gabriel pulled the silver-colored chain out from under his shirt and rubbed his fingers over the rune. Barney began chatting to himself, but Gabriel ignored him. The angel stood up, then paced back and forth in front of the couch twice before sitting back down next to Mira.

"I'm not sure what to do here," Gabriel said, keeping his voice low and for Mira's ears only. "I feel like I should be doing something." He took off the necklace. "You had one of these, and I think it would have stopped whatever this is."

He stared into Mira's eyes. She watched him, wondering what he was getting at. Her ward had been drained what seemed like ages ago, and he was right. There was a good chance it wouldn't have stopped a spell cast by so many.

"Anyway, this isn't going to help you. I know it's not. But I also know I have to try." Gabriel opened Mira's hand and closed it around the platinum medallion.

At that point, Mira felt so sorry for Gabriel that her heart ached. Mentally, she beat against the prison that her body had become.

"Yeah, I didn't think so," Gabriel said, sounding defeated.

He left it there for a while longer, as though hoping it would make a difference.

Bitterness began to well up and he yanked the chain away. "I knew that spell was a mistake. *You* should have known it was a mistake. It was a stupid stupid thing to do. I should have broken the damned chain the moment I left."

Mira would have liked to argue.

Argue, scream, cry. At that point, she would settle for anything.

Eventually, Gabriel's eyes landed on Barney again. "What about you?" he asked Barney. "Are you okay? The tea is on its way, but is there anything—"

"The voices don't stop. They lie and hiss out of the dark. They want—"

Gabriel nodded. "Hang in there, Ian's bringing your tea. Were you injured anywhere? Was she?"

"They trapped her with words. There was nothing anyone— why don't they stop? Why would John do this? I thought he was my friend." Barney drew his knees up, clutched at them, and buried his face.

Barney's rantings became muffled. The word 'voices' popped up repeatedly. 'Useless' was mentioned. Mira could sympathize with that feeling. How did she expect Gabriel to fight witchcraft without a witch? The words were already...

"The idea of magic is still too alien for me," Gabriel said. "I'm having a hard time really understanding it, but I think the words are important. Well, I guess with witch magic there's loads of other stuff—ingredients, symbols, language, the whole thing was wrapped together."

It was true, Mira mused. Everything was tied to the power of the witch. Even Della had to draw symbols in the air and understand the language of the spell.

But Gabriel had words as well. At least when he and Mira had been in the Ether, Gabriel's voice held power. Was it possible he could use his voice here?

"She looks uncomfortable," Gabriel muttered as though he needed an excuse. "I'm going to lay her down in the other room."

He carefully lifted Mira and took her into her bedroom. After laying her on her bed, he adjusted her arms and legs, then arranged her pillow.

Misery flooded Mira. She was trapped and Gabriel was wavering from upset to pissed off, to depressed, and back again. The whole situation seriously sucked, and she couldn't think of a thing to fix it. She really wanted to be left alone for a while to wrap her head around things—every noise and motion out of her eyesight felt inherently dangerous because she had no control.

She closed her eyes, the only part of herself she could move, and turned inward.

"I don't think you should close your eyes," Gabriel said softly. "At least not for long."

A part of her knew he was probably right. She opened them and stared at the ceiling, wanting to shut the world out.

"You can hear us," Gabriel said, sounding somewhat relieved. "Are you hurt anywhere?"

Mira stared at him, wanting to glare or cry—either would work.

"Once for yes and twice for no," Gabriel said. "Any pain?"

In the only way she was able, she told him no.

"This has to be hell for you."

She blinked yes and looked at the ceiling, tired of being stared at.

She felt the bed move as he sat down next to her and moved into her line of vision again. He took her hand—for her comfort or his, she wasn't sure.

"I don't suppose you have any ideas on how to fix this?" Gabriel asked.

Mira closed her eyes. Her frustration was running so high tears should have arrived, but she couldn't even cry properly.

Not that she wanted to cry in front of Gabriel.

"Right," Gabriel said, "stupid question. You probably have tons of ideas and nothing to do with them." After a while, he added, "Please open your eyes. I don't know what happens if you go to sleep."

Mira's eyes snapped open. She hadn't thought about that. Could it be possible that she'd be locked further inside herself?

"Since you can hear me, I guess I should ask first, but I'm not going to," he said, letting go of her, but setting her hand on his leg, as though not willing to lose contact with her. "I'm breaking the chain."

Mira blinked twice, which Gabriel conveniently didn't see, since he looked away.

She had been expecting to be able to feel the chain break, but she only heard it.

"It's funny," he said, "I almost wish you couldn't hear me, because I'm about to make a giant fool of myself." When he took her hand again, she could still feel the chain and ward in his hand. "Although, I guess it wouldn't work if you couldn't hear. Maybe, anyway."

Mira watched him closely.

"I'm not sure if this would work better if we were closer to the Ether, but I don't think that's even an option. Still, my voice worked there, maybe a little too well. There shouldn't be any reason for it not to work here."

Light dawned for Mira.

"Or maybe there's some reason I don't know," he continued, more talking to himself than Mira. "The word to use, that's important. We found that out the hard way. We won't know if it's the right word until we try, but I'll know if it's the wrong one."

He shifted on the bed as though uncomfortable.

"How does open sound?"

Thinking of all the ways open could go wrong, Mira rapidly blinked twice.

"Move? No," he said before she could answer. "I'm not sure what would happen if you didn't have the option of moving."

He thought for a while, and as useless as it was, Mira thought with him, trying to think of a word that would work.

"Well," he said at last, "they locked you in. How about unlock?"

Mira focused on the word. It made sense, and if it wasn't the right word, it didn't sound as though it could do much harm.

"It's worth a try, I guess. Now for the fun part. At least for you. If nothing else, it will give you something to laugh about later."

Mira blinked her eyes no, but she wasn't sure Gabriel noticed.

Gabriel opened his mouth to say something, but it looked as though he changed his mind. He closed his eyes and started once again before shaking his head.

After a moment, he laughed humorously. "It's funny. Over there, I had no trouble rambling things off. Granted, I nearly killed you, but here it feels stupid. It's as though that world wasn't real." He gently squeezed her hand. "Small price to pay, right?"

He closed his eyes again. "Remember what it felt like. That's what you said there, and it worked."

Mira could feel Gabriel's power swirl around him. The cool energy washed over her in a gentle wave.

"Remember what it felt like," he murmured to himself. With his eyes still closed, he adjusted his posture and situated himself directly facing her.

There was silence for a few moments, and then he said, in a loud clear voice, "Unlock."

Nothing happened, but Mira suspected Gabriel knew that because he didn't open his eyes.

"Unlock!" he yelled more forcefully.

There wasn't so much as a wobble from Mira. She could feel his power building, but not to the point that it should be.

He tried again with no effect.

Using one hand, he pointed at her. "Unlock!"

He opened his eyes, looking more than a little lost. Then his look hardened and his gaze darted around the room. He gripped Mira's hand. Then he stood, trying to look everywhere at once.

The shaking started moments later. Mira tried to tense, tried to move, but could only watch as the walls seemed to vibrate.

Gabriel's eyes locked onto the picture over her bed. He jumped on her, shielding her as it fell, smacking him on the back of his head. He grunted as it hit. Gabriel took her other arm and tucked it in under him, not letting go of her other hand.

Dishes rattled, books fell to the floor, and things broke around the apartment, but the shaking continued. He was tense from head to toe. Gabriel locked eyes with Mira for a moment before closing his own and resting his forehead on hers. Something inside him seemed to break.

"Dammit, Mira, come back."

It wasn't loud. He didn't yell or point, but Mira felt his cool power go through her, shifting something.

For the first time in what seemed like days, Mira took a deep, shuddering breath.

CHAPTER 16

L OUD CRASHES CAME FROM THE other room and it felt as though the whole apartment tried to come down, but at the moment, Mira didn't care.

She took another deep breath for the sheer joy of it, and gripped Gabriel's hand.

His eyes opened slowly, as though afraid.

Everything stopped moving. The dishes were unconvinced that the earthquake had ended, and a few more crashed to the ground.

Gabriel pushed the picture off and sat up. Mira wanted to hold him and not let go, but when she tried to grab his arm, her arm flopped around rather uselessly.

"Oh, god," Gabriel said, "what did I do?"

Mira laughed, but it turned into a sob.

Looking panicked, he grabbed her arm and started an inspection.

"It's okay," Mira said, her voice dry and cracking, tears running down her face. "It's asleep."

She sat up, buried her face into Gabriel's chest, and wrapped her arms around him as best she could.

Gabriel held her tightly. At first, she didn't care. She didn't try to stem her ragged breathing or tears. The pins and needles sensation spread through her arms and grabbed her attention. Sniffing, she tried to rein herself in. Gabriel didn't seem ready to let go, so she brought herself under control.

She wriggled her toes until the sharp stabs of pain suggested her circulation was returning. When she wiped the tears from her face, Gabriel loosened his grip.

"Sorry," she said, using the sleeve of her shirt to rub away the tears.

"Don't be," Gabriel said.

"Thank you." She had to grit her teeth to avoid falling apart again.

"I trust I wasn't asked here to witness this." Emmit's voice sounded serene, but he glared harshly at Gabriel.

Mira sniffed and shifted so that she could see Emmit.

The glare didn't entirely leave, but worry crowded most of it away. "What happened?"

"I should go," Gabriel said.

"What?" Mira asked. "No, you shouldn't."

"If all is well, maybe *I* should take my leave," Emmit said. "I was under the impression there was an emergency."

"There was," Mira said. "I mean, there is." She closed her eyes and rubbed her head. "I think I need a minute."

"Of course," Gabriel said, standing up quickly.

"I smell like smoke and need to move around a bit," Mira continued.

"Smoke?" Emmit asked.

"Of course," Gabriel said, ignoring him.

"Can you fill Emmit in on what happened?" Mira asked.

Gabriel's sighed. "Yeah."

"Thank you," Mira said, "because we really need to talk."

Gabriel shut the door, leaving Mira alone in her room. She wiped any remaining moisture from her face. Once again, she flexed her fingers and her toes, making sure they were still there.

They had trapped her inside her own body. Fuming, she grabbed a towel and shut herself away in the bathroom.

It had been easy for them to cast the magic. All her life she had been content in her own strength. Even in college when she let her life and her magic fall apart, she still knew the strength was there.

Today that had been taken away from her. She scrubbed from head to toe, taking her anger out on the bubbles. The fire had been stupid. She was ready to admit that. However, looking back, she wasn't sure she would have changed anything. Remembering John—a dead man—coming into the circle to get her, sent shivers down her body.

What did he want from her? *Why* did he want her? He hadn't really wanted her, had he? He would have been happy to use her, that was true, but she had blundered into his path.

Karma again? Mira turned off the water and let herself drip dry for a few moments.

It was one possibility, but there was too much about the day that karma couldn't explain.

What was she going to do now? John would come for Barney. She was sure of that. Barney was some sort of communication conduit from the other side. What they needed to communicate, however, she couldn't even begin to hazard a guess.

Mira dried off and put on a fresh set of clothes.

John coming after her was a possibility, but not a strong one. Mira getting in John's way was much more likely. Next time, though, she would be ready for them.

They had trapped her inside her own body and she was going to make them pay for that.

There was a chill in the air when she pulled on her socks. She wondered briefly how much damage the apartment had sustained, but was drawn from her thoughts when she heard yelling from the other room.

Shoving her other foot into her sock, she scuttled into the living room.

"I told you I didn't do anything!" Gabriel yelled.

Emmit went to grab Gabriel's arm and stopped inches away due to an invisible barrier.

"*She* doesn't have a ward, but you do?" Emmit asked. "Where did you get it?"

"Mira made it," Gabriel said.

Emmit stepped in and lowered his cold steel voice, intending for only Gabriel to hear. "And this is how you've repaid her?"

Mira felt as though she needed a ward, as power clashed around the two.

"Enough!" Mira yelled. "What the hell is wrong with you two?"

They appeared to ignore her.

"She wouldn't have needed the help if you were there." Darkness seemed to stretch up and around Emmit.

Alchemy hissed, his hair standing on end.

"She didn't want me there," Gabriel snapped.

The fire around them ebbed. "It's not magic she can break," Emmit said, although he sounded unsure.

"She didn't break it. She found a way around it."

Emmit stepped back and seemed to regain his composure, but his voice remained icy. "This is not how I intended things to go."

"Hey, SHE is in the room," Mira snapped.

"No one gives a damn what you intended!" Gabriel seethed.

It wasn't until Mira put herself between the two that they seemed to notice her.

This close, Mira could feel Emmit's power like a storm dammed up.

"What is it with you two?" Mira asked, glaring from one to the other.

The power that had built between the two slowly dissipated.

"We seem to be missing some information," Emmit said, calmly.

Mira shivered and rubbed her arms. "We have a lot to talk about." She looked around the room, feeling deflated at the sight of the mess. Then her eyes fell on Barney. He still sat in the corner. "Gabriel, will you close the window? Emmit, mind turning on the heat?"

She didn't wait for a reply, but went over to Barney and sat on the floor next to him. "How are you doing?"

"They won't leave me alone," he said.

"Is it coming from the Ether?"

Barney shook his head.

"The same people we heard earlier?"

Barney shrugged, and then nodded.

Gooseflesh broke out on Mira's arm. "I think I have something that can help, but I need you to move towards the middle of the room." She wanted those voices well away from anyone she knew.

Barney was reluctant, but moved out. Mira grabbed a long skein of silk yarn and began to unwind it as she walked around him.

"That's what *they* did," Barney said glumly, watching the string being placed.

Mira froze. "It's only temporary," she promised, "and you can step out of it anytime you want."

He nodded, but didn't seem convinced.

She finished the circle and twisted the strands together. "When you leave, step over the string, okay? Not on it." She traced symbols onto the carpet, and then touched the string, putting power into her spell. That little use of power had her wavering.

The effect on Barney wasn't instantaneous to the eye. For a few moments, nothing changed, and then he opened his eyes—which had been scrunched tightly closed. He breathed deeply a few times and started to relax.

"Later," Mira said, "I'll try to make you something you can carry with you that will have the same effects."

Barney was exhausted, but now he had a wide circle around him, enough to stretch out and get a break from the constant attack on his mind.

Mira waited until she felt steady before standing. Someone had stacked her fallen books up into a pile next to the bookshelf. Looking around, though, she saw that Gabriel and Emmit seemed as if they were conspiring together by the window. How could they go from yelling at each other one minute to another moment of being buddy buddy?

"What's up?" she asked.

Gabriel stood aside and motioned out the window.

Frowning, Mira pushed back her curtains. The world began turning white. Snowflakes blotted out the big house.

"No wonder it's so cold," Mira said, already missing the warmth. She stared out the window for a few minutes, thinking about the earthquakes, the heat, and now the swirls of snow. Life was complicated enough without the atmosphere fighting against you.

"We should talk," Emmit said.

Mira glanced at Barney, who seemed to be meditating in the circle. "In the kitchen. I'll make us some tea."

"Shoes," Gabriel said. "Trust me, you're going to need them if you go in there."

The idea of seeing her kitchen in such a mess made her cringe, but she figured, as she laced up her shoes, she couldn't put it off forever.

Even though she had braced herself for the mess, she groaned when she saw it. It seemed like everything had rattled itself off of shelves. It had caused more damage than the previous earthquakes put together. Trying to ignore the worst of the chaos, she waded over to the stove.

"I'm not sure I should chance the burners," Mira said. "At least not until the gas can be checked."

"There are a lot of blanks about the day that we need you to fill in," Emmit said.

"Yeah," Mira sighed, "I know."

The story unfolded while Mira made tea. Once that was done, she talked while starting to clean. The others helped where they could, organizing, stacking, sweeping. They managed to get much more done than she had anticipated. Mostly because it was a long story to tell.

Once she reached the part where she discovered John, Emmit interrupted.

"It couldn't have been John," Emmit said.

"You're right," Mira said, "it wasn't him. It was that thing that possessed him, wearing him like a costume. The moment he spoke, I recognized the voice, but I couldn't be sure it was him until he showed himself."

"How did he get here?" Emmit asked.

"We weren't exactly having a back and forth dialogue," Mira said. "John was going to toss me into the Ether for the enjoyment of his friends. He thought they could use me for something. I was more interested in keeping him the hell away from me."

"He couldn't have—"

"Trust me," Mira said, "he was intent on doing just that. Besides, if he's here, it means there is a way to get back and forth." Emmit opened his mouth, but Mira cut him off. "And if you're going to tell me again that it's not possible, you're deluding only yourself."

Emmit pursed his lips.

"It's not surprising," Gabriel said. "When we were at Barney's apartment the other day, it felt as though we were almost in the Ether again."

Mira nodded. "It felt as if something was right there with us."

There was a knock at the front door, then it immediately opened and Ian called out. Gabriel went to meet him in the living room.

"I know you don't want it to be true," Mira told Emmit the moment they were alone, "but he is back. It's not something I would lie about."

"Could you have been drugged?" Emmit suggested. "Hallucinating, perhaps?"

Mira shook her head and looked down. "He was having too much fun seeing my reaction while sober."

She didn't see Emmit move, but he was beside her in the space of a breath and hugged her briefly.

"I'm so sorry," Emmit said.

Not expecting the contact, Mira almost jumped, but the contact felt good. At least until Gabriel and Ian walked in. Then it turned awkward.

Emmit let go, but didn't move far away. "This changes a lot." Sadness filled his words, but Mira had no idea where it came from. "Everything, in fact. Is there anything else you can tell me?"

"You know the rest," Mira said. "John was the ninth person, but it was the chorus of six that, well, did what they did to me."

"John?" Ian asked.

"I'll fill you in," Gabriel said. "Maybe we should—"

"No," Emmit said quickly. "I'm leaving. Mira, would you see me out."

"Of course," Mira said. She couldn't look at Gabriel or Ian when she led Emmit through the living room.

"Are you going to be okay driving home?" Mira asked.

"I assure you," Emmit said, "Reinfield's men will see me safely home."

"Of course," Mira said.

"I am sorry this has happened," Emmit said.

"Any ideas of what we should do?" Mira asked.

Emmit glanced at the spot where the kitchen light streamed into the living room. "As much as I'd rather not say it, keep Gabriel close by if you can."

"I'm sure no one's going out in this weather," Mira said.

"Dead men have little to worry about," Emmit said. "There's a lot I need to do. I should be going." He was almost at the door, when he hesitated and turned back to her. "Would you..."

Mira's heart skipped a beat, but she had to urge Emmit to continue. "Would I, what?"

"I know this has been a trying day and you probably need your rest, but would you spend tomorrow with me?"

Mira's couldn't stop the smile from spreading across her face. "I'd like that."

Emmit's face softened. "I'll be here in the morning around ten." He gave her a rather chaste kiss before opening the door and disappearing in the sheet of white storming down.

When she turned to the kitchen, Mira's smile wavered. A week ago, she had wanted to spend the day with Emmit. As much time as possible, in fact. Now, the thought of telling Gabriel made her second think her date with Emmit.

That's silly, she scolded herself. *Gabriel hasn't shown any real interest in you. He saved your life several times, but he felt he needed to, more or less.*

To stall for time, she was going to ask if Barney needed anything, but found him asleep on the floor. She should have pulled the couch away from the wall, at least. Maybe she could get Ian and Gabriel to help with that. A circle around the couch wouldn't be any more difficult than on the floor, right?

For now, Mira grabbed a pillow and blanket for Barney before going back to the kitchen.

Mira's stomach growled at the smell of food in the air when she entered.

"It's good to see you up and around," Ian said. "I'm pretty sure Della would have a few choice words for us if we hadn't been able to get you fixed up."

"All thanks to Gabriel," Mira said.

"I brought food for everyone," Ian continued. "Want to see if Barney needs anything?"

"He's asleep," Mira said, sitting down at the mostly cleared table.

"Help yourself," Ian said.

"Thanks," Mira said.

"Gabriel and I were just discussing how this affects our case," Ian said. "Chasing a dead man isn't exactly something we can put in the case files."

"According to the case files, though," Mira said, "he's alive."

"True," Ian said, "but aren't people going to notice if we bring him in?"

"I think we're jumping ahead of ourselves," Gabriel said. "We have to find him first."

"What do you think he wants with the supernaturals?" Mira asked. "At least one of the chanters was a witch."

"Maybe he's recruiting them," Ian suggested.

Mira narrowed her eyes. "I don't think Tyler would have been hiding under a hood watching John feed me to monsters."

"Of course not," Gabriel agreed, giving Ian a 'stop right there' look. "But he disappeared a week ago, before the most current group of magic users. If John is recruiting witches, it's something new."

It was enough to mollify Mira partially. Her phone sounded with a text from Della, which distracted her from the aggravation.

Stuck in town. Are you at home? Everything okay there?

We're good here, Mira replied. *Only a little shaken up.*

We? Della asked.

Gabriel and Ian are here.

"Should I tell Della about Barney?" Mira asked the detectives.

Gabriel and Ian glanced at each other before Ian spoke. "If supernaturals weren't involved, I'd say yes. But now?"

"I think you're right," Gabriel said. "Not yet. We don't know who *is* involved."

Are they stuck there? Della asked. *I picked the worst day to be at the office.*

Mira smiled and texted back, *lol I don't know if they will leave or not.*

They can stay at the house if they need to. Just tell them my room is off limits. Who knows what I've left out in there ;) I need someone to check on it anyway. I think the heat is off and everything will freeze.

I'll let them know and text later, Mira replied.

"What are we going to do with Barney?" Mira asked, slipping her cell phone back in her pocket. "I mean, he can't go home. He could hang out here, of course, but would John expect that?"

"He definitely can't go home yet," Ian said. "I picked up a few changes of clothes for him and a few of his notebooks."

"I don't think here is a good idea, either," Gabriel said. "He could come home with me, I guess."

"Does he need to stay in one of the circle things that Mira makes?" Ian asked. "It doesn't exactly seem portable."

"I think I can make him something," Mira said, "but it would only be temporary."

"How long would it take?" Gabriel asked.

"Maybe a few hours," Mira said. "Although, I haven't checked downstairs yet. It may take a while to find everything. It may not matter much. I'm not sure anyone is going far tonight."

They looked at her quizzically.

"Della's stuck in town," Mira said. "The roads are getting bad."

Frowning, Gabriel got up and went to the window. "Christ, it's a blizzard."

Mira grinned and noticed Ian do the same as he joined his partner.

"I'll call in," Ian said.

Mira joined Gabriel while Ian called. "Della said you all can stay at her house tonight." The cars were completely covered. "How much do you think is out there?"

"Well over a foot already," Gabriel said.

Mira became very conscious of how close she and Gabriel stood. His arm brushed against hers and her heart beat faster. More importantly, she found that she didn't want to move away.

CHAPTER 17

T HE OFFICE SAID TO STAY put," Ian said. "They're going to call us if anything comes up in the neighborhood." Mira cleared her throat, but didn't move away. "You all are of course, welcome to stay here, but you'd probably be more comfortable at the house."

Gabriel didn't move, either, which was promising. Then she realized, if he stayed, he'd be here when Emmit came over in the morning.

How could she forget about Emmit?

She stepped away, breaking contact. "I need to go over there anyway. The heat's off, and in a house like that, the pipes could freeze fast."

Feeling more than a little confused about which direction her heart wanted to go, Mira woke Barney.

Barney was a problem. He didn't want to step outside the circle, and it felt cruel to make him.

"I promise I'll build a new one when we go to Della's," Mira said.

"No," Barney said.

"You can't sleep on the floor," Mira said. "Although, I guess I could pull the couch away from the wall."

"I think he'll be safer at the house," Gabriel said.

"I agree," Ian said. "Maybe Mira should stay over there as well."

"Mira will be okay," Gabriel said.

"I don't see how," Ian said. "She wasn't earlier."

"Which won't happen again," Gabriel said, his jaw set in a hard line.

"But—"

"I'll explain later," Gabriel said, cutting Ian off.

Ian changed tactics. "If we can't get Barney over there, we'll stay here."

"What about your string?" Gabriel asked.

Mira looked at him, puzzled. "What string?"

"The one you used last week. I think you kept it around your waist during a spell or something."

"Oh," Mira said, "I burned that." *Along with everything else that touched the Ether.* But she kept the latter part to herself.

"Would something similar work?" Gabriel asked.

Mira watched Barney and thought it over. "It might. It would be really temporary, but it might do the trick." She opened a cabinet and selected strands of pure, un-dyed, cotton, and considered the wool string as well. In the end, she decided both would work best.

The two materials, one having once been part of a living animal that listened to the world around it, and one from a plant, which could remember a time when it felt the vibrations of the world, would work to protect against a psychic attack.

If it were a circle, it could be made of almost anything. In this case, though, it would wind around Barney.

When she had the strings twisted together, she created a new circle on the floor, and then powered it; doing everything she could to lock the spell in the string instead of the circle itself. With that managed, she picked up one end of the string, handed it to Barney, and had him turn in three circles, winding the protection around his chest.

"Go ahead and test it," Mira said.

Barney was more than hesitant. Holding the end of the string like a lifeline, he stepped out of the circle. It took a few moments for him to be convinced that it was actually working, but when it sank in, he smiled.

"This will only work for a few hours at most," Mira said. "I'll set something up for you at the house."

Once Barney was settled, she bundled up for the great outdoors.

When she was ready, she saw that Gabriel and Ian were both weighed down with case files. She gave them bags so there was at least a chance the documents would stay dry.

When Mira opened the door, snow swirled into the apartment. Seeing the wall of white waist high that had drifted along the side of her apartment, she closed the door again.

"Let's go out through the garage," she suggested.

Mira ushered them downstairs.

"This room didn't take a lot of damage," Gabriel commented.

Mira, last in line, felt relieved when she was able to get a closer look.

Once in her workshop, she thought about what Ian had said—about her not being safe. It was relatively true. She had used two of her largest spells earlier in the day and hadn't had the time to replace them.

"Wait a sec," Mira said. "I want to grab something." She crossed the room, walking around the spot her circle sat, and picked through a few partially prepared items. They still needed some work, but it wouldn't take her long to get them started.

The hairs on the back of Mira's neck rose. She rubbed the spot and turned. Barney's eyes began to glaze over.

"Mira, does that thing you wrapped around him stop the Ether?" Gabriel asked while edging toward her, keeping his eyes on Barney.

Barney moved towards the center of the room. As he drew closer to Mira, she began to feel the Ether pressing into the room.

"No," Mira said. "A spell like that takes a lot more work. That's why he has the tea."

"I get the feeling that I'm missing something," Ian said.

Barney stopped in the middle of Mira's invisible circle. His eyes rolled back in his head.

Mira shivered at the sight of Barney and the feel of the room.

Gabriel reached Mira and pulled her farther away from Barney. "We need to get out of here."

"It shouldn't last long," Mira said, "it rarely does."

"This is different," Gabriel said.

Mira was more than happy to get away, so she didn't argue. She began to take a wide path around Barney, and the closer she got, the more powerful the pull of the Ether felt.

Gabriel grabbed her around the waist and swung her back into the corner, causing Mira to squeak in surprise. She was getting ready to tell him off when the room seemed to dim.

Shadows grew longer.

"Ian, go upstairs," Gabriel snapped. When his partner didn't move, Gabriel yelled, "Now! Go!"

Ian backed away toward the stairs. "What should I do?"

Static seemed to crackle in the air.

"Call Emmit," Gabriel said. "Tell him the Ether is trying to break through."

Ian pulled out his cell phone and moved into the stairwell, but didn't go upstairs.

Barney turned toward Gabriel and cocked his head as though listening to something on the other side.

The room grew bright, and then dimmed again.

The feeling of being watched began to build.

"Barney," Gabriel called, "whatever you're doing, you have to stop."

The seer grinned, showing more teeth than any normal smile should.

Out of the corner of her eye, Mira thought she saw something scuttle across the floor.

Why? Why here? Mira could almost understand the thinness at Barney's house. The Ether often made itself known there, almost as much as the real world, but Barney had never been here before.

What could cause...

It was the circle.

"Barney!" Gabriel yelled, trying to summon up as much command as he could. "Stop this now!"

For just a moment, Mira thought she saw the faintest glimmer of wings on Gabriel's back. Her hands felt the softness of feathers.

Then it was gone.

When Mira looked out from behind Gabriel, Barney sneered.

Would trapping Barney in the circle help? It had stopped Emmit from breaking through when she worked the Balance spell. She had been closing off the Ether. Something was here trying to open the path.

It could only be the center of the circle that was thin enough to breach. That was where the spell had taken place. That was where she had reached into Emmit and pulled a large part of him away from the other side.

She didn't have Push, Wind, or anything else that could help. There wasn't any time to cast even if she had had them.

Mira ducked out from behind Gabriel, dodged when he tried to grab her, and ran straight into Barney, knocking him out of the circle.

The world around her dimmed. She saw another figure in the room, one with patches of fur scattered over its form. When Gabriel grabbed her, though, it disappeared.

She stared at where the figure had been, vaguely aware that Gabriel was telling her off. It had been there. The Ether had been so close. Close enough to reach out.

To reach out and take them? To kill, maybe?

"Calm down," Ian said to Gabriel. "You're going to rupture something."

"How can I be calm?" Gabriel snapped.

"Whatever happened, it's over, right?" Ian asked.

"Maybe," Gabriel said. "For now, anyway. Until Barney decides to invite those monsters over for a chat again?"

Mira had been so focused on the creature that she had forgotten about Barney. She knelt down next to him where he had fallen to the ground.

"He was creating a monster?" Ian asked, sounding thoroughly confused.

"No, just bringing one here," Gabriel said. "Or taking us to them."

"If he did it once," Ian said, "can he do it again?"

"I don't think so," Mira said, brushing the hair out of Barney's face. "He's unconscious."

Gabriel crouched down and checked for a pulse.

"I'm pretty sure he's breathing," Mira said.

"I'm not certain that's a prerequisite for life anymore," Gabriel muttered.

"Let's get him over to the house," Ian said. "This place is giving me the creeps."

Sadly, Mira was thinking the same thing. She wasn't sure if she'd ever feel the same about her workshop again.

"I'll carry him," Gabriel said. "Get the rest of the stuff."

Mira grabbed everything Barney had dropped and led the way out of the workshop and into the garage. As soon as she stepped outside, she began to feel a little better. The atmosphere itself was stronger, not thinly stretched.

The snow was an issue, though. The howling wind brought frigid air that worked the flakes into a frenzy.

Being shorter than the others, Mira fell behind, letting Gabriel and Ian take the lead. She hadn't bargained for snow up to her knees and ice in her socks. She tried to catch up, since she was the one with the keys, but ended up face down in the snow for her trouble.

Never in her life had Mira expected to take so long to walk a hundred feet. Shivering from head to toe, she thrust the key into the back door and pushed it open, waving Gabriel and Ian inside.

"Crap," Ian said. "I didn't think about tracking all the snow into Della's house."

"It's okay," Mira said, brushing the snow off her coat and pants. "That's essentially what this room is for. Well, it used to be, anyway, and we're not going to hurt the kitchen floors. Gabriel, in the kitchen there's a large bench. You can set Barney down there for a few minutes and kick off your shoes."

Mira and Ian followed, and Mira went straight for the thermostat for that part of the house and boosted both zones. Then she kicked off her shoes. "I'll be right back." She dashed through the house, and with each turn of the dial, put a huge load into Della's heating bill.

When Mira dashed back to the kitchen, the men were in their socks. "Come through here," Mira said. "We'll put Barney down in the den."

"Does Della live in this house alone?" Ian asked as they wound through two rooms and into a third. He seemed afraid to raise his voice above a whisper.

"Most of the time," Mira said.

"Um... ah..." Ian stammered, looking around.

"Weren't you here the other day?" Mira asked.

"Not inside, no," Ian said.

"It's a family house."

"What does she do with all the space?"

Mira shrugged. "She entertains people several times a year for work, or charity, sometimes for the supernaturals as well."

"And the rest of the time?" Ian asked.

"Help me with this," Mira said.

Ian set down his pile of papers and helped her scoot a couch away from the wall.

"Most of the time, Della sticks to a few rooms and closes the others off," Mira said. "Let's put Barney here. I'll show you all where everything is and then I'll set up a circle."

After checking on Barney one more time, Mira gave a truncated version of the grand tour, noting earthquake damage in nearly every room. Upstairs, she turned on the heat for that level.

"There are a few bedrooms up here. These two are ready for guests," she said, opening two doors for them, one down the hall from the other. "Della's room is at the end of the hall. I'm sure I don't have to tell you not to go in there." She let her gaze flicker to Ian. "Remember, she's a sorceress, so you never know what you might set off."

"Bathrooms?" Gabriel asked.

"These rooms have a Jack-and-Jill. A shared bathroom," Mira added in case they were unfamiliar with the term, "but there's another across the hall, and I'll show you the one downstairs. Make yourselves at home. I'm going to create that circle for Barney."

As the tour progressed, Mira had grown more and more anxious about Barney being left alone. Who knew what John could put into his head now that Barney wasn't conscious?

Barney hadn't moved. Mira wasn't sure if that should be taken as good news or bad. She had to put it out of her mind. While she worked, she heard Ian and Gabriel's low voices as they talked on their way downstairs. They didn't say anything when they entered the room, but she could tell they were watching her.

It took a while to set the circle. Mira wasn't able to block the Ether, but she took extra steps to stop anything else that may go in and out of the circle.

"Barney is not going to be able to leave this one," Mira said when she was finished, still sitting on the floor. The long day and repeated magic use had left her feeling drained.

"Is that going to stop him from doing... whatever it was he did at your place?" Ian asked while Mira walked her circle around the couch.

"It should," Mira lied.

Gabriel raised an eyebrow at her.

Mira frowned and forced herself to her feet, not happy having to admit the truth. "What I mean is that what he did was tied to that location. I don't think that could have happened just anywhere."

"You mean it was tied to your apartment? Was it the magic?" Ian asked.

"Not exactly," Mira said. "It had more to do with the circle. That specific one, I mean."

"That happened because of him," Gabriel said.

"I don't think Barney—"

"Not Barney," Gabriel said, cutting her off, "Emmit. The spell you performed for him."

The accusation was clear in his voice, and Mira felt her embarrassment rise with her blood pressure. "Which you should know nothing about."

"When it nearly causes us to be dragged into another plane of existence, it damn well matters. I'm not going to turn a blind eye on it," Gabriel seethed.

Mira gritted her teeth. "When it's something you forced me to tell you, something you said you didn't understand, then you should mind your own business."

"He's tied to all of this!"

"So are you. That doesn't mean anything."

"Let's take a break," Ian said, keeping his voice smooth. "I'm still in the dark here, but something has obviously happened. We should step back and get a fresh perspective."

"I don't trust Emmit," Gabriel said, leaving the bite out of his voice.

"Maybe you should fill me in before he gets here," Ian said.

Gabriel looked at him, blank faced.

"You told me to call him," Ian said defensively. "He said he was on his way. To Mira's, I mean."

"Call him back," Gabriel said. "Tell him not to come."

"No," Mira said, "I think we need him on this."

Gabriel's eyes hardened. "Why am I not surprised?"

Mira tried to let Gabriel's remark roll aside, but it stung.

"It's not like he'll be able to make it through this snow," Gabriel said, shifting his tone.

"I don't think he cared much about the weather," Ian said.

"Yeah," Gabriel sighed, "he probably doesn't."

"I'll go home and wait for him there," Mira said. She couldn't bring herself to look at Gabriel as she moved swiftly by him.

She could hear the two talking in whispers as she yanked on her boots. She grabbed her coat and went to the back entrance, pulling the damp coat on as she went.

Going straight outside wasn't an option or she would have been out the door in a shot. Getting out of the house quickly wasn't worth frostbite, so she made sure she was tightly bundled up, with as little skin as possible showing. It was dark out the back window, but what little she could see showed the fierce weather was still raging. She had no idea if there was fresh snow falling, or if it was all old snow blowing around. Either way, it looked like the blizzard was set firmly in place.

CHAPTER 18

WHEN THE DOOR TO THE kitchen opened, Mira didn't look around.

"I'll go with you," Gabriel offered.

"No," Mira said. "You all should work on the case and keep an eye—"

A knock on the door startled Mira, who had been concentrating hard on her gloves so she wouldn't look at Gabriel. She opened the door to Emmit. Besides the snow whipping around him, he seemed untouched by the weather.

"I can't believe you got here in this mess," Mira said, ushering him inside.

"I was under the impression there was an emergency," Emmit said. "Although, had I known this would turn into a sleepover, I might not have left."

Mira wasn't sure how to take that until she turned and saw that his eyes were narrowed at Gabriel.

Gabriel's face was hard and his fists were clenched. Seeing how he had just accused Emmit of causing all this, Mira was in a hurry to separate the two.

"Let's go back over to my apartment," Mira said. "I'll explain things."

"No," Gabriel said with more force than necessary.

"What?" Mira snapped.

"I mean," Gabriel said, looking unflustered by Mira's anger, "he should see Barney first. We can tell him what happened here.

There's no reason to stand around your workshop, not knowing what might happen with him in the room."

Having Emmit check over Barney wasn't a bad idea, but Mira wasn't about to say so. Instead, she started peeling off layers of insulation.

Gabriel started the story, keeping things brief until he spoke of Barney walking into the center of the room.

"When he reached the center of the circle, it was almost as though it wasn't really Barney anymore," Mira said. "He was creepy."

They led Emmit into the other room and Gabriel told him the rest of the story. At one point, Emmit asked Mira to drop her protection in order to inspect Barney while Gabriel continued. Ian filled in a few blanks.

"At least it appears that this is Barney now," Emmit said.

His expression was downcast and made Mira uncomfortable.

"Is he going to be okay?" Mira asked.

"Until he wakes up, it's hard to say for certain," Emmit said. "Mira, would you take me to your workshop?"

"I can take you," Gabriel said.

"No," Mira overrode him.

Gabriel blew out a frustrated breath.

"Mira, would you give me a moment with Gabriel?" Emmit asked.

Mira frowned at both of them before shaking her head. "Whatever. I'll get my coat."

Gabriel started in on Emmit before she was out of earshot. "You know I don't trust you."

"For good reason, I'm sure," Emmit said, keeping his voice level. "But, will I be of any harm to her?"

Fuming, Mira went down the hall and started the whole process of dressing for the short trek across the driveway. They were talking *about* her instead of *to* her. She needed to nip that in the bud, but had no idea how to do that.

Deciding she would meet Emmit at her house, she opened

the door and stepped outside. Before she could close the door, however, Emmit was there.

Instead of saying anything, she turned and started to blaze a new path through the snow.

"It looks as if it's stopped snowing," Emmit said.

The flurry of precipitation swirled around them, though it did seem lighter. She supposed it could be blown snow now, but she wasn't interested enough to comment. The only thing she wanted was to get out of the cold.

Maybe to yell at someone, but she had no idea who.

The garage was almost as cold as outside, but the lack of frigid wind made it a hundred times more tolerable.

She hurriedly led Emmit to her workshop before she could say something stupid. When she unlocked the door, the warmth hit her, but she was still hesitant to enter the room.

"You can wait here if you'd like," Emmit said.

"No," Mira said, forcing herself to move on, "it's fine."

"Barney started from the door and went to the center of your circle?" Emmit asked.

"Yeah, I think he was having a vision. The Ether moved in, like it normally would around him, but then he kept walking and it stayed with him."

"I'm not familiar enough with seers to know if they typically move around while in a vision."

"I've never known him to. It wasn't until he reached the spot you were at when I cast the Balance spell that he stopped seeming like Barney." Mira took a deep breath and plunged on despite her fear. "I think it's related to the spell."

"Gabriel certainly thinks so," Emmit said. He didn't look at her while he walked around the room, staying as far away from the circle as he could.

"I didn't tell him," Mira said quickly, trying to reassure Emmit. "I mean, I did tell him. At least I guess I did. But it wasn't—"

"It's alright," Emmit said smoothly, "I understand."

But did he? Mira wondered. "I didn't mean—"

"Gabriel explained. Not in detail, but he is honorable enough to take the blame for what he did."

"It's not like he meant to," Mira said. When the words were out, she wondered how she'd ended up defending Gabriel.

"I assure you I understand," Emmit said. "Gabriel has a lot to process before he can truly take control of himself."

"Yeah," Mira said, "I think you're right. Did I mess something up with the spell?"

She hadn't meant to put it so bluntly, but it flew out of her mouth before she could stop it.

Emmit looked up at her for the first time since he'd come into the room. "This is not your fault."

"What can I do to make sure it doesn't happen again?"

He crouched down and stared at the empty space. "The path between this world and the Ether is thin here. Barney being in contact made it thinner."

"Can I seal it up?" Mira started wringing her hands. The Ether being closer was not an appealing thought.

"I don't know of a way for it to be sealed from this side," he said, more to himself than to Mira. "It is probably thin where you and Gabriel left the world last week, and where you entered."

"It's thin at Barney's house, too," Mira said. "I felt it while I was there. What can we do to put it back to normal? I don't much like the idea of living above a place that the Ether can slip through."

Emmit gave her a forced smile. "You won't have to worry about that."

Her brow furrowed. "There's a way to fix it? What can I do?"

He stood smoothly and walked to her with an almost exaggerated slowness. "I can see that you are uncomfortable here. Would you invite me upstairs?"

Mira smiled, despite the situation. "Of course."

She led the way, feeling good about putting some distance between herself and the circle.

"I had the most wonderful plan for us tomorrow, but I'm afraid that we'll have to forgo the day," Emmit said.

"Yeah," Mira said. "The weather is impossible for anyone to get out." Realizing what she'd said, she turned to him at the top of the stairs. "How did you get here?"

"I wasn't far," Emmit said as way of explanation.

"I'm sorry we dragged you here in this mess. For nothing."

"I'm glad I came. This is... unsettling."

The words should have sounded ominous, but he had moved closer to Mira. The way he stared at her made her heart beat faster.

"What did you have planned for tomorrow?" Mira asked.

Emmit smiled. "A couple of excursions. One perfect day out of all the madness around us."

"What type of excursions?" Mira asked, feeling genuinely curious about what Emmit Harker planned to do on a date.

"Just a few things around the city you might enjoy, or that we might enjoy together."

"What part do you think I would have enjoyed the most?" Mira asked.

His smile broadened. "There is a curator at the museum that collects occult antiquities from around the world. I arranged a meeting with him behind the scenes so that you could inspect the items."

"I didn't know they had anything like that," Mira said.

"It's not on display."

The thought of exploring the museum's hidden treasures—especially the occult artifacts—made Mira itch to find a spell strong enough to melt the snow. There wasn't one, but for what Emmit had planned, she felt it was worth looking, just in case.

"What part were you most looking forward to?" Mira asked.

His smile softened and his face with it. Emmit put his arms around her, drawing himself close, and kissed her. It was long and tender, quite unlike their first kiss.

Somehow, the effect was the same—Mira felt a fire ignite inside her.

It lasted forever, yet ended far too soon.

"That would have been a good part of the day," Mira mused when his gaze roved over her.

He cupped her face. "I quite agree."

She didn't say anything, and practically held her breath in anticipation of another kiss, another connection with him.

This time, however, he pulled her close and held her tight.

"But," he said, "the universe has conspired against us once again."

It was corny, but Mira loved it.

After a few moments, he sighed and tried to draw away. She tugged him back and enjoyed seeing the laughter that crossed his face.

"If you do that," he said, "it makes it more difficult to leave."

Mira bit her lip and nodded her head. "Yeah, I think that's the point."

"I'm afraid this new... development... in your shop might lead me away."

Mira tensed for a moment, guilt and confusion vying to take hold. "What do you mean?"

"I think if I... go away, it might clear up some difficulties."

"You think you being here caused this?" she asked, trying to make it clear how ridiculous that sounded.

"No, but if I go away, it's possible at least part of it could be fixed."

Mira wasn't exactly sure how she felt about that, but at the moment, she didn't want to think. "Stay for the night." She felt her face grow red at the suggestion, but she didn't care.

He stared down at her and Mira could see in his eyes that he warred with himself.

She wasn't sure what the result might be. Knowing Emmit, he'd be the gentleman and leave. Trying to end his battle of conscience, she kissed him. When he tensed for a moment, she gently tugged his body closer so they were pressed tightly against one another—tight enough for her to know what he wanted. Since it was exactly what *she* wanted—a night, at least one night, of forgetting the rest of the world existed—she didn't let go.

He relented, and they lost themselves in one another.

Mira woke to the unaccustomed warmth of someone sharing her bed and she treasured the moment. Emmit breathed softly next to her. She stretched and slipped out of bed, wearing exactly what she had fallen asleep in—nothing.

She wanted to hurry out of the room, grab a glass of water, and get back to Emmit. If she found a breath mint along the way, so much the better. At the door to her room, she hesitated, remembering that Gabriel, Ian, and Barney were only a house away. Her cheeks flared red at the thought of Gabriel showing up unexpectedly.

The thought of what Gabriel would say, seeing her and Emmit together, bothered her more than it should.

She switched gears and grabbed her jeans off the floor and a t-shirt from her dresser.

"Are you leaving?" Emmit asked quietly.

She couldn't place the tone of his voice, but she smiled at the sound. "Not a chance." She sat back down on the bed and leaned over, then kissed him in a way that indicated she wasn't about to run off. "I didn't mean to wake you. I'm only going to the kitchen."

He made a contented noise. "I'm glad you woke me. I'm pretty sure we have a few more hours of the night left together."

The reminder that it may only be a night made her smile not quite as bright as it should have been. "I'll hurry back then."

Maybe there's a way to get him to stay, she thought as she went through the living room. *He seemed intent on leaving, but would he after tonight?*

Pondering her future, she poured a glass of water and leaned against the counter.

Could she ask him to stay? Did she *want* to ask him?

Thoughts of Gabriel snuck in and she shook her head, trying to force the angel out of her mind.

A noise downstairs made Mira jump, and all thoughts of the men in her life were overrun with visions of monsters from the Ether clawing their way out of her circle. Her breath caught in her throat as she backed away from the basement door. She wanted to call for Emmit, but couldn't form the words.

A loud thump and a curse sounded out.

Gabriel.

Mira let out a deep breath and tried to calm her racing heart. When she heard him on the stairs, she gripped her glass, ready to give the man a tongue lashing for scaring her.

A hand clamped over her mouth. She froze.

The hand dragged her back and held her tightly against a heavily breathing man.

Mira dropped her glass and tried to pull away. The door to the basement opened at the same time Emmit arrived in the entrance to the kitchen.

A knife appeared at Mira's throat and she squeezed her eyes shut. She had forgotten what Gabriel showing up might mean, and now it was too late.

John gripped one of her arms, and Mira gasped as he painfully twisted it behind her. Never once did he move the blade.

"What is it with you two?" John snarled. "You weren't supposed to be here. I didn't see you here."

Mira tried not to swallow too hard, worried that the knife might break through skin. Emmit stood there in nothing but jeans, wearing a steely look, his focus solely on John. And there was Gabriel, who appeared to be analyzing the situation, trying to figure out what would stop the madness.

"You two make my life hell, you know that?" John didn't wait for a response. "Doesn't matter. The witch is with me. We've got things to do."

"You're not—"

"Shut up, Harker," John said, "and get out of my way."

Gabriel took a few steps away from the door to the stairway and stopped.

"You have to know, you can't win here," John said, watching Emmit.

Emmit took a step forward.

"Don't!" Gabriel moved closer to Emmit.

John twisted Mira's arm farther up her back. She tried to stifle the screech of pain.

"The bastard is right," John mocked. "Don't."

Emmit moved again.

Gabriel darted forward and, arm outstretched, blocked Emmit's approach. "You're going to get her killed."

"I already have," Emmit growled, shoving Gabriel aside. "You're too late."

John backed up a few paces. "You're going to make me do this the hard way, aren't you?"

"We're ending this here," Emmit said.

Emmit stalked forward. Mira tried to catch his eye, to catch a glimpse of some sort of plan, but he wouldn't look at her.

Mira felt the metal glide across her skin. Her eyes closed hard, expecting the accompanying pain, but it didn't come. She opened her eyes in time to see John take the blade away and wipe his hand across his neck. The discomfort that followed told her the cut wasn't deep. Still, his hand came away red.

Gabriel stopped Emmit's progress a second time.

"She's too valuable to kill here," John said. "But with a witch, there's always a way out."

The atmosphere began to feel thin, and the hairs on the back of Mira's neck rose.

Her eyes widened as the feel of the Ether approached. For a moment, Mira felt one foot in the Ether and the other in the real world. Emmit's only focus was John, so Mira turned to Gabriel. His face was pale, and his fear mirrored her own.

He lurched forward, seeming to forget that he had stopped Emmit from doing the same. Unlike Emmit, though, Gabriel's focus was only on Mira.

In a heartbeat, he was gone.

CHAPTER 19

D ARKNESS SPREAD OUT BEFORE MIRA, while John gripped her arm painfully.

"Christ," John spat. "Those assholes are a pain."

Mira tried to look around the darkness. In her head, a little voice began screaming. The rest of her wasn't ready to admit where she was.

"Come on," John snarled, towing her into the darkness.

Her breathing trembled and her chest tightened.

"Home sweet home," John chuckled as he strode through the dark shadow that her apartment cast in the Ether. He opened the door and shoved Mira out.

She gripped the handrail and took in the strange glow that came from nowhere, yet covered everything.

Shit! Mira's skin went cold and clammy. He had taken her into the Ether. An unmistakable haze hung in the air. Looking toward the big house, she saw there were no windows, only stretches of dirty wood that sided Della's home.

John grabbed her arm again. "Come on, princess. I think it's time for you and Tyler to catch up."

Mira clung to the name. "You have him here?" Her voice trembled, and it was all she could do to stay on her feet while John dragged her down the stairs.

"Not me," John said. "I've been out in the real world. In fact," he stopped almost at the bottom of the stairs, "I'm pretty pissed off for having to come back."

Mira only had the increased pressure on her arm as warning. John, using more strength than she would have expected, threw her down the last few steps. Pain lanced up Mira's side as she struck the ground and she cried out before having a chance to suppress the urge. She didn't want John to have the satisfaction of knowing he'd hurt her.

John laughed, proving she'd failed.

The landscape struck fear that bore straight to the bone. It wasn't just the windows missing. She knew from experience that there would be no mirrors or even water. A reflection had gotten her home last time.

She had destroyed that shard of mirror.

"Get up," John snapped, looming over her, "you've got work to do."

"I—what?" Mira stammered. "I'm not doing anything for you."

"You'll want to before the day is done." He kicked her and laughed again. "Things have changed since you were last here. Come on, I'll show you."

The little scream in the back of her mind grew louder, trying to take over. She saw no way to get out of this.

Shakily, she moved to her feet. John grabbed her hand this time, and like a kid wanting to show off a new toy, he took off running, giving her no other choice than to run as well.

Luckily, they didn't have to go far. At a neighbor's house, John pulled her up another set of stairs that took them higher than the stunted trees. Mira was already breathing more shallow than normal. Her chest felt as though it was being crushed, which didn't allow room for a lot of air.

"There," John said, dropping her hand and spreading his arms wide.

Mira stared out, seeing a small part of the city. She had no idea how she could see through the haze. Maybe the height or the strange light that distorted the world caused the effect.

"It's the city," Mira said. She was stuck here with John, but she didn't have to be. Well, she had to be stuck in the Ether—she couldn't think of a way around that, but would it be better *with* John, or away from him?

"Not just the city," he said, "watch."

She did as she was told, but the overriding thought was to get away. She took a few steps forward as though to get a better look. Her gaze traveled around the clearing below, looking for things that could trip her up.

A loud roar consumed the world. Mira shrieked and covered her ears, but she didn't dare shut her eyes. There was something out in the haze besides the buildings. A hint of movement caught her eye and she wondered what lurked in the shadows.

The sound swallowed her and reverberated through all the cells in her body. Ancient fears of darkness rose inside Mira. Shadows darted, and she badly wanted to see what moved out of the corner of her eyes, but she dared not look away from the city. Motion around one of the skyscrapers snagged her attention. A long tendril took shape and began to grow from the darkness. It wrapped a tower-sized root around a building. When it stilled and the movement stopped, she had a hard time making out where the building parted from the thing.

When the sound went away, Mira heard it continue in her mind. John said something, but she ignored him. Hands shaking, she removed them from her ears. Shrill sounds continued around her, and she glanced below and saw writhing in the grass.

Mira turned and ran.

Her mind blanked out and terror took over. The only thing she could do was run. The only place she thought to go was back to her apartment.

John yelled, but she didn't care. There was nothing else that she cared about. When she reached the garage, she ignored the stairs to her front door and rushed into the lower level, heading straight to her workshop.

When she slammed the door shut behind her, she locked it. The magic from her workshop had burned away most of the ethereal haze, but that barely registered. Seeing the darkness of the staircase, she ran across the room, slammed that door shut, and locked it.

There was loads of magic here. It was her magic, familiar and comforting in a small way.

Her mind feverishly fumbled through ideas on how to get back. What she kept coming back to was that there was no mirror. She seemed to fixate on that thought.

"Open up, witch!" John pounded on the door to the garage.

Mira's lungs froze, and she backed away from the door. In the middle of the room, she bumped into something. A terrified, squeaky scream burst out of her and she wheeled around.

An almost translucent form of Gabriel stood in the circle.

Mira reached for him, but the image faded away.

"Get the hell out here!" John roared.

Confused, Mira backed into a corner, trying to keep the door and where she had seen Gabriel in view.

When Gabriel flickered back into existence, Mira desperately wanted to run to him to have him get her out of there, but he wasn't solid.

"Mira? Dammit," Gabriel turned toward the door to her apartment as though talking to someone. "It's not working, Harker." The volume of Gabriel's voice fluctuated as much as his form. "Fix it."

"Don't come *here*," Mira squeaked. "Get me out!"

Gabriel became slightly more solid when he turned to her again. "Mira!" Hope lit up his face.

Mira didn't stop to wonder how they were making this work. She moved forward, ready to grab onto Gabriel.

The frame of the door shook. Something struck it, determined to get into the room.

Mira jumped, eyes fixed on the door.

Another shuddering bang and the door burst open.

John strolled into the room looking cross.

Mira reached out to take Gabriel's hand, but there was nothing of substance to grab. Not wanting John to get any closer, Mira backed into her corner again. John's eyes narrowed and he looked around the room.

His gaze went right past Gabriel, as though he couldn't see the angel. When John appeared satisfied they were alone, he smiled at Mira.

I must be going crazy, Mira thought, trying not to cry. *Wishful thinking.*

"I brought a friend," John said with a cruel cheerfulness that made Mira shiver.

From behind John, a moldy-looking creature stepped into the room.

"We just want to make sure you find your way," John said.

Gabriel yelled something, but he addressed a person invisible to her.

When Mira's attention wavered to Gabriel again, the moldy creature darted forward. Seeing the movement, Mira braced herself, expecting to be dragged out of her workshop.

As the monster reached the center of the room, Gabriel came into sharp focus. This time, he concentrated on the creature, not Mira.

It was the first time John realized they weren't alone. The apparition of Gabriel slashed out at the beast running towards her. For the space of a few heartbeats, a sword appeared in his hand and Gabriel's wings, hidden in the real world, shimmered.

The creature howled and scrambled backwards, and then Gabriel was himself once again. No wings, no sword.

"Leave her alone!" Gabriel yelled.

John tensed, expecting to be ordered away. When Gabriel's words didn't force him to retreat, John grinned. "Not even the bastard son of a god can straddle worlds for long. If you enter, your life is forfeit, same as hers."

Gabriel glanced at Mira and she saw his determination.

Another creature, previously unseen in the shadows behind John, dove forward, taking advantage of Gabriel's distraction. With seemingly little effort, Gabriel spun and the sword popped into existence again. This time, it remained for a short time after the beast screeched and ran away.

Once the creature reached the doorway, it screeched again, and Mira heard spirited movement in the garage. Remembering that the monsters ate their wounded, she pressed her hand tightly to her mouth and hugged her stomach.

John was right. Gabriel couldn't keep a foot in both worlds for long. Taking a few steadying breaths, Mira pushed herself away from the wall and moved to her worktable.

Hands shaking, she rummaged through ingredients. Maybe if she hurt enough of them, they'd be distracted and she could get away.

"Mira," Gabriel said, not taking his eyes of John, "I need you to help me over."

She stopped her search and gaped at Gabriel as though he were mad. "Not a chance. Stall them and I'll find a way to get past them."

"This isn't a debate," Gabriel said.

"You're right," Mira said. "If you can't get me back, I'll run." Mira turned back to her worktable, a fire of determination building. There was no way she could let Gabriel come here.

The fire dampened when she realized she had nowhere to run. Her last trip into the Ether hadn't been a success. If Gabriel hadn't been there, she would have died.

She began to tremble.

Magic was strong in the Ethereal Plane. She knew that now and she was in her own workshop. She could make this work, and if she was able to get to Tyler, she knew together they could stand against them all.

Remembering that something lurked in the shadows of the city, she amended the thought. She and Tyler could stand against most of them.

That would give Emmit and Gabriel time to figure something out.

Feeling eyes on her, she glanced at Gabriel, who watched her almost as intensely as John.

A scratching noise drew her attention. Another creature must have been behind the door to her apartment. John's smile returned, and staying clear of Gabriel, he went to the other door and opened it.

The creature that entered was a sickly yellow green with matted tufts of fur or hair in clumps around its body.

When it stepped forward, she automatically moved back. The thing wasn't erect, but low to the ground, looking almost like a person pretending to be a dog. It grinned at her, and more than one mouth appeared.

Mira shuddered and turned to Gabriel, but he was gone.

Panicking, Mira grabbed blindly at things on the table and moved toward the center of the room where Gabriel had been. She fumbled with the items she'd grabbed, and most of them fell to the floor, but it didn't matter, Gabriel had been stuck in her circle, unable to enter the Ether. She could use the same circle to keep everything in the Ether away.

Mentally, Mira reached into her core and let her power fall like a rock into the familiar lines of her circle. She saw the evil glint John had in his eyes, and then charged the circle, putting as much as she could into it. Growls and yowling erupted in the darkness. She could hear creatures running away as though scalded. Even John frowned and backed away.

For the first time since she'd entered the Ether, Mira was able to take a real breath.

"Your friend Tyler tried this trick," John said. There was an uncertainty in his voice that Mira clung to. "He's still recovering." John's face distorted and a too large grin appeared. His eyes were bright. "If you can call it recovering, now that we have him."

Mira desperately hoped that John was only trying to scare her. "Why do you even want us?"

"Harker didn't tell you? You'll find out soon enough." John cautiously moved forward and studied the bubble of power she held around her. He prodded it, and after a moment's thought, he whistled sharply.

When nothing happened, Mira tried to relax, but that was impossible with John in the room.

"Magic is only magic," John said. "If you don't know what you're doing, it will fail."

Two sharp bangs came from the dark interior of the garage. The sound of wood slowly splintering quickly followed.

"I know what I'm doing," Mira said. Her voice trembled, taking away some of her certainty, but she barely noticed when her attention was focused on watching the shadows in the garage.

John laughed. "No witch alive knows what they're doing. You're strong, you and Tyler both. Especially now that you've been in the Ether." John moved unconcernedly toward the entrance to her apartment. "This dump of a place has some benefits."

The doorway to the garage filled. The brown-green thing trying to get through couldn't fit, so it drew back. A club swung out of the darkness, widening the space, and the creature tried again, forcing its way inside.

"It has *several* benefits, now that I think about it," John continued.

The thing looked like a person that had been inflated past endurance. The skin was green mottled with brown. When it spilled into the room, there was a lot less space available.

"Now," John said, moving into the stairwell, "we're not going to kill you. Yet. But you're going to wish you'd come with me in the beginning. It would have gone easier on you."

The hideous beast lifted a knobby wooden club. Mira backed as far away as she could while remaining in her protective sphere. She poured more energy into her circle, wondering how long it would hold against brute strength.

The hunk of wood swung down, and Mira watched it connect with her magic. The blow spread through her magic and straight back to her.

Mira screamed as the force made her crumple to the ground. Breathing hard, she tried to figure out what had happened, but her mind could comprehend very little beyond the agony of the assault. Dazed, she saw her creation grow dimmer.

It wasn't her magic that was going to fail, she realized. It was her.

CHAPTER 20

SHE HADN'T EVEN SEEN THE creature swing a second time, but she felt the impact. Mira cried out, unable to stop herself. Her magic stuttered, and then stopped altogether. Tears ran unchecked down her face. She shut her eyes tight and tried to push aside the agony. If she was going to survive, she needed to be able to think.

"Go away."

The words were low, clear, and an obvious order.

There was a shriek. Mira heard something pounding against the wall.

Gabriel. For some reason Mira couldn't quite describe, his appearance made her cry more.

He didn't say anything else, but he didn't have to. After silence filled the room—the creature having pounded its way out of the garage, still he didn't make a sound.

Mira sniffed and tried to uncurl. She heard him walk across the floor and slam a door shut. He tried to shut the other, but had to push something in front of the door to keep it from opening.

She felt him kneel down beside her, and finally, Mira opened her eyes. Gabriel looked pale behind the pearly sheen to his skin. His wings were spread slightly behind him.

"Did that thing hit you?" Gabriel asked.

She took a few deep breaths and tried to sit up, but he gently pushed her back down and started running his hands over her arms, looking carefully for any damage.

It had taken a while, but Mira's brain pushed itself out of the cloud obscuring her thoughts. "I'm okay," she said.

Gabriel winced.

Mira's sighed, knowing that Gabriel caught the lie. "Would you buy, it's not as bad as it looks?"

He let out a small grin. "If you believed it, I would. Did it hit you?"

"Yes and no," Mira said.

"I don't know what that means," Gabriel said.

"It... my magic and... I don't know. It felt like I was being hit, but I wasn't."

"Anything broken?" Gabriel asked, his hand shifting to her legs.

"Nothing is broken." Mira gritted her teeth and pushed herself to a sitting position.

"Lie down," Gabriel said.

Mira found herself lying back down on the concrete without thinking about it. It took her a few moments to realize what had happened.

"Hey!" she snapped. "You can't do that."

"Sorry," he said, shifting to the other leg, "I'm not exactly good at control."

Mira winced when he pressed near her hip. "Still," she said, trying to find hints that he might be lying.

He pressed again, more carefully.

"Stop it," she said, "that hurts."

"I thought it didn't hit you."

She rolled her eyes. "It didn't. Can I sit up now? I feel stupid lying here."

He frowned uneasily. "If you're sure nothing is broken. You've got some nasty bruises."

Mira frowned and pushed herself up to a sitting position. "What are you doing here?" Seeing the hurt look on his face brought about by her words, she shifted gears. "I mean, I've never been so happy to see someone, but I hate to see you get stuck here again." She didn't add the 'because of me' part at the end.

"There was no way I was going to leave you here on your own."

"How did you get through?" Mira asked.

"Emmit helped." Gabriel's face took an angry turn. "Not that I gave him a choice. I don't know what you see in that guy."

Mira pulled her legs towards her and crossed them, sucking a pained breath when her hip protested. Her mind turned to Emmit, right before she was pulled to the other side. Emmit had already given up on her. He'd almost gotten her killed because he had already assumed she would die.

"Shit. Mira, I'm sorry," Gabriel said.

She forced a grin. "Liar."

He didn't appear amused. "I shouldn't have said anything. It's none of my business."

Mira frowned and wondered about that. *Was* it his business?

Only if she let it be that way.

"It doesn't matter," Mira said. "We've got more important things to worry about."

Gabriel nodded and looked around the room.

"I'm really sorry you're trapped here," Mira said.

"Not for long," Gabriel said, standing up.

"I destroyed the mirror. I don't know of any other way to get out."

"Emmit is covering that one for us."

"He is? How?"

"I may hate him, but I trust that he can help. He just needs time."

"How much time?"

"He said he'd try to have everything ready within twenty-four hours."

"One day?" The thought made Mira shiver. One day in the Ether. Then her thoughts turned to Tyler, and she wondered how long he had been stuck here. "I hope that's enough time. Help me up."

"If he takes longer, we'll just have to wait."

Gabriel grabbed Mira's outstretched hand and helped pull her to her feet. Mira flinched and wished momentarily that she had stayed on the ground.

"If that big green thing didn't hit you, what did?" Gabriel asked, looking at her side as though trying to see through her jeans to the bruise beneath.

"The ground," Mira said.

"You fell?"

"I was pushed down the stairs."

Gabriel frowned.

"John isn't a nice guy."

Gabriel clenched his fist and Mira was surprised to see his sword appear readily in his hand. Gabriel, on the other hand, didn't seem to notice.

Mira decided to move things down a different train of thought. "I didn't mean that Emmit may not have enough time. I meant we may not." She moved to her workbench to see what supplies their current world mirrored.

"You're right," Gabriel said. When Mira glanced his way, she saw that he seemed to turn inward, as though thinking through several different ideas at once. "If we can track John, maybe we can end this here."

"I don't think finding John is going to be easy," Mira said. "He may not even be in this world anymore."

"Can you locate him somehow using magic?" Gabriel asked.

"I doubt it. It's not exactly John anymore, is it? It's that leathery creature from here that's using him like a puppet now. I'm going to find Tyler."

"Tyler?" Gabriel asked.

"Yeah," Mira said. "He's apparently been stuck here for a while now."

"Weren't you concerned he was a part of this?" Gabriel asked.

Mira frowned at him. "He *is* a part of it, but only because he's been taken. They want to use him—all witches really—for something."

"What do they need witches for?"

Mira bit her lip, wondering how much to say. Then she realized if she held anything back, he'd know she was hiding something. "I don't know what they want us for, but John seemed surprised that Emmit hadn't told us."

"Harker knows? He let that asshole take you here and he knew what it was about?"

Mira felt deflated. Gabriel wasn't wrong. In fact, he'd probably been right all along about Emmit. She turned back to her worktable, unwilling to think about the man that had given up on her.

She also ignored Gabriel, who remained silent for a while.

Fire, Mira thought. *Fire can slow the creatures down.* She poured powdered charcoal in her mortar and added everything else she remembered from the fire spell she'd used most recently on John.

While she ground everything together, Gabriel came over and started poking through her supplies.

"What are you making?" he asked after he had checked out a few small bags.

"Something to create fire. I think it'll hold the creatures back if needed."

"I'm starting to get used to issuing commands," Gabriel said.

"I noticed," Mira said, not quite under her breath. "But if we get separated," she added in a normal voice, "it may keep me alive long enough to run."

"What about this?" Gabriel asked, holding out his hand.

Mira glanced at the ward she had made him. "You need to make sure it's touching skin."

"Harker said it was strong and that I should feel honored to have it," Gabriel said.

Mira shrugged noncommittally.

"Couldn't you use it while we're here?" he asked.

"It's very thoughtful of you to offer, but that's not the way wards work. It will only work for you."

He stared around the room. "You have a lot of supplies—can you make yourself one? Your old one came in handy when you were here last time."

"They don't work well when you make them for your own use. The ward is only as strong as the feeling the witch has for the person that received the ward. That one had been made for me by someone I went to high school with. We were close, and he gave it to me before he moved away."

"Oh," Gabriel said, closing his hand around the ward. He didn't say anything for a while so Mira got back to work.

Gabriel himself could keep everything away from them, assuming he had control. Mira knew she would be sticking with him like glue, but it was better to be safe and keep the fire handy.

"Is it only witches that can make wards?" Gabriel asked.

"What?" Mira asked, before she realized what he was asking. "Oh, no. Anyone can make them, even humans, but if the person making them has magic in some way, the ward is more effective. I don't think a ward made by a human would stop anything here."

"Oh," Gabriel replied, looking glum, "I was hoping I could make you one to keep you safe, but there's no point if it won't help."

Mira looked at him, feeling confused. Then it dawned on her that he still considered himself human. In a way, she felt sorry for him.

"I'm not sure if I could teach you how to make one, but I don't think creating it here would be a good idea, anyway," Mira said. "This place feels contaminated, no matter what it is you try to do."

"True."

"If you want to learn how to make one when we get back, though." Mira hoped he couldn't see the red creep into her cheeks in the strange light of the Ether. "I imagine you would make an excellent ward, even if you hated the person."

It was Gabriel's turn to appear puzzled until she motioned behind him. He turned his head, but if anything, the reminder of his wings seemed to depress him more.

Mira couldn't think of a thing to say to make him feel better. She managed to give him a half-hearted smile before getting back to her work. Concentrating hard, she charged the fire spell, keeping the magic on hold and stored into a crystal until it was ready to be released.

"Do you have any idea where Tyler is?" Gabriel asked.

"Not a clue," Mira said. "I'm going to create a spell to locate him. We'll need to go to his house before I can cast the spell."

"Why's that?" Gabriel asked.

"I need something from him."

"An ingredient?"

"You could say that," Mira said. "*He's* the ingredient."

Gabriel's nose curled up.

Mira could only shrug as she started the spell. "It is what it is. If a witch has a piece of you, they can do some pretty nasty things. That's why I picked up all your feathers the last time we were here."

"What?" Gabriel asked, sounding offended.

"To make sure no one did anything to you. Who knows what kind of magic someone could do with angel feathers. To the angel or to anything else for that matter." She shot Gabriel a disapproving glare. "You don't think I kept them to use against you, do you?"

"No," Gabriel said quickly. She didn't drop the glare, so he continued, "I just had no idea that anyone could do anything with them."

Mira suspected that at least for a moment he thought she had kept them for nefarious purposes. She turned her back on him and went back to work.

Before long, Gabriel started to pace. "Are you making anything else?"

"I should," Mira said, "but I don't think we have enough time."

"Good, we need to go." Gabriel went to the door and moved the table he had pushed in front of it.

"I'm not done with the spell yet," Mira protested.

"Finish it at Tyler's," Gabriel said. "We need to go."

"But—"

"Something's wrong, okay. Just trust me."

Realizing she trusted him probably more than anyone else she had ever trusted, she scooped up her projects and ingredients she might need and stowed them in a black cloth bag she used to hold ingredients that were more potent. At the last moment, she grabbed a ceremonial athame, and then followed the impatient angel.

"Slow down," she whispered to Gabriel as they made their way across the driveway.

"Tyler's house is a long way from here," Gabriel reminded her.

"Yes, but I'd like to make it there in one piece," Mira suggested. She stowed what she could in her pockets and attached the sheath to her belt buckle as best she could.

"I'm pretty sure I have the hang of my voice in this world."

"Will it work with something that can't hear, or something that's really big?"

Gabriel slowed his pace. "I'm not sure. It made that creature in your workshop run away."

"There's something you need to see," Mira said. She moved in the direction that John had taken her. "Keep an eye on the ground. I think there are things running around in the grass."

They moved up the small rise and the city came into view.

"It seems so far away," Gabriel said. "At least when you think about traveling by foot."

"Never mind that," Mira said. "Look at the towers." She watched him, not wanting to see the city.

"We already know there's no glass."

Mira sighed and turned. It took her a moment to spot what John had showed her.

"Concentrate on the large, dark skyscraper on the left."

"What am I..." His mouth gaped.

"Do you see it?" Mira asked when he stopped talking.

"Is it a root?"

"It moves," Mira said. Only hints of movement between the skyscrapers could be seen.

Gabriel grabbed Mira's arm and yanked her back.

"What the—"

"It's an interesting sight, isn't it?" John stood below them, about twenty yards away.

"Stay behind me," Gabriel said to Mira. Louder, he addressed John. "What is it?"

John shrugged. "Some call them monsters, some call them gods."

"But what is it?" Gabriel asked.

"Hungry," John said.

Mira looked around behind them, worried that something might try to sneak up from behind.

"Maybe we can make a deal," John continued. "Your witch for, say, six of mine."

"What are you talking about?" Gabriel asked.

"As a witch, she's easily worth six of mine, but to you, well, she's just one person. What's one person compared to six?"

"That's just twisted," Gabriel said. "Even for you."

"Is Tyler with them?" Mira called.

"He's not part of the deal," John said.

"Doesn't matter," Gabriel said. "There will be no trading people."

"It was worth a shot," John said. "In either my world or yours, I'll get the witch or more like her."

"Go away," Gabriel said. The pitch wasn't quite right for an order, but John disappeared around the side of the house. When it sounded like they were alone, Gabriel said, "Come on. We've got a long walk."

Mira took one last glance at the city, knowing they were moving toward the unknown monsters instead of away from them. John's offer had her worried, but she followed Gabriel without voicing them.

Six for one, Mira turned the idea over. *It's a deal in anyone's math. Can I trade myself?*

Lost in thought, Mira ignored the houses around them as they cut through yards that diminished in size with every street.

If she could get six people away, leaving her and Tyler together, she was sure they could work together to hold back the horde.

"You know people like him never stick to their word," Gabriel said, as if reading her mind.

"It's tempting to believe he would, isn't it?" She had meant it as a statement, but it didn't come out that way.

"Not really. You don't make deals with nut jobs, especially dead ones."

"They teach you that in police academy?" Mira asked.

"You bet. It was right up there with 'how to cope when you grow wings'."

Mira tried to laugh, but it didn't work. "Are you upset that you found out? About the wings, that is."

Gabriel shrugged, which caused his wings to extend slightly. "It's easy to ignore the truth in our world. Well, at least the feathered part. In this place, I can't say they've been useful, but everything that comes with them helps in some way."

"I guess it's hard to ignore the supernatural when it's a part of your case."

"Yeah, I can't wrap my brain around the magic part."

"And in our world, you're also dealing with chasing me around, making sure I don't stub a toe. I imagine that makes it harder to ignore the supernatural."

"I think the danger has to be a bit bigger than that," Gabriel said.

"But still. Maybe while we're here you could fix it."

Gabriel was shaking his head before the words were all the way out. "Not a chance. I vowed to protect you, and I will, even if it means I have to put up with Harker."

"It doesn't seem fair to you."

"I don't think it's fair for anyone to have to put up with Harker."

"You know what I mean," Mira said, giving him a wry smile.

"It's not a bad thing. Not many people can say, 'I saved someone's life today'."

"And yesterday and maybe again tomorrow."

"It seems like the bad karma is starting to wear off," Gabriel said. "Once we take care of John, maybe you'll be okay."

"And if I'm not?"

"Then we'll see a lot of each other." He appeared tense, but when he smiled at her, Mira couldn't help but smile back.

The screeching outcry thundered through the world once again. Mira covered her ears in useless defense. Gabriel did the same while looking around for the source of the noise. When he couldn't find the cause, he backed up close to Mira.

Sound rattled down to Mira's center and seemed to take root. When her ears told her the noise had stopped, her mind told her it continued.

"What was that?" Gabriel asked, his voice trembling.

Mira turned and got a face full of feathers. She backed up, looked at Gabriel, and backed up again so she could take the spectacle in all at once. His feathers had puffed up and out like a startled cat.

"What is it?" Gabriel asked, turning. "Do you know what made the noise?"

Her mouth opened and she snapped it shut again. He didn't seem to notice anything was wrong and it was... well, it was cute. It was something she'd never tell him to his face, but she wanted to run her hands through the fluffed-up feathers to see what it felt like.

"Are you okay?" Gabriel asked.

His concern snapped her out of it. "Fine. I'm fine. Sorry, I—" she cut off knowing he'd detect any lie. "I was taken off guard, is all. I think that noise came from the thing—whatever it is—in the city."

They couldn't see the skyscrapers from the street they were on, but they both stared in that direction.

"And here I was thinking this trip was going to be less terrifying than the first," Gabriel said.

"It'll be better when we find Tyler. He'll be able to help us," Mira said.

Gabriel gave her a sad look. "If Tyler's here, he may have been here for more than a week."

"So? John said he was starting to recover." Mira wasn't about to mention what else John had said about Tyler. John had just been trying to scare her.

"A week in a hostile environment. We haven't seen any water here and we know what passes for food."

She knew he was right, but she couldn't let herself think about it. What would they have done to her if she'd been here for a week? Would she have even survived?

"Shit," Gabriel said. "I'm sorry, Mira, I just meant that you should brace yourself."

Mira sniffed and wiped away the tears she hadn't immediately noticed. "It's okay. This place just gets to you after a while."

Gabriel nodded, looking miserable. Mira bit her lip, trying to rein herself in, but she was having a hard time.

He moved closer. "He may be fine, what do I know?"

The ear-piercing noise ripped through the air once again. This time the ground shifted under their feet. Mira grabbed Gabriel's arm, her heart frozen in her chest, and she closed her eyes tightly until it passed.

By the time it was over, she was trembling. They both stood still, waiting for something else to happen. When seconds ticked by, Mira began to breathe a little easier. The shaking started again, not as hard this time, but enough to make them aware that the ground couldn't be counted on to stay in place.

Mira swallowed hard and wrapped her arms around Gabriel. They held each other tightly, providing what little comfort they could until long after the earth stilled below them.

CHAPTER 21

W HEN THE WORLD WAS SILENT for more than a minute, Mira began to notice the comfort of Gabriel's arms around her. He had been gripping hold in terror, just like her.

Now, though, with their breathing starting to slow, it soothed her to hold him close. Neither of them moved for some time. Then, by some unspoken agreement, they parted. Unwilling to let go completely, Gabriel kept her hand in his.

"We should go," he said. Each word sounded like it cost him a lot.

She nodded, not wanting to say anything in fear that something else would go wrong.

He tugged gently and they moved off. They had only gone two blocks, walking between houses and through scraps of yard, when they neared a more industrial area. Gabriel let go of her hand, sword and shield appearing at the ready.

Mira saw nothing. Their way ahead was clear and nothing seemed to move.

"What is it?" Mira asked, keeping her voice low in case something listened.

"I'm not sure," Gabriel said. "Nothing specific yet. It just feels off."

They moved forward slowly. Mira listened so hard that she felt even her own breathing was too loud. Her heart pounded in her ears, and more than anything, she wanted to grab hold of Gabriel. He provided a strength that she hadn't noticed until it was gone.

Mira repeatedly watched behind them. The haze didn't allow her to see far, but she felt sure the odd glow would reveal something if it moved. A clatter made her glance up. A long black bar hung out over the top of the roof, but nothing moved.

When she didn't see anything else, she closed the gap between herself and Gabriel, then put her hand firmly against his wing.

He stopped. Mira kept her eyes up, checking out the rooftops. Looking back, she didn't see the bar, but thought it might be farther back than she thought.

"Do you see anything?" Gabriel asked.

"I... I'm not sure."

He turned and followed her gaze. He started breathing heavy and looking from roof to roof, glancing down from time to time as well.

"We need to—"

A thin, reedy whistle sang through the area and the rooftops erupted.

Creatures large and small jumped, climbed, and fell from above. Mira froze in face of the onslaught, but Gabriel dodged past her and slashed at the first beasts that greeted them.

"Back up to the wall!" Gabriel shouted, trying to be heard over the shrill noises that the beasts made.

It was either do what he said or be run over as he backed up. Mira pulled out her athame and held it, hands shaking.

You need magic for crap like this, Mira cursed herself.

She remembered the one spell she had made before coming to the Ether that she'd never used. Spark. It was a stupid spell and she wouldn't even admit to having it ready, but it had helped her in an emergency. Maybe it could help with this one.

Mira dug around in her pockets until she pulled out the matchstick she had used to attach the spell to, thankfully still in her pocket. Gabriel had her backed into the wall and he was faring well, but there were hundreds of them in all shapes and sizes.

Twice now, Mira had heard him order the creatures away, but only a few fled each time. Mira searched from left to right finding the highest concentration of creatures.

"Don't look to the right," Mira said, hoping Gabriel could hear over the cacophony of sounds.

Mira closed her eyes—trusting Gabriel would do what he could to keep her safe—drew her power, said the words, broke the top off the matchstick with one finger, and then blew across the top of it.

A ball of light larger than a basketball bolted forward and grew. The monsters shrieked and backed away from the path as shafts of energy—much like lightning—reached out to them as it neared.

Spark grew to the size of a small car, arched around, and disappeared. In the quiet that followed, Mira could hear the sizzle of the spell as it kept going.

Gabriel threw his arm around Mira, putting her between his shield and his body and yelled, "Run away and don't come back!"

The remaining few monsters ran.

Gabriel leaned back against the wall, panting, holding Mira to him. She still held the matchstick up, paralyzed over the result of her spell.

It took her a few minutes to wrap her head around what had happened. When comprehension started to sink in, she met the next realization, which was much more physical. She leaned back against Gabriel, who was starting to catch his breath.

Mira stowed the matchstick in her pocket with the intention of examining it further when they were out of this mess. When she gently pushed herself away from Gabriel, he let her go.

"I have no idea what that was," Gabriel said, not moving from the wall, "but, well done."

"It was unexpected," she said as she surveyed the damage around them. The smell of burning tar thickened in the air, but the corpses were what deeply troubled her.

She had killed them. Not all of them, but many. Instead of feeling strong or helpful, she felt sick to her stomach.

"Let's move out of here," Gabriel said. "The smell is going to attract something we don't want to deal with."

Mira nodded numbly, but didn't move.

"Come on," Gabriel said, gently tugging on her arm.

Realizing what she might step in if she moved, Mira yanked her arm away.

"What's—" he stopped short when he saw what she was looking at. "How in the hell do you not have any shoes?"

Gabriel's agitation brought out an irrational streak of anger in Mira. "How do you think?"

"Back home the snow is over two feet deep." He dropped the sword and shield and they clattered to the ground before disappearing. "And you're not even wearing socks."

In a huff, he picked up Mira and held her over his shoulder.

Mira tried not to inhale feathers. "How is this my fault?"

"You're the one without shoes," he snapped.

"I'm the one who was forced out of my house in the middle of the night!" Mira yelled back. She wanted to push away from him, but the urge not to touch the ground was stronger.

"You shouldn't even have been at your house. You should have been at Della's. You should have been with me. If you had been, we'd still be at home."

"That's not fair," argued Mira.

"But you were at your house because of Harker." Gabriel leaned over, dropping her on her feet.

Mira panicked slightly before she saw that he had set her well away from the carnage.

"This is not his fault," Mira said, trying to rein in her outburst. She knew she wasn't mad at Gabriel. She was upset about the situation, about where they were, and about all the bodies she had helped create.

"This is exactly his fault. He didn't even try to help you," Gabriel fumed.

Mira's face flamed red at the accusation and embarrassment. She had tried hard not think the same thing, so she couldn't argue with him.

Instead, she turned and walked away, so Gabriel wouldn't see that he had gotten to her.

Mira made a few random turns, intent on putting distance between herself and Gabriel.

In the back of her mind, she knew he wasn't mad at her for not having shoes. He might be mad at Emmit, and that part seemed to be genuine, but he wouldn't have said any of that if they hadn't been fighting for their lives.

Mira took that thought and mentally stomped on it until she felt better. At this point, she didn't know exactly where she was, but it didn't matter. She knew which direction Tyler lived in and started walking that direction.

It took her another two blocks before a tightness began to build in her chest. Sticking to Gabriel like glue; that had been the plan.

The haze and distorted light that came from everywhere were hard enough to live with. The windowless buildings appeared as though they were covered with ash, which made them creepy. The world felt empty.

At least until something made a sound. Each time she heard a noise, the world filled with monsters, at least in her mind.

Scuffling came from behind her and she whipped around. For as long as she lived, she swore she'd never tell Gabriel how glad she felt to see him.

To hide it, she turned and kept walking, although at a slightly slower pace. He jogged until he was level with her and started walking.

Neither of them said anything.

A hundred different things to say crossed Mira's mind over the next hour. All of them were discarded. She had a feeling Gabriel was doing the same thing next to her.

They were still a few miles away from Tyler's house when

Mira's pace began to slow. She felt drained, mentally and physically.

More importantly, she wanted water. It had only been a few hours and she was thirsty. Could someone actually last a full week?

The thought that Tyler wasn't alive slowed her down even more.

"We should take a break," Gabriel said half-heartedly.

Mira ignored the suggestion and trudged on.

"Listen," Gabriel said, "I understand if you don't want to talk, but if you want to rest—"

"Do you think he's still alive?" Mira asked.

"Who?" Gabriel asked, seemingly taken off guard by the question.

"Tyler."

Gabriel was quiet for a bit before saying, "I don't know."

Mira nodded, appreciating his honesty. "Me either. I think I took it for granted that he would be alive."

They walked silently until they neared Tyler's neighborhood.

"I'm sorry for what I said about Emmit," Gabriel said.

Mira sighed, but when Gabriel looked away from her, she immediately regretted it. "Should angels really be lying?" she asked, trying to bring some levity to the conversation.

It fell flat.

"Don't worry about it," Mira said. "You don't have to be sorry."

"I am, though," Gabriel said.

Mira arched an eyebrow.

It was Gabriel's turn to sigh. "I'm sorry I said it, but I'm not sorry I thought it."

"You weren't wrong," Mira said, taking her turn to look away.

She was grateful when they turned down the street where Tyler lived.

"How are your feet?" Gabriel asked.

"They're gross," Mira said, without thinking. "I don't know if they'll ever be clean enough when we get out of here."

"Did you step in, or on—"

"No," Mira said, not wanting to hear the end of that sentence. "It's just this place. I want to find Tyler and get home as fast as we can."

"We're not going back to your house," Gabriel said.

"What? Why not?"

"Something about the world being too thin there."

"Where are we going?"

"Emmit is setting something up at Lance's house," Gabriel said. "In the council's meeting room. Emmit said you'd know where that was."

Mira nodded and stopped in front of Tyler's house. "Do you think John knew we were coming to Tyler's house?"

"It's hard to say."

"We'll probably find out inside."

Gabriel followed her up the walkway.

"I guess it would be silly to knock," Mira said.

"Let me," Gabriel said. The door opened easily and Gabriel glanced around outside before stepping inside with Mira and shutting out the world. "Wait here while I search the house."

Mira had no interest in arguing. One look at the furniture was all it took to kill any expectation of comfort. The edges of the furniture blurred, and the dark colors appeared glossy in a way that made her anxious. It vaguely reminded her of the shell of a bug. Instead, she slid to the floor against the front door while listening to Gabriel move from room to room.

It was a mistake. How many miles had they walked? When was the last time she'd had more than an hour of sleep? Sleeping in the Ether wasn't an option, but she closed her eyes, trusting that Gabriel would have noticed by now if anything were in the house.

Tyler's house.

Mira's eyes popped open and she struggled back to her feet. This wasn't some pit stop on the way somewhere. This was where they started finding answers.

"The place looks clear," Gabriel said, coming back to the living room. "The way we left it back in our world, I expected the house to be trashed. But, I guess here there's no stuff to get damaged."

"There has to be something around," Mira said. Something about the house made her uneasy, but so did everything else in the Ether. There was no reason for Tyler's house to be any different.

"I didn't notice much of anything," Gabriel said. "Furniture, mostly."

"I thought there would be a spell book or two out." She moved into the next room and stared at blurred outlines of the bookshelves. The wood felt solid under her hands, at least. "Do you think it's the haze that makes everything seem blurred?"

When Gabriel didn't answer, she turned, finding him looking uncomfortable.

"What's wrong?" Mira asked.

"I'd rather not think about the haze," he said.

"Okay," Mira said slowly, giving him a questioning look.

Gabriel sighed. "There are no fires here, at least that we can see, and the only things that could be polluting the air are walking around."

Mira's nose wrinkled up. "Good point. Best not to speculate. At least magic seems to burn away… at least until now magic has burned away the haze."

"The things living here don't seem to like magic much, that's for sure."

It made sense to assume that Tyler had many hiding places in his house. Tyler loved being a witch, he loved magic, and he always had spells prepped. A sinking feeling engulfed Mira at the lack of clearer air. Surely, Tyler had enough stored magic that his house should be burning the atmosphere clean.

"What do we need to get from here?" Gabriel asked.

"For the spell to work I need a part of the person we're trying to find."

"A part of them. You mean like a finger?"

"Ew, no. Do I look like the kind of witch who'd use a person's finger?"

Gabriel let out a breath. "I don't know *what* that kind of witch would look like."

"Witches often keep vials of their own blood, hair, and sometimes even nail clippings. It's a fast way to add power to your spell."

"So Tyler's likely to have something left behind?"

"I think so, but I don't know how well it would be hidden."

"You don't think it would be someplace you know about?"

"We'll find out soon." Mira made her way through the dismal house, going straight to the spare bedroom.

"I thought you and Tyler were really good friends," Gabriel said, watching her carefully open the closet door.

"We are."

"Then how come you don't know where everything is?"

Mira rolled her eyes, but not where Gabriel would see. "I've told you, there are cases where spouses don't even know where spells and ingredients are kept."

"Yeah, but some mundane couples won't even share a candy bar with each other. I thought this would be different, somehow."

There was nothing in the way in the closet, but Mira felt uneasy about leaning inside. "Witches keep their secrets. People can turn on you." She took a breath, and then stepped in the dim light of the closet. It only took her a few seconds to open the baseboard.

"If the situation was reversed," Gabriel asked, trying to watch over Mira's shoulder, "would Tyler be able to find something of yours to work the spell?"

"In the real world, yes. For something like this, he could grab hair from my brush or something and work with that. But he wouldn't find anything overly useful." Mira wrinkled up her nose before plunging her hand into the seemingly empty space.

"And here?" Gabriel asked.

Mira pulled her hand out quickly, and then steeled herself to search. "I think you could find it here. Magic affects the surroundings in this world. It makes itself known. At least to us."

"Why should anyone else be any different?"

"They may not be, but we're magic people, so it may affect us differently."

"Here, let me do that," Gabriel said.

Mira gratefully gave up her fright-filled search and turned it over to Gabriel.

After cursing a few times, he situated his wings in a way that prevented them from bending awkwardly and he explored the space.

"There's nothing here," Gabriel said.

"I don't know how that's possible," Mira said. "It was in there the other day."

"What happens to magic in this world, if we use it in our world?" Gabriel began inspecting the rest of the closet for hiding spots.

"I think it goes away," Mira said. "But that's just a guess. I made your ward recently and the materials I used aren't here."

"And what happens to magic there, if the stuff is used here?"

"I have no idea. This world seems like a reflection of our own, so maybe nothing happens. But, no one comes here. Magic isn't used in the Ether."

"Until recently."

"You think someone used up Tyler's supplies in this world?" Mira asked.

"Or took them."

A roar erupted from the city and the ground began to shake. Gabriel jumped out of the closet. He tried to say something to Mira, but no sound could penetrate the outcry. Mira began to tremble and grabbed Gabriel's hand.

The moment her hand was in his, Gabriel pulled Mira to himself and held her tight. The movement of the ground ceased and the noise abated, leaving the world in a deep silence. Mira had no idea where her trembling stopped and Gabriel's started, but neither let go until their hearts stopped racing.

"You okay?" Gabriel asked when he pulled away. He spoke in a whisper, as though not wanting to alert anything to their presence.

Mira sniffed and nodded. "I think so."

"I'm not," Gabriel said. "Let's get what we need and get the hell out of here."

The house felt more empty to her than it had before. It was as if knowing there was no magic here left a vacancy that struck deep.

"Let's keep looking," Mira said with no real feeling. "How much time do we have?"

"Emmit won't get started for another twelve hours."

Mira gaped at him. "We walked for twelve hours?"

He gave her a wry smile. "More like eight. Even if we have a smooth trip back, I think it'll take longer. And I don't think John will let us have an easy time of it."

The sheer amount of time, along with thoughts of the walk back, dragged Mira down, but she nodded and moved to the kitchen to search for any traces of magic.

Gabriel trailed behind and started to search with her. Mira felt more and more hopeless the longer they looked. When she gave up on finding anything in the kitchen, she moved to another room.

"If you can't find anything," Gabriel said, watching her explore the laundry room, "is there anything you can use in place of something of Tyler's?

Mira shook her head and didn't look up. "To find a person, you need to have a piece of them."

"But what if you focused on something besides Tyler?"

"What do you mean?"

"If you used your own hair or whatever, would that be able to find another witch?"

"It might work," Mira said, turning all the spell ingredients and side effects over in her mind. "I couldn't do it in our own world. Too many people have a bit of witch in them. But here, it's worth a try."

Bolstered by the idea, Mira sped through the rest of the house before going once again to the kitchen. She laid out her supplies on the counter and tried to think through adjustments in the spell.

Gabriel leaned back against the counter to watch. He was forced to ruffle his wings to adjust. For once, he didn't seem to be disgruntled about the fact that they were in the way.

"How does this work?" he asked.

"I'm not really sure," Mira admitted. "It usually involves a map, but beyond spell books, I haven't seen any paper in this world. We're also dealing with the fact that magic seems to work a lot stronger here."

"I've noticed. That was a hell of a spell you cast earlier."

Mira remembered the bodies lying all around her and the smell of burning tar and she shivered.

Gabriel didn't appear to notice. "If something like that could happen in our world, I'm pretty sure the secret of magic wouldn't be kept for long."

She wondered briefly how much bad karma had been stacked against her.

"You really saved us back there," Gabriel said.

CHAPTER 22

M AYBE SAVING AN ANGEL HELPED *balance the scales*, Mira thought. Then she tried to push the idea out of her head.

"What I have to do is make the spell work, but instead of using a map, we need to adapt it for a pendulum."

"Pendulum?" Gabriel asked.

"Something heavy attached to string or chain. It's sometimes used to scry."

"I've head of scrying," Gabriel said. "I have no idea what it is, but I've heard of it."

"Divination, fortune telling, finding lost things."

"Do you read fortunes?" Gabriel asked.

Mira raised an eyebrow at him, but noticed the small grin he wore. "No, I suck at reading fortunes, so I don't. My nephew is pretty good at it, though."

"How old is your nephew?" Gabriel asked.

Mira got to work on the spell, thankful for the dual distraction of Gabriel and altering her enchantment as she went. "Mark is twelve."

"Kids start using magic that early?"

"It starts around four or—" Mira stopped dead, her breath caught in her throat at the sound of a door rattling.

"I'll check it out," Gabriel said, his sword already materializing in his hand. "How much time do you need?"

"Maybe ten minutes," Mira said, turning quickly back to her work.

Gabriel strode out of the room.

Something banged on the wood that had replaced the kitchen window in this strange world. A shrill scream escaped Mira.

Gabriel ran back into the room. "You okay?"

Mira bit her lip and nodded. Hands shaking, she tried to concentrate on her project again. Gabriel stalked the rooms as noise was made in different spots outside.

"This place really needs windows," Gabriel muttered on his fourth trip through the kitchen.

"It would make getting home a lot easier," Mira said.

"I can't tell if there's one thing outside running around or two, or a hundred."

Mira gasped and a new wave of terror began.

"It's probably not that many," Gabriel said.

"How do you know?"

"No one in this world ever seems worried about making noise. I can't imagine these things not yelling or taunting if there were a bunch of them together. You ready?"

"Yeah," Mira said.

"Can you cast it in here?" Gabriel asked.

"Better here than in the streets."

"As soon as you're done, we're leaving."

A jarring noise from Tyler's office made them jump.

Gabriel went to the doorway of the kitchen and watched the other room.

"What happens if—" Mira stopped, not wanting to finish the thought.

"If what?" Gabriel asked, looking tense.

"What happens if Tyler is in the city?"

Gabriel looked as if he was doing some quick calculating in his head. "Let's not invite trouble," he said after far too long of a pause. "Find out the direction, and then we can decide what to do."

He left the room before Mira could respond. In truth, the answer had been written across his face. If Tyler was in the city, Gabriel didn't think they should go.

Mira took out a silk thread she had taken from her workshop and used it to help cast her circle. While she sat inside casting the spell, she could hear Gabriel's constant patrol of the house.

When she was finished, she broke the protection, then scooted back to lean against the cabinets. For a moment, she closed her eyes and tried to imagine that she was at Tyler's house in the real world. The strain of constant terror was starting to take its toll.

"You ready?" Gabriel asked from the doorway.

Mira's eyes snapped open with a start.

"Sorry," he said. "I wish we could take a break, but now is not the best time."

She nodded and moved to stand.

"Wait," Gabriel said. He scanned the rooms behind him quickly before sitting down next to her. Then he began to pull off his shoes.

"What are you doing?" Mira asked.

"Giving you my shoes," Gabriel said.

Mira let her head fall back against the cabinet. "I'm not wearing them."

"Of course you are." He slid a boot over to her and started to untie the other.

"That's really nice and all, but not practical. You're going to be fighting—you need to keep them."

He didn't say anything, but tugged off the second boot.

"Look at my feet," Mira said.

"I have been, which is why you're wearing my shoes."

"No, look at their size. I'd walk right out of your boots, or worse, trip over them and fall when I need to be running."

Gabriel squeezed his eyes closed and rubbed one of his temples. "Nothing is ever easy."

"Sorry."

"No, it's not you, it's this place. This whole damned world."

Mira sighed and closed her eyes. "Sorry."

"I just said—"

She cut him off. "I'm the one that dragged you to this side. Again."

"John did this." He glanced up at the sound of rattling again in the other room. After listening intently for a few moments, he continued, "You can't be blamed for what that asshole did."

Mira sniffed and closed her eyes tighter. If she hadn't brought Gabriel over the first time, this never would have happened.

They sat in silence, Gabriel twitching each time a sound came from the other room. It took a few minutes before Mira would open her eyes.

"Here, take these," Gabriel said.

"I told you—" Mira looked down. "Oh."

Gabriel held out his socks. "It won't stop anything from scraping up your feet, but it may keep out whatever grime we step in."

"You won't need them?" Mira asked.

"They're just socks." Gabriel sighed. "Put them on and let's get out of here."

The fact that she wouldn't be directly stepping into the dirt made her feel moderately better. She put them on while Gabriel laced his boots back up.

"How are we getting past the things outside?" Mira asked. "However many of them there are."

"Same way we get anywhere in this place," Gabriel said. "I'll yell at them until they run away, and if that doesn't work, you break out the big stuff."

Mira grinned at him. "I don't have much ready, but I think it'll work."

"Which way are we going?" Gabriel asked.

"Let's find out." Mira closed her eyes and held the pendulum— in this case, a piece of crystal tied to a string. She concentrated hard, kept her hand steady, and waited for the pendulum to swing.

The stone jumped, throwing itself at the wall, pulling the string out of Mira's hand.

"Was that supposed to happen?" Gabriel asked.

"I wasn't expecting it. I'll just have to remember to keep a tighter hold next time."

"Any idea how far away we're going?"

"Sorry," Mira said, "I have no idea. I'd like to say close, since the spell was so lively, but I can't say for sure in this world."

"Well, it's not the direction we were going, but it's also not the city, so I guess we have that in our favor."

Mira picked up the crystal and stowed it in her pocket. "You're okay with going after him?"

Gabriel looked at her, surprised. "That's the whole point why we came this way."

"Yeah, but Emmit will be ready in, what, around eleven hours? You're not afraid we'll miss our chance to get out?"

"No, I'm not concerned with that. I *am* worried about one of us falling over exhausted if we take too long, though, so let's get moving."

Mira gathered her stuff. Since she had no idea what she might need in the next eleven hours, she kept everything, just in case. Then she followed Gabriel to the front door.

"Remember how we did this last time?" Gabriel asked.

"Yeah."

Gabriel wrapped an arm around her, holding her between himself and his shield. When Gabriel opened the door, he took a deep breath.

Then did nothing. No creatures stirred outside. He looked up, just in case something might be lurking on the ceiling of the front porch.

"Maybe there was only one of them," Mira whispered.

"Could be," Gabriel said. "Hold the shield."

Mira took it and held it in front of them, making it easier to walk, since they weren't crushed together. It surprised Mira that she wanted to stay that close to Gabriel.

Well, no, Mira thought, *not surprised that I wanted to be pressed up against him, but a little startled that I'm thinking about it here of all places.*

"You good?" Gabriel asked.

"What?" Mira asked, snapping back to their current predicament. "Oh. Yeah."

"Go slow," Gabriel said. "There could be something on the roof."

Mira swallowed hard and began to move down the steps, waiting for something to fall on them at any moment.

When they reached the road, Gabriel was watching the house, intent on finding the slightest movement.

"Do you see anything out of place?" Gabriel asked.

"No," Mira said. She was starting to feel strung out and jittery. "Not that the haze lets us see far."

"Maybe we should go around and check the back of the house," Gabriel suggested.

Mira looked at him as though he'd gone crazy. "No way," she hissed. "There's no reason to. Let's just get out of here."

Gabriel seemed reluctant, but moved with her when Mira tugged on his arm.

They walked quickly, but in silence, each lost in their own thoughts as they walked parallel to the city. Mira concentrated on her magic and their direction while Gabriel tried to watch every direction at once. After a few blocks of nothing more than the acrid haze, their pace started to slow.

"You know," Gabriel said, keeping his voice low, "it's the silence of this place that really works its way into you."

"I'd rather hear nothing than something in this place," Mira said.

"It's so alien to our world. I mean, the city is never quiet, but even in the country there's noise all the time. People, cars, animals. Here, there's nothing."

Mira unconsciously moved closer to Gabriel.

"And the light," Gabriel said. "There's no night or day, at

least that we know of. And where the heck does the light come from?"

"And the things here?" Mira asked, wondering how they couldn't be the worst thing.

"Between the two of us, I think we'll be okay against them."

She gaped at him. "You know I don't have the same spell with me now, right?"

Gabriel shrugged. "Will they chance it after what you did to them last time?"

"I guess it depends on how much choice they have. And if they're people or animals."

"Or both."

Mira frowned. "In our world, you can't be both."

"I've run into a few that might make you disagree."

"But they're smart," Mira said. "Okay, maybe not smart as in intelligent, but they have a brain and can make their own choices. It's not all instinct."

Gabriel shrugged, but didn't argue.

"The thing in the city freaks me out more than anything else," Mira said, changing the subject.

They both stared in that direction. Even if the haze had been lighter, the buildings would have blocked their line of sight.

"I can't wrap my brain around that," Gabriel said.

"Me either," Mira said. "Did you believe John when he said some people called it a god?"

"It looked more like a root the way it was twined around the Borgo building. I can't imagine anyone calling it a god."

Mira gazed bleakly around them. "I really want to get out of this place."

"We will."

"How far out of the way have we walked?"

"Not as far as you'd think," Gabriel said.

Mira held out the pendulum, still following the direction it led. "Do you think we'll make it back to Lance's in time for Emmit to bring us through?"

"He'll wait."

Remembering how he had acted when John took her, Mira bit her lip and tried to keep her eyes from welling up.

"He'll wait," Gabriel repeated, more insistently.

"Emmit was quick to give me up for dead," Mira said.

"Yeah, well, he and I had words about that."

The pendulum began to swing wider, which gave Mira the excuse to concentrate on something besides Emmit.

Gabriel pivoted on the spot. Mira's attention jumped to Gabriel as something brown and black cannoned into him, knocking him to the ground. The thing screeched in triumph and brought its head down, ready to sink razor-sharp teeth into its prey.

As Gabriel's hand raised, the sword appeared, slicing the thing open.

Within seconds of Mira looking away from the pendulum, Gabriel had dispatched the creature. Dark brown blood dumped itself onto Gabriel before he could push the beast off him.

Mira wanted to help Gabriel, but instead took up her post as lookout to ensure that nothing else was poised to attack. Her heart thundered in her chest and she started to feel sick to her stomach.

"I don't think there are any others," Mira said shakily.

"What I want to know is how the hell did I not sense that one?" Gabriel asked, getting to his feet and staring at his shirt in disgust.

"It was quiet," Mira said. "I didn't hear it at all."

"Yeah, but if it was going to attack I should have sensed it, since it could just as easily hurt you."

"Unless it specifically targeted you," Mira said.

Gabriel frowned. "That's a dirty trick."

"Where's your ward? It should have prevented the brunt of the attack," Mira said.

"I can't hold it, the sword, and the shield all at once," Gabriel said.

"You're not wearing any socks," Mira reminded him. "Put it in your shoe."

Gabriel looked like he was going to argue, but then shook his head and pulled out the ward, putting it in his boot.

Mira took another look around before holding her trembling hand up to get the pendulum swinging once again.

"Christ, this stuff stinks," Gabriel said, curling his nose up.

"Do you think it will attract more of them?" Mira asked.

"I know it will." With a sigh, he started to take off the shirt, only to find that he was trapped in it. He struggled for a minute before giving up and ripping the shirt off his wings.

Mira had a wan smile, remembering that their last time in the Ether, she had been bemusedly upset because Gabriel had taken off his shirt and had another on underneath it. This time was no different.

"You okay?" Gabriel asked.

She shook her head. "No, but I will be when we get out of here."

"Is it safe for me to drop this?" Gabriel asked, lowering his voice and leaning in.

Mira searched around again, worried that he had sensed someone listening. "I think it will be safer to leave the shirt here than to keep it with us. If it had your blood on it that would be a different story."

They moved another block before Gabriel tossed the shirt into an alley that was just as silent and grimy as the main streets. Mira adjusted their course a few times; happy it took them slightly away from the city and not toward it. The buildings were lower here. One and two story, mostly, with the occasional taller building.

"Do you know where we are?" Mira asked, watching the blank buildings closely.

"Um," Gabriel turned around, "I think this is Short Street."

Mira stopped and took a closer look at the buildings. "That's not good."

"Why not?" Gabriel asked. "We're making good time at the moment."

"I found Barney on Short Street. That's where Ian picked us up yesterday." Just saying the word 'yesterday' made her feel tired. It felt like she had lived a lifetime in this world. "John was going to send me to the Ether, but had to settle for trapping me inside myself."

"That's good, though, isn't it? Not about John, but if they were around here in our world, maybe they're holding Tyler there in this world."

"It also means it's probably well-guarded."

"Probably," Gabriel said, shrugging the idea away. "We can take care of anything that might be there."

Mira wished she could be as confident as Gabriel was about their abilities. His abilities, sure—she was certain he could take care of himself. She knew she was a liability.

CHAPTER 23

"LET'S JUST TAKE IT SLOW," Mira said.

Gabriel allowed Mira to set their pace. Despite his certainty there would be no problems, he was on edge with sword and shield at the ready.

Although she could put it down, Mira held the pendulum out as though it were a shield of her own. Since she knew where they were going, she didn't feel as though she needed it, but aside from fire, it was her only magic.

As they neared their destination, they hugged the buildings across the street, looking for movement.

"At least there are no windows," Mira whispered. "We can't see in, but they can't see out either."

"I thought this place burned to the ground," Gabriel said.

"In our world it did. Maybe it takes a while for the Ether to catch up."

"Let's go."

"Now? Just like that? Don't you want to watch to see if anyone comes and goes?"

"No, I want to find your friend and get out of here. It's not like we need to know who's behind this."

Mira gripped her stomach. She didn't trust her voice, so she nodded and followed Gabriel across the street.

He hesitated at the door. "Keep your hand on my shoulder if you can, so I know where you are."

Mutely, Mira put her hand on his wing. Gabriel gently pushed the door open after glancing quickly around. Then he slipped inside. Mira watched their back, knowing that whatever was in front of them, Gabriel could handle.

They left the door open behind them. The light inside was almost no different to the amount of light outside.

When Gabriel moved forward, Mira moved with him. They slowly made their way across the entry.

"Do you think we have the wrong place?" Gabriel whispered.

"Through that door is where I found Barney." Mira's voice trembled almost as much as she did.

"Keep an eye on the staircase."

"If it's behind you, I've got it covered," Mira reminded him.

Gabriel said nothing. He opened one side of the double door to what in their own world was a sanctuary of sorts and checked the room.

"There's a lot of places where something could hide in this room." Gabriel backed out. "I don't suppose that pendulum could tell us if what we're looking for is in there."

Mira let go of Gabriel and dug the crystal back out of her pocket. "It should at least give us an idea."

She let the crystal drop from the chain. With Gabriel watching, she closed her eyes and said the phrase she needed. Instead of a steady shift, the pendulum tugged frantically against its chain.

Mira looked over the glow of the magic, down the hall. "It looks like we're in luck. We don't have to go in there."

"I think we're due some luck," Gabriel said. "Lead the way."

The pendulum swung back and then lurched forward again as though urging them on. The last thing she wanted was to be in front of Gabriel.

You can do this, she told herself. Mira took a deep breath, stood up straighter, and followed the trail. At each door they passed, Mira's breathing slowed. She wasn't exactly holding her breath, but was afraid even the noise of the air moving would alert something hiding behind closed doors.

As Mira walked, the pendulum shifted its trajectory slightly with each step. At almost the end of the hall, it swung side to side, the crystal straining against the chain to go either left or right.

"Which door?" Gabriel asked.

"Um, both, I think."

Gabriel sighed. "Left first. Step back."

Mira watched as he checked the doorknob.

"Locked," Gabriel said. He turned and tried the other side and found it locked. "Shit."

"Wait," Mira said, "in our world I found a key in a frame next to the door. It seemed like a decoration."

"Nothing like that here," Gabriel said.

"No, but they left the key where anyone could use it. Maybe they did that here?"

Gabriel grinned. "Makes sense. Then you can send anyone to check on whoever you have inside."

Despite what Gabriel had said about the decoration, Mira checked the walls while Gabriel checked the doorframes. When neither found anything, they did the same down the rest of the hall until Gabriel found the key above the first door in the hallway.

Hearts buoyed slightly, they hurried back and unlocked the first door. Gabriel thrust it open, shield up in front of him.

Nothing happened.

He lowered the shield and stared around. From the corner, someone burst into wailing and tears.

It didn't sound like Tyler, so Mira peered around Gabriel.

"What did you do?" she hissed at Gabriel, pushing him aside, going to the young girl in the corner. Mira approached, but didn't move too close. This was the Ether, after all.

Besides, the girl—who Mira estimated was around six—cried louder when Mira got too close.

Something thumped against the door across the hall, followed by an indistinct yell.

Mira ignored it and spoke gently to the little girl in the corner. "It's okay. We're here to help you."

"I didn't want to die," the girl sobbed.

"Don't worry, we're going to get you out of here and back home," Mira said, trying to keep her voice soothing. "What can I call you?"

Mira had assumed that the girl was a witch and that was why the spell had led her here. Asking a witch's name might not be the best idea in the circumstances. A witch's true name had power and Mira didn't want the girl to get the wrong idea.

"Andrea," she said after a few uncertain moments.

"My name is Miranda. Mira for short."

Andrea sniffed and looked up at Mira with watery eyes. "Are you an angel, too?"

Something slammed again against the other door.

"What?" Mira asked, distracted. "Oh! No, I'm not an angel. I'm a witch."

"Did you die, too?" the girl asked.

"Die?"

The little girl nodded at Gabriel, who appeared uncomfortable.

"I see," Mira said, squatting down. "No, I'm not dead, and neither are you. He's not that kind of angel."

"Does that mean—" Andrea hesitated, watching Mira closely.

"That means we're going to help you get out of here," Mira said when the girl didn't continue.

"And my brother?" Andrea asked.

A voice behind the closed door started cursing. Mira couldn't make out the actual words, but the tone suggested swearing.

"And your brother and anyone else we can help," Mira said. She approached the little girl again, but she cringed back into the corner and Mira stopped. "Gabriel, go let her brother out."

"Maybe I shouldn't be the one," Gabriel said.

When Mira gave him an appraising look, Gabriel seemed self-conscious. The sword and shield had disappeared and he had moved back out into the hallway. His wings were hunched down further than Mira had ever seen them.

Mira squatted back down, facing Andrea once again, and lowered her voice as though telling a secret. "I'm going to go get your brother. That guy out there, his name is Gabriel." She lowered her voice even further, leaning in to the girl. "He's my guardian angel." Mira paused, giving an extra moment for that to sink in. "I'm going to ask him to watch out for you. Is that okay?"

Andrea's eyes widened, and for the first time since Gabriel had opened the door, she looked hopeful.

"What should I call your brother?" Mira asked.

"Kevin," Andrea said, "Kevin Henderson."

Mira tried to keep the same look of concern on her face. "I'll be right back."

Out in the hall, Mira whispered to Gabriel, "How long have the Hendersons been missing?"

"Three days," Gabriel said. "She didn't mention her parents."

Mira swallowed hard and gave a nod before going across the hall.

"Kevin, are you in there?" she called, trying not to be too loud. "I'm opening the door. Your sister wants to see you."

There was no reply from inside.

Mira fumbled with the key, but managed to get the door unlocked. She had worried about being rushed at by an angry little boy. Instead, she had a furious teenager standing in the middle of the floor, clenching and unclenching his fists, but also with tears shining in his eyes.

Kevin said nothing, and Mira was at a complete loss for what to say. She opened the door wider and stepped aside, but the boy didn't move.

"My name is Mira. Your sister wants to see you and then we need to get out of here."

There was still nothing from Kevin.

"She's okay," Mira said. "Only scared."

"Are you with them?" Kevin asked with as much acid as a teenager could put into his voice.

"I'm a witch," Mira said. "My friend and I are here to help."

"You'll help him?" Kevin asked, the anger not abating.

Mira glanced around the room, trying to figure out who 'him' was. Her eyes landed on the man on the floor, lying next to the bed.

"Tyler?" Mira asked. Then she left the boy alone and rushed into the room. "Tyler!" He didn't stir at her voice, so she crouched down next to him, looking him over for injuries.

Tyler appeared gaunt and frail. Mira put a hand to his neck to check for a pulse. Tyler's eyes popped open, and with more strength than Mira would have thought possible in his state, he punched out.

The assault was easily fielded by Gabriel.

"Mira?" Tyler asked, his voice hoarse. "Shit, they got you?"

"Not exactly," Mira said.

Gabriel dropped the hand when Tyler's strength faltered.

"Are you injured?" Mira asked.

Tyler let out a mirthless laugh that fell into a hacking cough.

Mira glanced out the door to see Kevin and Andrea across the hall. Then she looked meaningfully at Gabriel.

"I just had to make sure you were okay," Gabriel said. "I've got an eye on the kids."

When Tyler's hacking subsided, Mira turned her attention back to him.

"Do you think you can walk?" Mira asked.

"To where?" Tyler asked. "Those things will tear you to pieces."

"We're getting out of here," Mira said. "Come on, I'll help you up."

"I don't think you understand—" Tyler started to protest, but it turned into a groan when Mira helped pull him to his feet. He leaned against her, panting, trying to catch his breath.

To Mira, he felt dreadfully skinny. "How far do we have to go?" she asked Gabriel.

The angel gave Mira a worried look. "Mira," he said, keeping his voice soft, "it's a long way."

She watched Gabriel struggle and she was genuinely curious as to what he would say. After Emmit had given her up for dead, before she was even hurt, she felt the need to know what Gabriel would do now.

"Let me search the rest of the rooms," Gabriel said. "I'm going to need you to watch him and the Hendersons until I get back."

Gabriel called the kids over while Mira helped Tyler into a chair. Once they were all together, Gabriel pulled Mira aside.

"I don't like the idea of shutting the door," Gabriel said, "but it may be safer to keep it closed. You have a way of stopping anything you need to, right?"

"I burned this place down in our world," Mira said. "I have no problems burning it down here as well."

Gabriel smiled. "I'll be back soon."

Once the four were shut into the room, Mira listened intently at the door, trying to hear Gabriel make his way through the building, but any traces of noise he made died in a few moments. There was no way she would use her fire spell if there were any chance Gabriel could get caught in the flames.

"Who was that?" Tyler asked.

"A friend," Mira said.

"He's going to get us home," Andrea said.

"I don't suppose he has any water in his bag?" Tyler asked.

Mira frowned and looked closely at Tyler. "What do you mean?"

"The white bag he has on his back," Tyler said.

"Those are his wings," Andrea said knowingly. "Every guardian angel has to have wings."

"Guardian angel, huh?" Tyler said, trying to smile at Andrea.

"Yep, and he's come to take us home," Andrea said.

Mira moved closer to Tyler and watched him carefully. He wasn't looking at Andrea, she realized. He was looking in her general direction.

"Tyler," she said softly, "how did you know it was me?"

He lost all semblance of a smile. "Your magic. That and you were close enough. I figured they'd be after you."

"Why, though?" Mira asked. She kept her voice low and glanced at Andrea and Kevin. Both of them watched her closely, as though she may evaporate.

"Water?" Tyler asked.

"Sorry," Mira said, feeling crushed that she could help no one, "but we'll be out of here in a few hours."

He lapsed into silence, closed his eyes, and slumped in the chair.

She turned to the kids, but didn't have the heart to ask them any questions about what might be going on. Mira was afraid of how much they knew and didn't want to hear the answers from people so young.

The door burst open and Mira jumped and stuck her hand in her pocket, ready to lash out with magic. When she saw a wide-eyed Gabriel, she glared at him.

"A little warning would have been nice," Mira snapped.

"Sorry," Gabriel said. "We need to get out of this place."

"Did you find anyone else?" Mira asked.

Gabriel glanced up and down the hall. "No, let's go."

Even though Gabriel had all but crashed his way into the room, Tyler hadn't moved. Mira took hold of his arm, which caused Tyler to jerk awake and try to push her away. Once again, it took him a few moments to catch his bearings.

"Mira?" he croaked.

"We've got to go," Mira said, afraid to recognize that her friend might not have remembered the past thirty minutes.

After Mira had helped him to his feet, she tugged his arm over her shoulder to help support him.

Gabriel looked like he was doing some fast calculations, watching the two. "That's only going to work for so long." Before Mira could get upset, he continued. "We're going to need to trade off. Right now, you cover Tyler and set our pace. The quicker the better."

His sense of urgency was infectious. "Is there something I should be looking for?" Mira asked as she maneuvered Tyler out of the room.

"In this place?" Gabriel snorted. "Everything, as far as I can tell."

"I meant," Mira said, agitated, "did you see anything lying in wait for us?"

"No."

Mira slowed at the front door. "Then why are you so freaked out?"

"Being here is enough," Gabriel said.

Mira's temper began to rise, but there wasn't much space for it around her fear. "Will you just—"

"No!" Gabriel closed his eyes and took a deep breath. "I'd rather spare you the details," he said, his voice restrained.

Her anxiety ratcheted up and she stood aside to let Gabriel get the door. When the angel had confirmed it was safe, Mira hobbled Tyler out as fast as she could manage.

Despite feeling the eager need to move, her pace began to falter after a block or so. The party fanned out in the street, Gabriel on one side, her on the other, and the kids in the middle. Tyler's weight became heavier, but she worked hard to hide the fact from Gabriel.

It was hard for her to admit the uneasiness she felt when she thought about letting Gabriel know the full extent of Tyler's condition. A mixture of resentment toward Emmit and fear of being left behind was at the root of it—none of which was Gabriel's fault. When Tyler slowed further yet, Mira pushed them another block before calling for a break.

Once she helped Tyler down on some steps, she turned to Gabriel. "We need to talk." It came out more resolute than she'd intended, but Gabriel seemed not to notice. "Kevin and Andrea, can you two take care of Tyler for a few minutes?"

Neither of them said anything, but they moved closer to Tyler in a show of agreement.

Gabriel's scan of their surroundings never rested as they crossed the street, keeping the others in sight.

"How's he holding up?" Gabriel asked.

Mira bit her lip. "Not well."

Gabriel's wings twitched and he looked down at her, dropping his vigilant search of their surroundings. "Are you okay?"

"No, I'm not." She sniffed and gave him a semblance of a smile. "None of us are."

Concern filled his face. "We're going to get out of here."

Mira nodded and turned away, pretending to scan the street, but not really seeing anything. "Tyler's really bad off. Weak and nearly blind." She sniffed again, her eyes watering. "I wanted to make sure you knew."

Gabriel pulled her into a hug, which startled her.

She stiffened for a moment, but then fell into it, hugging him back and soaking up the comfort. She could feel the soft rustling feathers over her hands.

"We'll get him back to our world and to the hospital," Gabriel said.

"And say what?" Mira asked, trying not to break down completely. "We found him wandering the streets?"

"We'll figure something out," Gabriel said. "Let's concentrate on getting out of here first."

The outcry from the city punched out and the ground began to shake. Gabriel held Mira tightly and looked over her shoulder at the kids. Mira followed his gaze and the pair broke apart, but Mira kept a firm grip on Gabriel's hand as they ran across the street.

Andrea had her hands over her ears and her eyes were shut tight. Kevin tried to remain stoic, but wasn't managing it well.

Even Tyler seemed terrified. He didn't get up, but his eyes were wide and roving and his hands were clenched into fists.

When the sound continued, Andrea's mouth dropped open into a cry that Mira couldn't hear. When the creature that lurked in the city stopped its screech, Andrea's sobs replaced the sound.

When the ground stopped moving, Andrea threw her arms around her brother and wailed.

Kevin hugged Andrea until his sister calmed down.

Mira was at a loss as to how to comfort anyone. The only hope she could offer was getting the hell out of there.

"How far away are we?" Mira asked.

"Still a few hours," Gabriel said. "I'll help Tyler for a while."

The group didn't spread out quite as far as they previously had. Gabriel and Mira kept on either side of Kevin and Andrea. Mira repeatedly patted her pocket, reassuring herself that her crystal holding the fire spell was still there.

"Does this seem strange to you?" Mira asked after a while.

"Yes," Gabriel said without thinking. "Which part in particular?"

"The first time we were here we couldn't move more than a few steps without being attacked," Mira said. "Don't get me wrong, this time hasn't been a walk in the park—but it seems easier." She stopped when she realized that Gabriel had fallen behind.

Tyler had stopped dead, forcing Gabriel to a standstill, and he stared in Mira's direction.

"Are you telling me you're one of the ones that started this?" Tyler asked.

CHAPTER 24

MIRA COULD FEEL TYLER'S ANGER, even if he didn't have the energy to yell.

"Started what?" Mira asked. "I still don't know what's going on."

"How did you get here before?" Tyler asked.

"It wasn't by choice," Mira said. "We were yanked over by whatever is living in John now. Well, they pulled me over—getting Gabriel with me was an accident."

"You weren't with the witches that came here?" Tyler asked.

Mira stared at Tyler in disbelief. "Witches don't come here." She glanced at the kids. "No one should even know how."

Gabriel got Tyler moving again, taking advantage of Tyler's more energetic, if angry state.

"Someone managed it," Tyler said.

"John would know who," Mira said.

"He's a psychic, not a witch," Tyler reminded her.

"Actually, he's not even that now," Mira said. "He's dead. What's in his body isn't him anymore."

"I don't know what you're talking about," Tyler said. His voice started to fade again.

"Maybe it's best not to go over this here," Gabriel said. "We have enough in front of us."

They all lapsed into silence. Mira's attention began to fade as they plodded across streets, through yards, and down alleys that Mira would have avoided back home.

"Maybe they decided they couldn't fight us in this world," Gabriel suggested after a while.

"What?" Mira asked, feeling groggy.

"I mean," he continued, "the fight we had earlier took a lot of them out. Maybe they've decided it's too risky to attack here."

"Maybe he's done with me." She didn't believe it, but it would be nice if it were true.

"They're not done with any of the witches," Tyler's voice came out scratchy and dry.

Mira wanted to ask more, but didn't want to make Tyler talk. She saw that he leaned much heavier on Gabriel than he had earlier.

The houses began to grow larger, signaling they were getting closer to their destination.

A flash of black disappeared around the corner, and Mira stopped, wondering if she had actually seen something. No one else seemed to notice, so she went on. She hadn't slept in what seemed like ages, and that little jolt of fear left her even more tired.

She caught more movement out of the corner of her eye, but when she turned, she saw nothing.

"Hold up," Mira said.

"Just a little further," Gabriel said.

"I don't think that's a good idea." Mira studied her surroundings, but still, she could see nothing out of place.

Gabriel sighed heavily and moved Tyler to where he could lean against a wall. Tyler didn't last long there before Gabriel had to grab him and lower him to the ground. Kevin and Andrea went to sit with Tyler, Andrea laying her head on her brother's shoulder, looking almost as exhausted as Mira felt.

"Lance's house is close," Gabriel said, pulling Mira aside. He seemed cross, but then it had been a long day for everyone. "We really should press on."

"We're being watched." Mira rubbed her forehead and tried to wake her brain up. "Or followed, or something."

"What makes you say that?" Gabriel asked.

"I saw something a little while back."

"And you didn't say anything?" Gabriel asked before she could continue.

"No." She didn't have the strength to get aggravated with him. "I thought I had imagined it, but then I saw something dart around the building over there."

Gabriel looked around. "Last time we were here, you thought they were herding us somewhere. Do think that's what they're doing now?"

"No, but I don't think they need to." Mira tried to get her thoughts lined up. "Does John know where we're going?"

"How could he? We could be going anywhere."

Mira thought that over. "There was no magic at Tyler's house. Maybe he assumed we'd be going back to my place for spells. He couldn't know we'd be going to Lance's house. Only John couldn't be sure about it. Like you said, we could have gone anywhere, so he'd have someone report back to him."

"So, you think he's laying a trap?"

Mira rolled that idea around. "Yeah, I think he is."

"And Lance's house is only a few blocks away from yours." Gabriel sought out the others. Tyler and Andrea appeared to be asleep. "And I'm not sure what we could face like this. Why is nothing in this place easy?"

Mira didn't bother with a reply.

"You have a spell, right?" Gabriel asked.

"Yeah," Mira said, feeling uncomfortable about the spell, "but this one is strong even in our world. I'm afraid of what it could do here. If we aren't together, it could affect any one of us."

"It's fire, right?" Gabriel asked.

"Yeah, it was a stupid idea—"

"No," Gabriel said. "If John wants you this badly, and he's had the time to plan something, then we'll need all the strength we can get."

Mira knew that a strong spell wasn't a great idea when you were worried about it hitting the wrong target. A brief memory of her last spell rose, filling her sleep-deprived mind.

"Here's what we're going to do," Gabriel said. "We need to try to find out what's in front of us. I'm going to scout ahead and see what we are facing. You all can stay here. Can you make a circle?"

Mira shook her head. "If we were in my workshop, it would be easy. The circle is permanent there and the magic is so ingrained that I don't need anything but willpower to raise it. But here?" She looked around. "I'm not sure what I would end up with."

Gabriel ran his fingers through his hair and his wings rustled. Mira tried to kick her sluggish brain into gear, but she couldn't think of anything useful.

"It's still going to be safer if I scout ahead," Gabriel said. "I want you to take this and look after everyone here."

Mira blinked in confusion at the sword he tried to hand her. "What am I supposed to do with that?"

He grinned weakly at her and wrapped her hand around it. "The same thing I do. Stick the pointy end in anything that's trying to kill you."

She wanted to smile, especially since his hand was wrapped around hers, but she was too tired and worried about the idea. "But it's yours. Will it even stay with me when you're gone?" She'd held the sword once before, but she was once again surprised with the weight of the thing. It was heavy, and she couldn't imagine waving it around the way Gabriel did.

"It seems to know what I want, so it should stay. If things get bad, don't forget about your spell. Use it if you have to." He dropped her hand and walked away.

"Wait!" This was happening way too fast for her. She wanted to say something to Gabriel, but couldn't find the words.

He turned back to her and a lump formed in her throat. They'd never been apart in this world. Not for more than a few minutes. When she was here, Gabriel was with her. He kept her safe and sane in this nightmare.

Gabriel looked at her questioningly and walked back to her.

What could she say? She had been taken from her own world

and he had crossed between the worlds for her. What do you say to someone who does that? Especially before he went off on his own to face who knew what.

"I'll be back," Gabriel said. "It shouldn't take long."

She grabbed his hand before he could turn away. Carefully pointing the sword back and away from him, she pulled him closer and hugged him.

He was hesitant at first, but after a few moments, he wrapped his arms around her as if it was the most natural thing in the world.

In this world, Mira told herself, *it is natural.*

He breathed deeply, gripped tighter, and then unwound himself from her, keeping her hand. "I'll be back shortly."

She nodded, afraid her voice would crack if she spoke.

He squeezed her hand and hurried away.

Mira watched him, and when he disappeared behind a building, she stared at the last spot she had seen him.

"Where's he going?"

Her mind jumped back to where she was. Kevin watched her expectantly, keeping his voice low so he wouldn't disturb his sister.

"He's going to look ahead," Mira said. "He'll be back."

Kevin looked at her, deadpan. "Why should he come back?"

Mira tried to reassure him. "It's what he does."

"Is he really an angel?" Kevin asked.

"Yes, but probably not like the ones you've heard about. Kind of like witches. We're not old ladies living in the woods, cursing anyone who comes by. He's not going to be wearing a halo or playing the harp."

Kevin watched her for a while, until Mira became unnerved by his lack of expression.

"But he does help people," Mira continued to fill the silence. She started to look around as an excuse to stop watching Kevin. "He doesn't have wings in our world. In fact, very few people in our world even know he's an angel."

Kevin watched Mira silently scan the streets.

Mira caught sight of a creature, but it was too far away for her to make out any details. She gripped the sword, holding it down and away, afraid she'd cut her leg, and rammed her other hand in her pocket, grabbing the crystal.

When the creature disappeared, Mira tried to relax. She rolled her shoulders, which had begun to knot up.

"My aunt is an old witch," Kevin said.

When Mira glanced his way, he still watched her. It was as though he'd fixated on her, not bothering to look around.

"She has a big mole on her face, too," he continued. "And my mother says she curses way too much."

Mira grinned at him. "To be fair, I've never actually asked Gabriel if he plays the harp."

For the first time since he'd sat down, Kevin's blank facade cracked.

His smile was weak, but it was there. Mira's heart panged when it didn't last. Kevin sniffed and looked away, only glancing back when his face was blank and distant once again.

He's trying to cope, Mira thought. She figured there wasn't enough money in the world to cover the psychiatry bill these kids would have over the next few years.

"You should get some rest while you can," Mira told him. "Once we leave this spot, I don't think we'll stop again until we're back home."

He glanced down at his little sister, sleeping against him. Then he looked at Tyler. "One of us needs to be awake," Kevin said.

"I'll keep watch," Mira said.

Kevin's face turned into a scowl. "One of *us* needs to stay awake."

He spoke in such a vitriolic way that it took Mira aback. Then she really took in the three of them. They'd gone through a sort of hell that she probably couldn't cope with.

"Thank you for looking after Tyler," Mira said sincerely. "That means a lot to me."

That seemed to mollify Kevin a little and they both lapsed into silence.

Mira started to pace, but soon began to totter. Only the twist in her stomach about the thought of what might be happening to Gabriel kept her moving. Mira saw movement, so she jerked the sword up in that direction. A creature moved down the street, only a block behind them.

It ambled towards them, seeming to be in no real hurry.

Kevin got to his feet and stared at the beast. It had a reddish-brown color and three legs, though whether this was by design or by an accident, Mira couldn't say.

Mira's heart thudded in her chest. She felt an urgent need to turn around, but was afraid to look away from the known threat.

"Kevin, I need you to help me." She worked to keep her voice calm and level. "I need you to be on the lookout for anything else. I see this thing, but I need you to start keeping an eye out for anything else." When he didn't say anything, she went on, "Can you do that for me? For us?" she added, knowing that he'd be more apt to help if it meant protecting his sister and Tyler.

"I'll look," he said, his voice betraying his trepidation.

"Let me know if you see anything," Mira said.

"The angel! I see Gabriel," Kevin's voice raised to a yell, the relief obvious.

Mira had no idea where he was, but knowing he was nearby made her feel stronger. The creature stopped. Pounding feet could be heard behind her. Gabriel, running.

He must have seen the thing in front of her.

Another scream tore out of the city. Mira flinched at the sound.

The monster in front of her lunged forward and Mira flung the sword up. The thing bounded forward twice and then leapt. She screamed, but the noise from the city swallowed it. She saw claws coming towards her and realized that it didn't matter if she stabbed it—it would still tear her to shreds.

Her sword was thrust aside and the creature disappeared behind Gabriel's shield. When it hit, Gabriel stumbled into Mira from the impact. His wings shot out, steadying himself.

A wing caught Mira in the chest, and she was flung back and landed hard on the asphalt. She saw the sword fall to the ground beside her, but the clatter was lost to the sound that pierced through her.

She laid there, stunned. The sword disappeared, and she shut her eyes and tried to block out the sound.

"Shit."

Her first thought was that Gabriel sounded frustrated. Then she realized she could actually hear his voice. She struggled to open her eyes. Once they were shut, she wanted to do nothing but sleep.

In fear that she'd be tempted to do just that, she opened her eyes wide and tried not to blink. Gabriel's face hovered above hers and she smiled.

"Dammit, don't scare me like that," Gabriel said.

She grinned wider. "When I can see the wings, hearing you curse takes on a whole new level of amusement," she said.

He looked puzzled. "Did you hit your head?"

Mira frowned, her mind a jumble of mixed-up emotions and memories. "Maybe," she muttered.

Gabriel began running his hands over her head.

It took a few moments for her to remember where she was and what was happening. She wanted to close her eyes again and go back to that dazed feeling.

"Is she okay?" The voice was as indistinguishable as Tyler's that she had to look around to see who spoke. It sounded as though he were sixty years older.

She winced when Gabriel hit a sore spot. "I'm okay."

"I can't handle a lie right now," Gabriel said in a voice only for her ears.

She sighed and felt even more tired. "I'll be okay after I get home and get some sleep."

"You're sure?" Gabriel asked, standing back up.

"Yes," she said, reminding herself that it was true, since she didn't say how much sleep it would take before she started to feel like a normal person again.

She grabbed his hand and let him help her to her feet. When her head spun, she gripped his arm for a moment and closed her eyes until the vertigo passed.

Gabriel started to say something, but Mira spoke over him to avoid further questioning. "What are we looking at?"

"We're going to have to go out of our way a few blocks, but I think we can get to Lance's," Gabriel said. "I'm going to need my hands free, though."

"I can help Tyler," Kevin spoke up.

"I've got a special job for you," Gabriel said. "Mira, get Tyler ready and I'll chat with Kevin."

She raised an eyebrow, suspicious about what the task might be, but she knew Gabriel wouldn't ask Kevin to do anything that would lead to more peril.

Andrea stood next to Tyler, looking like she could curl up and go right back to sleep. Mira envied Andrea's short nap.

"Come on," Mira said to Tyler. She leaned down and put his arm over her shoulder, ready to pull him up.

"Leave me," Tyler said, still sounding much older. "Get them out if you can."

"Not a chance."

Tyler looked her straight in the eye, despite his visual deterioration. "I can't do this anymore."

Mira met his gaze. "You're coming with us or I'm staying with you. Take your pick."

He closed his eyes and leaned his back against the wall. When he opened them again, Mira felt his grip on her increase, and she helped pull him to his feet.

Was it possible for him to be lighter? Mira thought. Her friend was wasting away, but help was around the corner. Or near enough, anyway.

"This way," Gabriel said, waving them on. "Until we get to Lance's house, don't talk unless you have to. We're going pretty close to some of these things, but it can't be helped."

Gabriel's shield and sword never left his hands as he led the way through the streets. Kevin gripped his sister's hand, and Mira walked with Tyler as fast as she dared push him.

Every now and again, they would hear a noise that would make them freeze. It was always in the distance, though.

How much power does John have here to keep a bunch of these monsters that quiet? Each time the thought rose, Mira squashed it back down.

She was so exhausted that she could cry, but didn't dare do so. If she started that now, she'd never stop. The terror had built to the point that she felt sick and shaky. When she caught herself slowing down, she refocused her efforts.

Hope spurred her forward when Lance's house came into view. Her eyes bore into the gate with each step, as though she were afraid it might disappear. She attempted to gauge the distance. Five hundred steps away. Then down to 200.

When she mentally hit double digits, a wail rose up from behind the gate. Mira looked nervously at Gabriel, wanting him to tell her what to do, but he was running forward, pushing open the gate.

Blocks away, screeches rose up. Hundreds, maybe thousands of voices gathered in response to the cry.

Mira urged Tyler forward. When they reached the gate, Gabriel dispatched the lookout that had called to the others.

"Let's move!" Gabriel yelled. His knuckles had gone white from the pressure he put on his sword.

Kevin and Andrea hurried forward while Mira followed as quickly as she could.

The noise grew louder. Whoops and snarls mingled with growls. For a moment, Mira thought about looking behind her, but she realized it would do her no good. Instead, she focused on the door where Kevin stood waiting.

"Get inside!" Gabriel hollered near Mira's back.

Kevin pushed open the door and disappeared inside with his sister.

They had just reached the steps when the faster, more eager beasts caught up with them. She could hear Gabriel wielding his sword while something banged into the shield.

Mira gave up getting Tyler to move faster. Instead, she gripped him tighter and dragged him up the stairs and into the house.

Kevin stood just inside the door.

"Go down the hall and find the double doors," Mira directed, never stopping. She sucked in lungfuls of air, but it was beginning to feel as though she couldn't breathe. "Open one side and get in there."

Kevin, still gripping his crying sister, ran to follow her orders. When Mira reached the hallway, he stood outside the door.

Mira chanced a glance behind her. She could still hear Gabriel fighting, but she couldn't see him yet.

Getting Tyler to safety had to happen first, and then she could help Gabriel.

"Go inside," Mira snapped at Kevin.

When he dragged his gaze away from the room, she could see pure terror written across his face. There was no way for her to move faster to help with whatever he faced.

"What's wrong?" Mira asked, although she reached the door moments later.

The room was lit, not by the dim, strange light of the rest of this world. Instead, it was a light that was bright and clean where it had already burned away the haze.

In the center of that bright light was Barney.

He was talking, but she couldn't hear anything.

"It's okay," Mira told Kevin. "This is our way back." *I hope,* she added mentally.

Barney waved them forward, and then disappeared.

The glow grew brighter.

"Take Tyler," Mira told Kevin. "Take him and your sister, and move straight to where you saw that man."

Where Barney had been, a pulsing yellow began to form.

"But—"

"Just go. Everyone on the other side is a friend. Go!" Mira leaned Tyler against Kevin and ran back to the double doors.

Down the hall, it sounded like the front door slammed shut.

Mira didn't leave the room until she saw Kevin enter the magic. All three of them began to fade as he moved into the glowing yellow.

Gabriel ran toward her. Behind him, Mira heard the door being smashed down.

When she turned back to the room, Kevin, Andrea, and Tyler disappeared completely.

The glow went with them.

CHAPTER 25

N O!" MIRA SHRIEKED WITHOUT REALLY meaning to.

Gabriel pushed her into the room and slammed the door shut behind him. Panicked, his eyes darted around the room.

"We need to put something against the door," Gabriel said.

The door shuddered and they both backed up.

"Where'd they go?" Gabriel asked.

"Gone," Mira said, "back home."

The door crashed open and there was no time for further discussion. Gabriel hacked and slashed while using his sword to push others away.

"Go away!" Gabriel yelled.

Shrieks followed. Some creatures ran out, but retreated straight into more moving inside.

Gabriel breathed hard. When the retreating creatures had all been replaced, Mira could see her ward at work.

There were too many for one person to fight.

Mira drew her athame and held it out like a dagger. A beast, low to the ground, jumped out at her. It grabbed her leg, and pain lanced out as she slammed her athame into its flesh. When she scrambled backward, it didn't move. Two more faced her.

Before one could reach her, Gabriel stepped in front.

"Go away!" Gabriel's voice boomed through the room.

A frenzy rose up around them and the beasts trampled each other in their need to follow his command.

She could see him panting heavily before he rushed to meet the next wave. Something huge lumbered in, blocking the path.

Gabriel hacked at the beast, hitting it once. When he tried to pierce the beast again, hundreds of tendril-slim hands shot out and gripped the sword. The sword sliced through anything that touched its blade, but the monster stopped the swipe by gripping the hilt. It roared and swung down a club.

"Go away!" Gabriel shouted.

The club still came, but the tiny hands retreated. The wood smashed into Gabriel.

The magic in the ward she had created winked out.

The beast trampled everything in the hall on its mad rampage out of the house, but more came from another direction. Mira wanted to cry. They kept coming.

Smaller creatures entered in a swarm. Tiny claws slashed through Mira's clothes, slicing the skin beneath. Blood poured down one side of Gabriel's face, and in a few moments, his shield dropped from his hands.

"Go—"

Gabriel breathed deep and tried again. "Go away!"

His strength was fading.

Mira was doing what she could with her athame, but it wasn't enough. Not near enough. A chunk of wood flew into the room from the hallway and hit Gabriel.

The world slowed for Mira.

Her heart shattered when he fell. Mira stabbed the beast that had jumped on top of Gabriel before it could do any more damage.

Mira had the crystal in her hand before she realized it. She fell down next to Gabriel and released her spell.

Fire sprouted around them and burst in all directions. The intense heat scalded her skin in a flash that quickly receded. Mira numbly watched a wall of fire speed away, using the creatures as fuel.

Gabriel didn't move. His skin appeared sunburned from the burst of fire. She leaned over him, trying to find his pulse and check his breathing at the same time. She held onto her breath until she felt air blowing across her skin. It took her longer to find a pulse. She was shaking so badly it was hard for her to sense anything.

When she felt his heart beat, she left her fingers against his neck and glanced around.

Nothing moved. Charred lumps could be seen here and there, and the remains of a house burned next door.

It took her disorientated brain a while to figure out what was wrong. Mira stood up and turned slowly in a circle.

Large parts of Lance's house were gone, and the rest was black, smoldering remains.

A roar went up through the city and the ground shook.

Mira sank to her knees, tears running freely, and tapped Gabriel on his cheeks.

He didn't stir.

Mira let out a sob, and bleary eyed, she looked around at the watery glow that rose around them. She rubbed her face and blinked several times until she saw the magic that had returned. As she watched, the swirling yellow mass began to form. She shook Gabriel, but wasn't having any luck getting him to wake up.

Her heart beat madly in her chest. She was almost home. *They* were almost home. A few steps away the noise, haze, and smell of burning tar would disappear.

Mira forced herself to her feet, grabbed Gabriel's arm, and pulled. He moved a few inches and stopped.

It didn't take her long to realize his wings were getting caught up.

Frustrated, Mira rolled him over, wincing as a wing bent in a way she was sure wasn't good for it. Once he was on his stomach, she grabbed both his hands.

"You are coming with me," she said, moving a few inches. He stopped again, and she took a few deep breaths and tried once more. "You're coming with me or I'm staying here."

She closed her eyes, dug her feet in, and pulled back step by step. When hands reached out and touched her, she screamed, let go, and then fell backward onto the floor.

Everything went fuzzy. Mira had no idea how long it stayed that way. Emmit was there the moment she opened her eyes.

Mira had never used the word hubbub, but she figured this is exactly what it would look like.

"The doctor is seeing to Tyler," Emmit said, his face unreadable.

Mira winced when something was pressed hard against her arm.

"Tell me where you are injured," Emmit said. "I'll call the doctor over."

She tried to shrug him off, but it seemed to be a fruitless endeavor.

"I'm not hurt," Mira said.

Emmit raised an eyebrow. It looked out of place with the rest of his impassive face.

"Not badly, anyway" she corrected. "Where's Gabriel?"

"His partner and one of Reinfield's men are with him," Emmit said.

"Is he..." Mira wasn't sure how to finish that thought. She didn't want to breathe the word 'dead,' for fear that it might be true.

"Unconscious," Emmit supplied. He turned to someone else. "Hold this tightly."

Mira nodded and closed her eyes. "And Tyler?"

"His arrival and that of the children was a surprise," Emmit said.

Mira cried out when someone else gripped her arm. She inhaled sharply, trying to bite back the pain. Emmit moved to the other side and began to clean blood away from the numerous cuts.

"That's why the portal closed so suddenly," Emmit continued. "Mr. Singer thought he was bringing *one* of his witches back, not four witches and a detective."

Hearing Mr. Singer's name should have worried Mira, but she was so tired that she was beyond caring.

Mira tried to leverage herself up, but with men holding her arms to check for injuries, she didn't get far.

"Don't move around until the doctor has a chance to see you," Emmit said.

She saw Tyler lying on the couch, eyes closed, with what must have been the doctor and two other people over him. Andrea was sobbing and being comforted by someone unfamiliar to Mira. The little girl clung to her brother's hand as tightly as she could.

"I want to see Gabriel," Mira said, searching for him as best she could. *He has to be all right.*

Three witches familiar to Mira, including Mr. Singer, seemed to be wavering in different spots around the room.

Ian's voice began to rise, even over the sound of Andrea's sobs. "I said, call an ambulance!"

Emmit gave him a dark look from across the room. "We have another doctor on the way."

"That's not good enough!"

Mira struggled with more effort to sit up.

"Lie still," Emmit snapped.

Mira's eyes narrowed. "What?"

"You were lost once, it's not going to happen again," Emmit said, his face showing hints of pent-up anger. Tight lines appeared around his eyes and his lips pursed.

"You didn't lose me, you gave up on me! I want to see Gabriel now."

Emmit didn't look abashed, but he stared at her for a few moments before glaring at the man holding Mira. "Keep pressure on her arm." Turning back to Mira, he spoke in a more gentle voice. "We'll help you."

The world spun for Mira when she sat up. Emmit didn't say anything, but waited until she was ready to stand. When she finally got to her feet, she wished she hadn't tried. The exhaustion threatened to overwhelm her, and the stinging pain of hundreds of cuts became more pronounced.

Tiredness fled her mind, however, when she spotted Ian's beet-red face. He was seething and Mira didn't blame him. She didn't say anything when she joined Ian. There was nothing she could say that would help.

Ian didn't feel the same way. "You can talk some sense into these people."

"How's he doing?" she asked, ignoring the comment.

"He's unconscious, what do you think?"

Mira knew the answer, but she had to ask Emmit the question anyway. "Why aren't we calling the ambulance?"

"We might have to," Emmit said, looking across the room to the doctor. "But we can't exactly tell anyone what happened. I'm not certain we can get away with that due to Tyler's condition. Especially when an injured detective comes in at the same time."

"You people should be good at lying by now," Ian said. "Call the damned ambulance."

"You people?" Emmit asked.

"And what about her?" Ian asked. "You're willing to let her bleed out?"

Emmit had Ian by the throat before anyone knew what was happening.

"You are trying my patience," Emmit said quietly.

The noise in the room seemed to die away. Mira held her breath and watched, hearing only her heartbeat for a few seconds. That was all it took to have her wavering.

"Emmit," Mira tried to sound stern, but couldn't make it work. The room began to spin around her. She reached out and grabbed the man that was holding her arm, trying to steady herself. "Leave him alone."

The room began to dim. Mira's muscles felt watery. She saw Emmit turn to her before the noise died away and the world went black.

Mira woke for short periods of time. She was coherent enough to know that she had suffered blood loss and exhaustion. It felt like ages before she woke up and felt like a person again.

Looking around, she first noticed that the bed wasn't hers and she had never seen the room before. Then she noticed that she wasn't alone.

A man stood nearby, facing the door and seeming to ignore the bed.

Mira sat up slowly. She didn't get any sense of danger, but she jerked back when the man moved toward the door and out of the room. He said nothing.

When she threw off the covers and moved to get up, her muscles felt sore and tight and her bones were stiff. She'd only made it as far as the edge of the bed when Oracle jumped up beside her.

The cat rubbed against her and she scratched his ears. As Oracle began to purr, Alchemy joined them. Seeing the cats calmed some of the building trepidation.

There was a knock at the door and Emmit entered. Mira quickly made sure that she was covered, only to realize that she was in a long white night gown. Something that definitely didn't belong to her.

"You should be resting," Emmit said, striding across the room.

Mira had to clear her throat before she could talk. "I feel like that's what I've been doing." Still, she eased back in the bed and Oracle curled up on her lap.

"For good reason."

"Where am I?"

"You are in my apartment," Emmit said. "The doctor is on his way."

"Where's Gabriel? And Tyler? What happened to them?"

"Tyler is in the hospital. Gabriel has been released."

"He's okay?" Mira asked, feeling a sense of relief so deep that she teared up.

"He will fully recover," Emmit said. "Unfortunately, he hasn't been willing to go into detail about what took place on the other side."

Mira let herself fall back into the bed. "I don't blame him."

Emmit steepled his hands in front of him and leaned forward. "I do need the details."

Alchemy sat up straighter and watched Emmit closely. Mira didn't want to remember the tar-like smell of death that had surrounded her in the other world.

"How did you get us back?" Mira asked.

"I was hoping to wait on that part." When Mira didn't respond, Emmit leaned back and sighed. "I didn't. The witches did. I just helped... move things along."

"We don't know how to do that."

"That's where I played a part."

"I bet Mr. Singer flipped."

Emmit cleared his throat and appeared uncomfortable. "There is a message for you related to that."

"What message?"

"A letter." He nodded toward the bedside table.

When Mira went to grab the message, Emmit reached it first, and then handed it over. "You really do need to rest."

"You were ready to interrogate me a minute ago," Mira said, trying to keep the pang of sadness out of her voice. "Don't deny it." He had given her up for dead, and now he wanted her for information. *How did I ever think dating Emmit Harker was a good idea?*

"If I could avoid it, I would, but everything in the Ether is stirred up, and I need to know how bad it is."

"Why?" Mira asked.

A flash of irritation crossed his face. Mira sat back up and turned her attention to the letter in an effort to avoid Emmit's gaze.

Mira popped open the wax seal and pulled out a piece of cream-colored parchment.

If Mira were honest with herself, she would have expected a thank you for finding the kids and Tyler and bringing them back. She had never been so wrong.

The first time through, the words didn't really sink in. She read the lines again:

The witches council has formally requested that all witches avoid contact with Miss Mira Bluebell Owens, unless she is accompanied by an elder or a member of the police department on official business. On the night of the next new moon, full judgment on her status in the community will be decided.

But... why? Stunned, Mira couldn't follow the logic.

"What is it?" Emmit asked, still looking cross.

"I've been shunned," Mira said, staring down at the paper and seeing nothing.

Emmit took the letter from her numb hands. "Surely such a thing isn't done."

The room became as silent as a grave.

"It's only for a week or so," Emmit said, at last. "I'm sure the council won't—"

"Are you sure?" Mira broke in. "Actually sure?"

"I'll speak with them," Emmit said, putting his usual confidence back into his voice.

"I should let Gabriel know," Mira muttered. "It may slow things down during the case."

"Ian," Emmit said, "you should let Ian know."

Mira's forehead wrinkled. "Gabriel will let him know."

"Ian will let Gabriel know," Emmit corrected.

Mira's eyes narrowed.

"I think that Gabriel would prefer a little time," Emmit said. "He's taking a step back, you could say."

"He's not on the case?"

"He's not returned to work yet, but he will still be partnered with Ian." Emmit looked as though he weighed every word before saying them.

As realization rolled over her, Mira's heart sunk, and she hated the fact that her eyes started to burn. "He's stepping away from me, you mean."

"Don't worry," Emmit said. "You'll have a guard on you at all times. Gabriel has direct access to them in case of anything unforeseen."

Mira nodded. If she spoke, she knew she would cry. Being shunned by the witches meant her family would have no contact. She had lost both them and Gabriel in the space of a few minutes.

"I'll give you some time," Emmit said, standing quickly and stepping away. "Let Thomas know if you need anything."

Mira looked quizzically at Emmit, glad for the momentary distraction.

"He'll be in here on guard," Emmit said.

"*In* here?" Mira managed to ask.

"Don't worry," Emmit said, stepping into the hall. "Reinfield's men are very discreet."

He was gone for only a few moments before someone else—Thomas, she supposed—replaced him. The man assessed the room, then took up station where he'd previously stood, staring at the door, away from her.

The room was now uncomfortable. She felt crowded, as though the man took up more space than a normal person did.

"Could you, um, wait in the hall?" Mira asked.

"Sorry, Miss Owens." He didn't even turn around. "I have to be here."

Mira got unsteadily to her feet and gazed around the room. *He can't do this,* Mira thought fiercely. Not Thomas, of course, but Emmit. The man in her room was only doing what Emmit had ordered.

"Do you need any assistance?" Thomas asked, still looking away.

"No," Mira said quickly. "I just need to, um, find some clothes, and um, get cleaned up."

"There is clothing in the dresser and the closet," Thomas said. "Your bathroom is the door to the left."

Keeping an eye on Thomas, Mira found a mixture of clothes that were hers and others that were merely her size. When she walked to the restroom, Thomas moved to follow.

"You're not following me in there," Mira said, more shocked than angry.

"I'll inspect the room before you enter and wait at the door," Thomas said. "I'll only enter the room if required."

While Thomas searched the room, Mira thought over what might 'require' the man to enter, but she gave up. When he left, Mira went in, Alchemy and Oracle trailing after her. She closed the door firmly behind them and looked around, finding a fairly modern bathroom.

After splashing water on her face, Mira grabbed a thick, heavy, white cotton towel. Numbly, she sat on the floor and covered her face, letting the towel soak up the tears and muffle her sobs.

Creating a new series has been nerve wracking and a lot of fun! Mira was a fun character to write and I love watching her get to know Gabriel.

If you enjoyed this book, please leave a review on the site where you made the purchase. Leaving a review helps the reader and author in many ways. Your support is appreciated!

Thank you for reading!
Amanda Booloodian

Interested in information on upcoming releases?

Sign up for the Hidden World Newsletter to receive information on upcoming releases, news, and more!

ACKNOWLEDGEMENTS

The first book in the Spellbound Murder series, Oath Bound, made the USA today bestsellers list in The Shadow Files box set. Thank you to all my friends and family who helped make that a reality!

Special thanks to Christina Benedict for giving me feedback! I'd also like thank the ARC readers for Grim Magic and Oath Bound. Special thanks to Sarah Landis for being an awesome cheerleader! I also need to thank JD Book Services and Frankie Sutton, my editors, for their feedback on the book.

Deranged Doctor Design has done another amazing job with this series! They've provided the entire series with wonderful covers. I love their work and their flexibility.

Many, many other family, friends, and acquaintances have been incredibly supportive.

For all the people who gave reviews online, you are amazing! Thank you so much for taking the time to leave a review.

ABOUT THE AUTHOR

Amanda Booloodian lives in Missouri with her loving, and often times peculiar, husband. In 2006, she took part in Great Beginnings and was awarded first place in the Mystery/Thriller category. Amanda has been passionate about the written word throughout her life. Now, much of her spare time is spent at the computer, delving into worlds accessible only through vivid imagination. In warm weather, when she isn't pounding on the keyboard, she can often be found wandering through the wilderness. Occasionally she gets it into her head to SCUBA dive or to sit back at home and make wine, which can have interesting results and inspire her writing.

You can find out more about Amanda and her writing, including upcoming releases, on www.Booloodian.com. You can also find her on Facebook: Amanda Booloodian - Author, Twitter: @ajbooloodian, and Instagram: AJBooloodian.